THE LOST HISTORY OF STARS

The

LOST

HISTORY

of

STARS

a novel

DAVE BOLING

ALGONQUIN BOOKS
OF CHAPEL HILL
2017

Published by
ALGONQUIN BOOKS OF CHAPEL HILL
Post Office Box 2225
Chapel Hill, North Carolina 27515-2225

a division of
WORKMAN PUBLISHING
225 Varick Street
New York, New York 10014

This is a work of fiction. While, as in all fiction, the literary perceptions and insights are based on experience, all names, characters, places, and incidents either are products of the author's imagination or are used fictitiously.

LIBRARY OF CONGRESS CATALOGING-IN-PUBLICATION DATA
Names: Boling, Dave, author.
Title: The lost history of stars / a novel by Dave Boling.
Description: First edition. | Chapel Hill, North Carolina :
Algonquin Books of Chapel Hill, 2017. | "Published simultaneously in Canada
by Thomas Allen & Son Limited."
Identifiers: LCCN 2016047224 | ISBN 9781616204174
Subjects: LCSH: South African War, 1899–1902—Concentration
camps—Fiction. | Concentration camp inmates—South Africa—Fiction. |
Afrikaners—Social conditions—Fiction.
Classification: LCC PS3602.O6539 L67 2017 | DDC 813/.6—dc23
LC record available at https://lccn.loc.gov/2016047224

10 9 8 7 6 5 4 3 2 1
First Edition

For the victims of the Anglo-Boer War,
and those many who suffered
in its unsettled aftermath in South Africa.

AUTHOR'S NOTE

I set out to write a novel based on the experiences of my grandfather, a young British soldier in the Second Anglo-Boer War in South Africa (1899–1902). I discovered that twenty-two thousand Boer children died in British concentration camps—more than the combined fatalities among soldiers on both sides. It wasn't on the scale of the Holocaust, nor was it of genocidal intent, but it is nevertheless a twentieth-century atrocity—a war against children—that has been largely forgotten.

The Boers were mostly descended from the Dutch who settled in the Cape Colony and later migrated north to the remote interior of South Africa to escape British colonial influence. But the Brits sought to take over the small Boer republics of the Orange Free State and Transvaal after the world's richest diamond and gold deposits were discovered there late in the nineteenth century.

The vastly outnumbered Boers changed the way in which future wars would be conducted, introducing the hit-and-run guerilla tactics that allowed small commando units to prolong costly wars against world powers. The tenacity of the Boers caused the British to resort to scorched-earth tactics that led to the burning of thirty thousand Boer farms. Suddenly homeless Boer women and children were then installed in poorly managed and disease-plagued concentration camps, in which a total of twenty-seven thousand fatalities were recorded. Many thousand native Africans also died in separate camps that the British established, but no one bothered to count them.

[The Boers] must obviously be one of the most rugged, virile, unconquerable races ever seen upon earth. Take this formidable people and train them for seven generations in constant warfare against savage men and ferocious beasts, . . . give them a country which is eminently suited to the tactics of the huntsman, the marksman, and the rider. . . . Then finally put a finer temper upon their military qualities by a dour fatalistic Old Testament religion and an ardent and consuming patriotism. . . . Combine all these qualities . . . and you have the modern Boer—the most formidable antagonist who ever crossed the path of Imperial Britain.
—SIR ARTHUR CONAN DOYLE, *The Great Boer War*

The fatality rate of our soldiers on the battlefields . . . was 52 per thousand per year, while the fatalities of [Boer] women and children in the camps were 450 per thousand per year. We have no right to put women and children into such a position.
—DAVID LLOYD GEORGE,
British member of Parliament and future prime minister

The women are wonderful: they cry very little and never complain. The very magnitude of their sufferings, indignities, loss and anxiety seems to lift them beyond tears. . . . I can't describe what it is to see these children lying about in a state of collapse—it's just exactly like faded flowers thrown away.
—EMILY HOBHOUSE,
British activist and reformer, on life in the concentration camps

THE LOST HISTORY OF STARS

PART I

Weeping Love Grass

1

September 1900, Venter Farm

The first warning was so delicate: Moeder's hanging cups lightly touched lips in the china cabinet. By the time we turned to look at them, stacked plates rattled on the shelves from the vibration of hoofbeats.

"Ma . . . they're coming," Willem said, his voice so calm I didn't believe him. "It's them."

"Is it just our men again?"

"Too much dust, it's them . . . the British."

"Lettie, take your sister. . . . Willem, turn out the stock. . . . Bina, gather food," my mother said with rehearsed precision.

"I'll get your point-two-two," Willem said, retrieving the rifle my mother kept in her bed on the side where my father had slept before the war. The weapon was almost as tall as my little brother.

The British swept upon us like a grass fire, and by the time we reached the *stoep*, two dozen soldiers had dismounted; more were pouring into the barn and rounding up stock. Mother had drilled us for this moment every day since the men left almost a year earlier. Her first rule was that the children were not to speak. Not a single word, no matter what the Tommies did. Say nothing, she told us, pointing her finger as if to jab the rule inside us.

"Where are your men?" the officer at the front of the group shouted.

"Out killing British," I yelled, my silence lasting no more than five seconds.

My mother and the soldiers focused stares on me.

"We know they've been here. . . . You've been supplying them and that makes you spies," the officer said. "They destroyed the rail line near here . . ."

"Were many killed?" I asked.

"Lettie . . . shhhh." Mother turned to me with such force that I feared she'd aim her rifle at me.

"Yes . . . Lettie . . . shhh," the officer mocked, approaching the stairs. "We've been getting sniped at for miles, and you give them support. We could hang you from that tree. All of you."

I was enraged. They were at our house, with their fat British horses and their knives on the end of their British rifles. Here . . . in *our* country, at *our* house. They were no longer a vague threat, some distant rumbling in the night. They were here, looking into our faces. I stood tall and narrowed my eyes at the officer. The fool. I took a step toward him, sending hatred in my gaze. I am small . . . but dangerous.

"Do you have more to say, little girl?"

Little girl?

I raised both hands above me and shook my fists at him . . . and made a growling noise through my teeth.

The officer laughed. "Will you hurt us with your dolly?"

I had gathered my little sister's things when the soldiers rode up. I still had Cecelia's doll, Lollie, in my shaking hand. The British were not threatened.

"Stop laughing at her, *rooinek*," Moeder shouted, turning the .22 at the officer.

"Put it down, missus . . . ," the officer said. "What—"

A pebble bounced off the officer's shoulder. Willem had fired his slingshot at him from the corner of the *stoep*.

A dozen soldiers lifted weapons; half aimed at Mother, the others at Willem. Two Tommies twisted at her rifle, a small-caliber shot pinging into the sky before they could wrench it from her.

"We'll shoot her right now," the officer said to Willem. "You've attacked us with a weapon and she fired a shot. We could hang you all right now. Or put together a firing squad."

Willem waited, considering . . .

"Put it down, Willem," Mother said. Willem turned and cocked his head to her. He placed the slingshot on the *stoep*.

"Bring him here . . ."

He looked so small, a barefoot eight-year-old under a too-large hat, wiggling as two soldiers dragged him by the arms. They stood him in front of the officer, and when they released their grip, Willem straightened into a post.

"Where are the men, boy?"

Silence.

"Where are the men, boy?"

Silence, with a defiant stare.

"You know the penalty for being a spy . . . and for attacking an officer," he said, signaling for men to come forward. "Firing squad."

I screamed and Moeder pulled at the soldiers holding her arms. She tore free from one, but another came from behind and coiled an arm around her throat. My mouth dried so quickly that I couldn't speak. I turned to pick up little Cecelia and shield her eyes.

Five aligned in front of Willem in such a straight line it was clear they had been drilled.

"Stop it, he doesn't know where they are. . . . None of us knows," Moeder said. "They haven't been home. . . . They could be anywhere."

The officer ignored her, focusing on Willem.

"Where are the men, boy?"

Silence.

"Brave officer . . . threatening a little boy," I said, barely able to raise a sound.

Willem broke his focus on the officer to glare at me.

"It's no threat. . . . Where are the men?"

Silence.

"Ready . . ."

Moeder twisted again, and the soldier lifted so hard against her neck he squeezed out a choking gasp.

"He doesn't know," I said. "They never tell us where they're going. No, wait, they never come home. They haven't been home."

"Aim. . . . Where are the men?" The officer screamed it this time.

Silence.

Soldiers' rifles angled toward his center, Willem inhaled to expand his chest toward their rifles. He curled his bottom lip over his top.

The tension in my arms pinched Cecelia so tightly she raised a wail, so long and at such a pitch that the officer and the men recoiled from their rigid stance.

"As you were," the officer said.

The squad lowered weapons.

"Fine boy you have there, ma'am," the officer said to Moeder. "They usually start crying and tell everything they know the second the squad lines up. He's the first one to just go mute." He offered his hand to Willem to shake but withdrew it empty when Willem sneered. "But you're still spies, and we're taking you in. You have ten minutes to get what you can from the house."

Mother spent the first moments staring at the officer, and then at every Tommy who walked past her, studying each man's face as if memorizing it for later.

Willem and I scrambled into the house to get our bags as two of the soldiers carried our chests and tossed them from the *stoep*. In the parlor, a soldier started up at mother's organ, a man at each shoulder. Offended by their nerve, Moeder rushed at them. She was blocked by the men. The Tommy played so well I stopped to listen. His playing was equal to Moeder's as he read off the sheet music that had been open on the stand. Three sang in ragged harmony as Moeder stood helpless.

> Rock of ages, cleft for me,
> Let me hide myself in thee;
> Let the water and the blood,
> From thy wounded side which flowed,
> Be of sin, the double cure;
> Save from wrath and make me pure.

The singing felt so out of place but struck me as the perfect prayer.
Let me hide myself . . . yes, I thought, please, dear God.
Save us from wrath . . . yes . . . yes . . . now, please.
Another soldier pushed through and smashed the keys with his rifle

butt, startling his fellows, and the organ rendered a death moan until the soldier beat it breathless.

"Stop . . . ," Moeder screamed. She had promised never to satisfy them by showing emotion. But the organ . . . how could they?

I pulled Cecelia tighter to my hip when the Tommies became more violent. One smashed the glass of the china cabinet and crushed the contents with repeated rifle thrusts. The force of the sound stunned me, as if the glass shards themselves had flown into my flesh.

Pictures of ancestors were ripped down, and the painting of Jesus was knocked to the floor when they tore into the walls with their axes. It took them only a few wild ax chops to discover the silver setting and valuables we'd hidden behind a false wall.

"What did you think you were saving?" one asked. "We're going to dynamite the place in a few minutes, anyway."

"Get them out of here," said the officer, now bored by our presence.

They herded us with the tips of their bayonets. Our native girl, Bina, carried the largest basket of our belongings on her head. We stepped outside into a chorus of death wails. The pig produced a heartbreaking squeal as it was speared; one sheep after another raised pathetic pleas that turned into bloody gurgles when the knives were pulled across their throats. And beheaded chickens spun through their frantic death dance by the dozens.

I ran toward the sheep until a soldier turned and pressed his bayonet hard to my breastbone.

"Don't you touch that child," Bina yelled, dropping the basket to come to my side.

"It's not your war," he screamed at her, although the rifle pointing at her chest seemed evidence that it was. "We're not here to fight kaffirs, too."

Men dragged several freshly killed sheep to the well and threw them down. At the house, nails screamed when boards were pried loose from the walls and floors. The wood was hauled out and orderly stacked on a wagon—treated with more respect than we were.

Appetite for destruction peaking, the officer yelled a command and the Tommies dispersed. The explosion sucked the air from my lungs and sent pieces of the house splintering into the sky. I could feel the heat on my face and was convinced I could see the sound waves roll across the tall veld grasses. The house burned black and loud, the uprights groaning like a wounded thing before it collapsed in upon itself.

THE THINGS OF OUR life rose as smoke and faded into a high, gray haze. Fire consumed in minutes what had taken generations to accumulate. Had it really been just half an hour since the teacups betrayed their approach? Twenty-five minutes since I had shaken a doll at a British officer? Fifteen minutes since the organ cried and Jesus once again held his silence while beaten to the ground? Half an hour by the clock . . . a week's worth of heartbeats . . . a lifetime's tears?

The Tommies rejected most of the things we tried to bring and heaped them on a pile burning near the barn. We were left with some bedding, clothing, and a few other small things we could carry. To the open mouth of her satchel, Moeder had tossed whatever food she could that would not spoil—biltong and rusks, mostly. She packed the family Bible and swept some personal things off her bureau before the khaki-clad locusts swarmed in to devour the rest.

Oupa Gideon would have been so disappointed if he'd seen us; we had maintained less order than our headless chickens. I had gathered up my notebook and some bedding and then helped Cecelia with her clothes and her doll. Willem carried his slingshot in one hand and his little *riempie* stool that Vader had made him in the other. Moeder shouted at him to put on his boots, which he wore only in the coldest months. The Tommies snatched his slingshot and tossed it on the fire. One tried twisting the stool from his hands, but Willem's kicks made it not worth his bother.

They marshaled us toward an ox wagon. A soldier pushed my mother with a hand low on her hip.

"Don't . . . push . . . me . . . " She turned on him with her fists. Our house was burning, our stock being slaughtered as we watched, and that push was a final insult.

He swung his rifle off his shoulder so that the bayonet was at her throat, the tip still wet with sheep's blood, dripping a roselike pattern onto the front of her dress.

"Well, you're not staying here."

He pulled the bayonet back, but only an inch.

"We'll find somewhere," she said after a deep breath.

"Have you heard of the families that tried to stay out . . . women with children who thought they could live off the land? . . . You know what happened to them?" the soldier asked. "Bands of angry kaffirs raped the women and killed the children. You want to be used like that, missus?"

"No . . . no such thing," Bina shouted.

"Want to risk it?" he asked Moeder. The soldier slung his rifle back over one shoulder and attempted to lift her onto the wagon.

"Don't you touch her," Willem yelled.

He ignored Willem and put both arms around Moeder's waist to lift her so that her thrashing boot heals could not threaten his shins.

Willem glared and closed in.

"Tucker . . . that's enough," shouted another soldier, of sufficient rank to cause the Tommy to release her. "Back away, or help her climb up. They're not animals."

She made one last shove at the Tommy's arms, handed her bag to me, and mounted the wagon on her own.

Bina came last, our large basket on her head.

"Go . . . ," a soldier said, making small stabbing motions with his bayonet. "Go to your people."

Bina's eyes showed white and she tried to push around the soldier to get to the wagon, but he caught her across the throat with his rifle stock. She dropped in a pile, our things scattering around her. On her back, bayonet now at her throat, she could only watch as our wagon pulled away. I held both arms toward her, hugging the air between us, and focused on her eyes until they faded with distance.

I recognized the family in the wagon. We did not know the Prinsloos well; they were Doppers who lived near the railway and stayed to themselves. Their kind rarely joined in Sunday sermons or Nachtmaal services and struck me as joyless by choice. They were already backed toward the front of the wagon with their few possessions, eyes fixed on our flaming house. The children squeezed closer to their mother, as if trying to hide beneath her skirts.

I lost my footing and arrested my fall with a hand to the greasy cart bed. It had been used to haul livestock and was still slick with wastes. We stood holding on to the back gate of the wagon, staring at the burning farmhouse and at the gray mounds of dead sheep.

Cecelia had been a little trouper, only four, but doing as she was told, staying close to me. But when the Prinsloo children started wailing, she gave in and did not stop until the jerking of the oxcart forced her to hold on. We collapsed into our pile of belongings—except for Willem, who vomited over the side of the wagon. Embarrassed, he kept his back to us, but I could see the pumping motion of his head. Staring down a firing squad and then watching our home destroyed warranted a purge, I thought. Sapped of emotion, he collapsed in place and slept without stirring.

I was ashamed that he had been the strong child. I was older; it should have been me standing up to the officer, defiant against a firing squad. Instead, I shook a doll at them. I did nothing but make them laugh and provide them with an amusing story to tell over supper.

We had not eaten since breakfast, and Moeder apologized for having forgotten water. She asked a soldier where we were being taken and was told only "a place of concentration."

When she turned her back to the fire cloud above our house, I recognized her look, staring without focus. She was making a plan.

"At least we're together," I said to her. She did not seem to hear. And we weren't all together, anyway. What would happen to Bina now? What would happen to Tante Hannah, my aunt, and her nearby house? Surely they would burn her farm next.

My stomach became unsettled with the rocking of the wagon, and I thought of our ancestors, the Dutch sailors accustomed to the motion of ships at sea. I studied my mother again. I knew she would soon tell us to be smart and calm; God would guide us.

Our wagon merged in line toward the end of a caravan of perhaps a dozen others. The heat wilted Willem and Cecelia. I took off my white pinafore and spread it like a buck sail on the back corner of the wagon to shade them. I began to tell them a story, just something I made up to try to take their minds off what had happened, to distract them from the smell and the filth, the heat and the hunger. Moeder fed us biscuits. It took some effort to gnaw them soft before swallowing, and that made them seem more filling. It would tire our jaws if not fill our stomachs. I was soon so dry I could not go on with the story.

By dusk, the soldiers outspanned and we were allowed off the carts. Many children, driven by thirst, ran to roadside puddles, fell on their bellies, and drank muddy standing water, even as their mothers shouted for them to stop. The soldiers handed out tins of bully beef as supper for the hundred or so women and children. We were allowed no fires to cook, as it might draw the attention of our scouts. The night was beautifully clear, and I pointed out my favorite constellations to Willem, who sat on his little stool as if he were displaced royalty on a portable throne.

It would be four days in the open wagon before we reached the "place of concentration." After climbing from the wagon each evening, I could turn in all directions and see a dozen pillars of smoke rising to join the stained clouds. But my eyes were gritty with dust, so that sometimes it looked not like smoke on the rise but like dark, punishing storms raining down with devilish accuracy on farmhouses and barns.

More wagons joined our caravan each day. By the time we were off-loaded, some of the children who had drunk from the puddles were already sickened with a disease whose name I had never heard. And perhaps confused by the ordeal, I was certain I had seen an apparition in our new enclosure: a man who looked a great deal like Oom Sarel—my father's brother.

2

September–October 1900, Concentration Camp

A sprawling city of white bell tents spread in a grid across the valley, row by row, column by column—densely concentrated. We had eaten little on the trip and had such a small ration of water that my insides were like dry leather. My eyes stung from fatigue, but each time I closed them I saw the colorless outline of our house aflame. I had stared so hard that the image was etched onto the surface of my mind.

The Tommies shouted at us to gather and make ourselves orderly for an officer's remarks. We would soon see the rules of the camp posted everywhere, he told us, and it was his job to be certain we understood them from the start. He would read them in detail for the benefit of "the many illiterate" among us.

Moeder remained straight and solid while Willem and I cleaved tight from opposite sides. Cecelia slept through it all in Moeder's arms.

The wagon had been so crowded, and I so reluctant to lie in the animal wastes, that I had held on to the back gate, standing much of the trip. When we were off-loaded, the ground continued to roll beneath me and I strained to keep from faltering.

The officer cleared his throat and resumed shouting.

"No letter shall be posted without being read and approved by camp censors," he announced. He turned his head across the span of our group, but looking above us rather than at us. We had no idea where to write to our men, and no means of getting a letter to them. I would have no problems following that rule.

No bad language was allowed, he said. My parents were more strict about that than any British officer might be, so I did not curse as it was, except in my mind, and I doubted the British could police that. I thought a damnation of the officer as a test. He did not respond, so I was safe. I committed to silently cursing them every day.

No critical remarks were to be made against the British sovereign or government. I broke that one on the spot. Moeder gave me her "hush" look.

No lanterns could be burned after 8:00 p.m. except in case of illness. I knew I would want to read and write at night but soon discovered that candles were too scarce to allow it.

Tents were to be kept clean. My mother was already meticulous to the point of annoyance. She might work around the clock trying to sweep dirt off a dirt floor.

And nothing could be hung on the wire or fences, he said. I was not sure why we would need to or why it was forbidden, and it was not a controversy in camp until I made it one.

That first morning, they called us refugees, which I didn't understand and came to despise once I did. Refugees, we were told, were not allowed to leave the tent after dark. I would break that rule often because I could not check on the stars in the daylight. They could force me to live inside these fences, I supposed, but they would struggle to keep me from studying the stars. I had promised my grandfather I would always do that when possible.

I was used to rules; from as early as I could remember I'd followed the guideposts planted by Oupa Gideon and my parents and by the Bible we studied every night. I saw them all as commandments, and I respected them, mostly, because I respected those who made them. But those were *our* rules.

The British neglected to provide rules regarding the ways in which many thousands in this camp were to live in an area roughly equivalent to the space we had used for planting oats on the farm. Oupa Gideon always said that no one should live within sight of his neighbor's hearth smoke. But I would see the faces of more people on my first day in camp than I had in my entire life. More frightening to me was the idea that they were looking back at me, judging.

The camp rules became meaningful to me in only one way. I discovered that these British guidelines were printed on one side of a sheet of paper. I had brought along my notebook for a journal, but those pages were limited and dear. The sheets of rules provided an almost inexhaustible supply of paper for anyone brazen enough to rip them off the posts at night, when no one could see.

The British army may have created a vast empire, but my reading of the news led me to know that its leaders showed poor understanding of conducting a war in our vast country. So it should not have surprised me that camp organizers had not recognized the need to make a rule prohibiting the stealing of the rules.

. . .

THE GALL OF THE British to call this a refugee camp, portraying themselves as humanitarians providing food and shelter to thousands of homeless, when they were responsible for our being homeless in the first place. I would not hide my contempt. Whenever I saw a guard, I twisted my face tight and shot him through with looks of scorn.

They treated us like stock from the first moment, herding us into separate fenced kraals. Among those now imprisoned, we were called the Undesirables because our men were still on commando and refused to surrender. Some of the British called us Irreconcilables, which I preferred, as it sounded more defiant. I did not appreciate being considered undesirable, but I would proudly admit that I would never be reconciled to the British presence on our land.

A fence inside the fences kept us from the Boers who were there under British protection. They went by different names, too. The Tame Boers were those who would not fight. The Hands-Uppers were those who had surrendered to the British. And the Joiners were the worst, being traitors who not only surrendered but agreed to help the British, in actual combat, or with scouting and spying. We considered them all traitors and decided that they were fortunate to be protected from us. If they did not fight against the British, they might as well be British, we believed. In exchange for selling their country to the devils, they received more and better rations in camp, and soap and candles and small things to make their lives easier.

We heard talk of the British putting ground glass in the flour, or fishhooks in the bully beef. The meat was such gnarled gristle that we might not have noticed hidden glass or metal if it were in there. Meals were an unchanging series of mealie pap, canned beef, meal or samp, condensed milk. No vegetables. No fruit.

The maggots were not large, but they glowed starry white against the leathery meat. My throat seized shut the first time I saw them. But as proved true with so many of the worst things, familiarity eased disgust. Bina used to talk of eating bugs and beetles, and she certainly did not appear to be underfed. It taught me how spoiled I had been at home, where the smell of Moeder's cooking pulled at me like gravity. At first I surrendered myself to memories of the flavors and textures— the loins, the chops, the ham, the crunch of bacon, the saltiness of biltong—and each memory caused a different part of my mouth and mind and stomach to react. Every day felt like the brink of starvation until I realized how much I was punishing myself with the memories. Better not to think of those things. Eventually I relinquished the words for them.

Our flour was flecked with black weevils, but they were not as obvious or bothersome as the maggots. I still did not enjoy coffee, since the smell reminded me of Oupa Gideon, which caused my chest to ache. Moeder sometimes made a sour look when tasting her coffee. But when she sipped from a rusty tin that previously held the processed meat, she gripped it in the same delicate fashion she did her china teacups at home, her grace undiminished.

She coped without complaint, and seeing her strength, the rest of our family adapted. It was not the case with the family already occupying the tent. Having had the space to themselves for a month before we were billeted among them, the Huiseveldts treated us like intruders. We four cautious Venters joined the begrudging Huiseveldts in a space the size of a small bedroom at home. It was not as if we had chosen the tent of our own accord so that we could siphon off their luxuries.

A quick friendship among the children added to the civility but contributed to the clamor. In so many ways, Klaas Huiseveldt and

Willem were the same little boy, their slightly different bodies covering common internal devices. Every stick became a rifle, every stone was hurled, and every incidental contact an invitation to do battle as if to the death.

They played fivestones and knucklebone and chased each other and hid between tent rows with no regard to the weather or the well-being of bystanders. Communication was limited in form: either a shout, a whisper behind a shielding hand, or a fistfight. Klaas was thicker and Willem taller, but they were equally committed to their apprenticeship for manhood. It was harmless in open spaces, but dangerous in a crowded tent. And when one boy took a scolding from his mother, the other looked on in knowing sympathy or slipped out of the tent for fear of getting winged in the crossfire of blame.

The two mothers, trying to appear respectful of the other's domain, would often target their own son for punishment just to send a message to the other boy. But we often sensed the tone that said: I wouldn't have to correct my son if you corrected yours.

On some days, Klaas and little Rachel Huiseveldt sat in when I schooled Cee-Cee and Willem. Their mother, Mevrou Huiseveldt, listened and offered sour criticisms or faulty corrections. While I was bothered by her ignorance, I most deeply resented her ignorance of her ignorance. The woman believed the world was flat. I could not even go into it with her.

She had been so dramatic in her claims of being on the brink of perishing that I did not expect her to survive our first day in the tent. But she lived to complain anew the next morning. Rheumatism one day, indigestion the next, painful "blockages" on the third. She rendered foul winds that filled the tent and disgusted even the two young boys, who took pride in such matters.

Often she would not move around the tent or venture outside for a whole day, and when she did, it was with a limp of one leg or the other or both, which caused her to stoop as she walked, making her look twice her age. Yet she was no older than Moeder. At times, though, she would disappear from the tent without a word, leaving her children unwatched for hours.

Her head, she repeatedly warned us, "feels like it's about to explode." The third time she announced this, I began immediately dropping to the ground and covering my head. Once I was sure she recognized my act, I would peek out to see whether the danger of explosion had passed. She yelled at Klaas, hoping to chastise me by ricochet. Willem and Klaas caught on to the "explosion" response, and the three of us would fall as if we'd been shot. After a few times, she at least reworded that complaint.

"My head feels . . . ," she started, as the three of us eased toward the ground, "achy."

She was such a contrast to my mother, who greeted hardships with an appropriate scripture or a reminder that our sufferings were trivial when held against the sacrifices made by our men in defense of our independence. I expected as much from her. I had seen her suffer unspeakable pain. Moeder knew Mevrou Huiseveldt's complaining wore on us all. Sometimes she would remind us—in polite tones directed at Mevrou Huiseveldt—to "think of the men, think what they're going through."

"At least your Matthys is still alive and well," Mevrou Huiseveldt jumped in, missing the point. "My Jan has been captured and sent to prison on an island . . . Saint Helena."

Meneer Huiseveldt was always "my Jan" to her.

"Our men are still fighting," Willem countered. He stressed the word "fighting" as a point of pride that our men had avoided being taken prisoner. Klaas tore into him, and they wrestled until Moeder pulled them apart.

"But . . . but . . . Saint Helena," Mevrou Huiseveldt said. "I don't even know where that is."

"It's an island in the South Atlantic more than a thousand miles from here," I said. "It is so remote that the British used it as a place of exile for Emperor Napoleon of France, and he died there in 1821. After that, slave ships headed toward America were captured and taken to Saint Hel—"

"Aletta . . . not now," Moeder said.

"But Ma, she said she didn't know where it was. . . . I thought she might like to learn something . . . factual."

"Aletta!"

"She brought it up . . ."

Mevrou Huiseveldt began wailing, "My Jan . . . my Jan . . . a thousand miles from here."

"The Lord God shall wipe tears off all faces," Moeder said, the words sympathetic but stern.

"I wish they'd shoot me," Mevrou Huiseveldt moaned. "It would hurt me less. And this food. They are trying to kill us all."

"Mathilda . . . please," Moeder said.

Indignant, Mevrou Huiseveldt pulled her children up on her cot and held them like a shield. They wriggled free from her grip. I didn't blame them for wanting to be away from her. She was one reason I tried to escape the tent at every opportunity, and I think it was why Moeder so readily allowed it. She did not need the stress of my comments triggering more conflict.

The woman's crying—loud and dramatic—would start as soon as

we all turned in. When the sobbing ceased, the snoring began. When she was not in the tent, Klaas amused us with his imitation of her thunderous snores. He shook the canvas of the tent flap as if it were a bellows powered by her fluttering exhalations. Willem skittered back and forth as if being sucked toward the sleeping woman and then blown back by wind. The real thing was less amusing at night.

These early challenges of camp caused me to see that I was not quite the frightened weakling I had suspected. "Blessed is the one who perseveres under trial," my mother quoted almost every time she could sense I was readying to voice a complaint. As I developed the will to persevere, I lost an equal amount of tolerance for those who had not found that will. But the promise of God's reward failed to subdue my disgust with a few things in camp. The latrines in particular.

Almost five thousand people were now crammed into our camp, and they all used the latrines. But the pits had been neither redug nor moved. Each time I used them, I brought my scarf to my face and breathed through the filter of cloth, but it did little to mask the stench. At times the air was so thick with bluebottle flies you might breathe them in. They clustered in your ears, where their buzzing would madden. And they fought one another for places at the corners of your eyes, where they sucked for moisture. All the while they spread the filth upon which they had trod with their many thousand twitching feet.

Bothersome, too, were those with no shame over their sounds . . . no better than barnyard animals. Perhaps it had been sapped from them over time, but I resented their absence of modesty and consideration. Yet I coped without comment, my stoic mother as inspiration. All adaptations required a balance, I learned. As I gained some control over my loathing of difficult circumstances, I grew less patient with difficult people.

At times the little ones clustered like a litter of playful puppies. They would roll and shove, and I withdrew, preferring to sit alone, pressing against the sidewall of the tent to find my own space. Sometimes I was so sensitive to touch that the rub of my clothes felt like a burn. I grew tender, as if swollen beneath my skin. I wanted to shout or cry or slap someone, uncertain which from minute to minute. But as an adult, I felt obliged to be mature and stable. Still, sometimes as little as a sharp word would pierce me. I watched Moeder, strong as if wearing armor. But I so often felt transparent as gauze.

As much as I despised the mud and the food, and the flies at the latrine, they were all just unavoidable parts of being in this place, and I had no choice but to adapt and to do so in a manner befitting the mature, thirteen-year-old adult I'd become.

3

Early October 1899, Venter Farm

Silent as a spirit, Oupa Gideon would steal me from my bed to take me outside and teach me the wonders of the sky. I was seven or eight the first time. I startled when he touched me; he sealed my lips with a rough finger. His eyes said, Quiet . . . trust me. He scooped up the blanket around me and carried me in a warm bundle. The scratch of his whiskers convinced me it was not a dream. He turned sideways to slip me through the bedroom door and somehow avoided furniture as he navigated the dark parlor.

"Can you see?" I whispered.

"You're safe," he said, and I was convinced I was.

The night air on the *stoep* always cleared my head. And on nights when it was cold enough to see my breath, I would exhale "smoke" from the corner of my mouth just as Oupa did, opposite the side where he held his pipe with clenched teeth.

Oupa Gideon was so forceful during the day that I feared him at times. But he lifted me from bed with such a tender hand and spoke to me with such a peaceful voice on these nights that he seemed a different person. No one discovered us exchanging whispers during those many nights together, and we told no one. It was my first conspiracy.

He passed along the lessons of the sky that he learned from his grandfather, the captain of a Dutch merchant ship. From a sky iridescent with stars, he would point out specific points of light, and they brightened at his mention. When he spoke a constellation's name, it took shape, and the stars connected so that I could see a cross or a bear or a throne. He had the power to make the sky come alive.

"And God made two great lights, the greater light to rule the day, and the lesser light to rule the night . . . and God set them in the firmament of the heavens to give light upon the earth."

The first time he said "firmament," it sounded like a mix of "firm" and "permanent." That was how I came to think of Oupa, firm and permanent. No one could be stronger or more reliable. Except maybe my father. Or my mother. They were the living firmament of my world.

"Look . . . ," he said on one of the first nights, opening his arms wide, pointing long, knotty fingers from horizon line to horizon line. "The sky is as wide here as it is on the seas, but we are a mile closer to it on the high veld. A mile closer to heaven. Think about that: we're closer to God here."

"Can he see us better here?" I whispered.

"He can see you everywhere," he said, raising his unruly eyebrows.

He often propped me on a chair and returned moments later with cups of coffee and hard-baked rusks for us to eat. I shook my head to help choke down the bitter drink, but he taught me to soak and soften the oblong biscuits so that they would fall apart in my mouth. Oupa would not even blow on the steaming coffee but just brought it to his mouth and drank it down. I was certain he could breathe fire if he wanted. When others were around during the day, I pretended never to have tried coffee and to be disgusted by it. I wanted Oupa to know that I was a trusted guardian of our secrets.

The sky is always changing and the change is wrought by God's hand, he said, and that made this an opportunity for mortal man to watch God work miracles every night. Who is so unwise as to sleep through God's miracles?

With wide eyes and uplifted palms, I always answered, "Not I."

I was proud that he singled me out to share these lessons. It was my duty, he said, to memorize my ancestry, back through the line of sailors and captains who had fought wars against the British and explored the world's seas.

"That is your cargo," he said. "You will carry these stories to your many children. You will be like your mother . . . God's chosen vessel."

Most of the stories came from his *oupa*, recalling storms and perils, and travel to exotic lands, and settling in the Cape to handle trading for the Dutch.

"Through the centuries, their two constants were the Bible and the stars. . . . Both taught us to navigate through life. Both guided us to this place . . . our own place . . . away from others."

He introduced me to the moon first.

"Twice a day the seas swell in the direction of the moon," he said, using one fist to symbolize the earth and the other the moon as they moved through space. "The moon always shows us the same face, and it pulls at the oceans."

"I've only seen oceans in a book."

"I know, *skattebol*, but you can see the sky from everywhere," he said. "There's your connection. It's the same sky my *oupa* taught me."

His stories built such a powerful connection to my ancestors that I believed it my destiny to be a ship captain. I would learn the stars first, then navigation, and the seas and the ships later. I would stand behind a giant wheel to steer a ship, guiding the family legacy across the seas.

"Can women be ship captains?" I asked.

"No." He took a sip of coffee. "Don't be silly."

Well, I would be the first. I would surprise Oupa and make him proud. People around the world would know my name. So I studied the moon. I thought about its strength, pulling the oceans toward it, making the earth go lopsided. And when I concentrated on that power, I was certain I could feel it pulling at me, too, almost lifting me from my chair. After all, how could it be strong enough to pull the ocean but not raise up someone as little as me?

"Some of the tribes believe the moon is a god," he continued. "Unbelievers—that's what *kaffir* means—they can't think as we do because of the Curse of Ham."

"Bina and Tuma are cursed?" I asked.

"Blackened for their sins . . . destined to serve even the lowest peoples," he said. "That is the Holy Word."

"Bina saved my life . . . killing a snake . . ."

"She did, but some of their kind throw animal bones on the ground rather than read the Bible."

On the first night he took me out, I asked about the brightest stars, the three in a perfect straight line. He put his arm around me and pointed so that I could follow his line of sight.

"Some call it Drie Susters. I learned it as Orion, the Hunter," Oupa said. "The three stars are his belt, and those four at the corners are his feet spread and his arms raised for battle."

Oupa stood, taller than any man I knew, legs apart and arms open as if he were drawing a bow. The stance of the Hunter came into focus.

"And there is the Pleiades, the Seven Sisters." He pointed to a cluster of blue stars that seemed nearer to us. "It is written in the Bible: 'Seek him that makes the Pleiades and Orion, and turns the shadow of death into the morning,'" he said.

On an October night not long before the men left for war, Oupa plucked me from my bed. I had long been old enough to walk to the *stoep*, but his carrying me was the first part of the ritual. Rains had blown through in the early night, leaving the air moist and the sky looking as if the stars had been scrubbed clean.

"We're leaving soon," he said. "You and I won't be able to do this for a while."

The coffee scent chased the sleep from my head. He relit his pipe, drawing the flame into the bowl, flicked the match to the dirt, and started the evening's lesson. This night, he told of the most amazing sky he'd ever seen, when he and his young wife traveled by wagon to buy horses. He called it the Southern Lights.

He described the colorful display, but I wanted to hear more of my *ouma*.

"Will you tell me about her?"

He repacked and relit his pipe.

"She died when your father was young."

"How?"

"Your *oom* Sarel killed her."

I had never heard this and was stunned.

"Killed her?"

He moved on without answer.

"It was just the three of us after that . . . me raising the boys."

"By yourself?"

"We had a girl who looked after them, who cooked for us."

"Before Bina?"

"Yes."

"Where is she now?"

"She left."

"What was her name?"

"I don't remember much about her."

"And then Bina and Tuma came?"

"That was later. Look, a meteor." He spotted a long, bright flash.

"What was Vader like when he was my age?"

"Good boy . . . but your father and his brother always scrapped."

"Fought?"

"Brothers always do. . . . The younger always wants to overtake his older brother, so Sarel always tested your father. . . . It was good for them. . . . I encouraged it. And then Sarel grew jealous of him, of course."

His story was interrupted with pointing and then wordless scanning of the bright pinpoints.

"Enough," he said, taking our cups to the kitchen to wash and put away, to hide the evidence of our secret ritual. Back in bed, I considered Oupa's stories of our family and realized how much I didn't know and how little I understood. From the life of the adventurous ship captain all the way to our living on the remote veld, the message was this: There is a giant and exciting world out there, but we seem driven to get as far away from it as we can.

4

October 1900, Concentration Camp

Oom Sarel slouched in without sound or statement. He was smaller and bent, as if his bones had gone soft. He looked twenty years older than the man we'd seen eagerly ride to war a year earlier.

"Out," Moeder shouted, rising and pointing to the tent flap so quickly it seemed a planned response.

Within our first few days in camp, we had heard that Oom Sarel had not only surrendered but was working for our keepers. Moeder declared him a traitor, putting him at a level of shame lower even than the British.

"He's family," Willem argued at first. "You always say family is the most important thing."

"That, *seun*, is what makes it worse," she said. "That's beneath the lowest."

"But—"

She slapped a red mark on his cheek and forbade the speaking of his uncle's name.

Oom Sarel had not approached us in our few months in camp, nor had we seen him on our side of the fence. Not until this day. He instantly thrust a palm toward Moeder as if to hold her back.

"This is for you, Lettie, from Tante Hannah," he said, handing me a small sack.

"Let me explain," he said to my mother. "Give me one minute."

Even the Huiseveldts quieted to hear.

"I was injured . . ."

"We don't care," she said.

"I was captured and they took me to their doctors."

He opened his collar and pulled back his shirt to unveil a scarred and misshapen shoulder, still discolored, with knots raised like tiny fists under the skin.

"This is not a camp for prisoners," she said. "You're not a prisoner. We respect prisoners who were taken. . . . You surrendered."

"I was injured," he said. "This arm is almost useless now."

He lifted his right arm like a broken-winged bird. It was withered to half the size of the other arm.

"Were you shot?"

"The doctors said they had never seen anything like it. Bones were sticking out of the skin. I got separated and was captured. I tried fighting with my left arm but couldn't load my rifle. The pain . . . I can't . . ."

"Are you saying that your father and brother left you behind? Of course not . . . they would never leave you."

"I was scouting, and they didn't know what happened to me."

"And the Tommies brought you here?"

"This is where they could tend my shoulder."

I had no idea how such things worked, but I was surprised that a fighting man would be taken to a camp for the families of those burned from their homes.

"Liar . . . you surrendered . . . didn't you?" Moeder shouted now. "Didn't you? You gave up . . . didn't you?"

"I had to get to a doctor. . . . I was dying."

"Nobody dies from a broken bone. . . . You signed the oath, didn't you?"

"I couldn't lift my arm."

"But you surrendered."

"I would have died."

He paused, awaiting her next assault. She stared.

"I fought . . . but they have half a million soldiers. . . . We have a few thousand farmers."

"And fewer once the cowards give in."

"More Tommies are dying of disease than from our rifles. They're bothered more by lice than by our commandos."

"You lie. . . . The British lie."

"It's only a matter of how many have to die."

"You disgraced us."

He sagged, shrinking into his boots.

"I want this to end before everyone is dead. . . . The God of Hosts has turned against us."

"That's a sin . . . sinner."

"We're all sinners. . . . This is my redemption. . . . This is the right thing. You can see God's will in all this. . . . His will is that we stop now . . . to save lives . . ."

"What about the others? Are they quitting? Your father, at his age?

That old man you're always trying to impress? Schalk, at his age, a young man, is he quitting? Is Matthys quitting, your brother, your rival? . . . Is he going to surrender? Never."

"They weren't wounded. . . . They weren't captured," he said.

The two were a foot apart; their breathing sounded like horses after a gallop. I inched forward to help my mother in case of blows.

"Men fight with arms shot off," she started up again. "Matthys would . . ."

"I'm a farmer, not a soldier," he said.

"There is only one reason to stop fighting," Moeder said. "Because you are dead. I wish you had died out there so we could have been proud instead of ashamed. At least we would have mourned you. How can Hannah live with this?"

"She is my wife."

"She vowed to marry a man . . ."

"When this is over, we'll get our land back. . . . We'll start over again. . . . They don't want our farmland . . . just the gold mines. It will be like before."

I knew that was the wrong thing to say to her.

"There are women who have escaped camps and are chasing down cowards like you . . . forcing them to go back," she said. "And if they won't go back, the women shoot them. . . . That saves their husbands from having to waste ammunition on them. There are even some women on commando, fighting to their death while you give up. Women fighting, but not you. Old men fighting, but not you. Young boys fighting, but not you."

I had not heard of the women fighting but had no trouble imagining Moeder leading a column of avenging women. I knew of boys as young as twelve and men in their eighties who were on commando.

"I'm not . . . a soldier . . ."

"That's an excuse, not a reason. . . . Get out of here. . . . Get out of here, coward. I can't stand the sight of you. Don't go near my children, they shouldn't have to look at you . . . to be reminded you're of their blood."

"This is why I came," he interrupted.

He held out a pencil and some paper. He explained in little more than a whisper: the women were being allowed to write to their husbands and tell them about life in the camp. "A man deserves to know what his family is going through."

"How would you know what a man deserves?"

"They promise the messages will be delivered," he said. "You can tell him how the children are."

Moeder's eyes flared as if she had heard the voice of the devil. She stepped closer, tilting her chin toward his face.

"Matthys would gut you if he saw you." She made a motion of a knife starting low on his stomach and rising up to his breastbone. She stepped forward so quickly he flinched and raised his good arm.

Mevrou Huiseveldt shouted for her to stop, and her children cried from behind her.

Moeder paused and then reached for the paper. "Yes, I have a message."

She wrote a few words and gave it back, careful not to touch his hand.

"Read it," she demanded.

"Susanna."

"Read it."

He read aloud: "Matthys, better to die in battle than return in defeat. Susanna."

He folded it and put it in his pocket.

"I worry about you . . . and the children."

Moeder inhaled for such a long time she seemed to swell. She looked at his right arm, which hung limp at his side. She moved the pencil to her left palm, with the point forward, and then closed her fingers around the base of it. She stared at his face—no, specifically at his right eye. Taking aim.

Mevrou Huiseveldt shouted again and began crying herself. Moeder turned to her. "Quiet . . . woman," she shouted.

Oom Sarel had slipped from the tent by the time Moeder turned back. She seemed stunned that he had run off. She tilted her head back and growled toward the peak of the tent—not a word, not a scream, just a sound from deep inside. And when she had emptied her lungs, she inhaled and turned to me with unexpected calm.

"Here, Lettie . . . this is for you."

She handed me the pencil to keep. I later used it to write about the day, and my mother's hatred, and the way it was turning her into someone I had never seen.

5

Early October 1899, Orange Free State

The soil smelled of old bones baked by the sun; I imagined them the dusty remains of the natives who had lived here long ago, although they could have belonged to animals, since bones are all the same once they've been gnawed bare.

It was my first time sleeping on the ground in the bush, and I strained to conform to the uneven earth. A steady drumbeat, soothing as a mother's pulse, calmed the night. But drums from other native villages soon alternated, as if questions posed by booming, deep-chested men were being answered by distant women with rattling wood-on-wood voices. A night of tribal passages, I assumed. I pictured frenzied dances by firelight to celebrate someone's coming of age.

The hypnotic rhythms surrendered to a rumble that seeped from the core of the earth and rolled in waves across the veld until it clenched a deep, vague place low in my gut.

"Pa . . ."

"Go to sleep."

"But Vader . . . what's happening?"

My father sat up in his bedding and leaned toward the campfire, his face emerging shadowy gold from the darkness.

"Lions," he said.

"More than one?"

"Yes, Aletta, it usually is."

Several roared at once, knotting that place inside me.

"They'd probably go for us first," said my brother Schalk, so calm he didn't roll over. "You would be . . ."

Another roar muffled his words of comfort.

I would be . . . what . . . safe from harm?

I would be . . . what . . . in no danger?

"Schalk . . . I would be what?"

"You would be their little dessert."

"Dessert?"

"A sweet *melktert* after they made a meal of Pa and me," Schalk said.

Only my brother would laugh at the possibility of being eaten before dawn.

"They won't get you," my father said, "or us."

"What do we do?"

"Go back to sleep."

Given the pace of my heartbeats, I believed myself capable of running the many miles to the safety of home or springing to the very top of a tree if necessary. But the one thing I knew I could not do was fall asleep. I told myself to be brave; I had promised not to be a bother if they allowed me on this hunting trip, which was expected to be the last for a while, as the British were said to be gathering at our borders.

A lion punctuated a roar with several deep coughs and a softer grumble: Yesssss, I thought it said. Sleep, sleep, sleep . . . if you dare.

"May I sleep by you, Pa?" I was already on my feet when he answered.

"No . . ."

I froze in place. My face chilled.

"Stay there," he said.

"But—"

"Aletta . . . we'll be gone soon; you can't be such a little girl."

"I'm not, Pa, I'm twelve."

"Aletta."

"Fine."

Schalk could tell by the tone of that single word that I was about to cry.

"Be brave, little one," Schalk said.

"Schalk . . . ssstttt." My father silenced him with a whistle through his teeth. "They won't come near the fire."

With a poke stick he speared the coals at the core of the fire, and it flared bright and angry. I stared into it and it made a crackling laugh at me, and ghosts dancing in the smoke waved their wispy gray arms. I tried to look beyond the radius of the firelight, but the night was as I'd never seen: not merely black, but thick and textured, like the felt of my father's hat. And as I squinted, spots flashed . . . reflections off the great cats' yellow eyes.

The spots moved. They circled. Stalking outside the curtain of light. Pacing, waiting for the fire to fail, patient, quiet and patient, until the moment they could pounce. I pulled myself tighter. I gasped and blinked with force. They scattered.

"They're here, Pa, I see them."

"No, they're not, Aletta. Go to sleep."

I blinked again, as hard as I could. They withdrew. Waiting.

"What if . . . the fire goes out?"

Several lions roared, each louder in succession. They were not within striking distance of us after all. At least not the ones we could hear.

"Lettie, those may be, what, Pa, five miles away?" Schalk asked.

"Maybe."

"You can hear them that far?" I asked.

"Sure, I almost wish one would attack me sometime," Schalk said. "Men who live through it always say the same thing."

"Praise God Almighty for his salvation?" I whispered from the tight ball I had become.

"All they talk about is the lion's breath," Schalk said. "They say you'll never smell anything so awful. You'll never forget the stench. More than anything else, they remember the sickening breath."

I looked at my father for his confirmation that Schalk was insane. But he only stirred the fire.

"Lettie . . . it's fine to be afraid," my father said. "The Book says: 'The lion hath roared . . . who will not fear?' "

He pulled his small Bible from his chest pocket but by firelight could not find the passage.

"In the morning, I'll read from Peter . . ."

"Be watchful, the devil is a roaring lion . . . ," Schalk said, quoting the line Father referenced.

"The devil 'prowls' like a roaring lion," my father corrected.

"Except if they're stalking you, they often don't do you the favor of offering a warning," Schalk said.

"Neither does the devil," Father said.

"So I'm to be frightened when they roar, because the Bible says it is to be so," I said, "but I should be frightened even more when I don't hear them?"

I vowed never to leave the house again.

"But," my father said, "the rifles make us the dominant animal."

My grandfather Oupa Gideon preached the "dominant animal" theme for many occasions. You stand taller and you assert yourself. You let them know that taking you will come at a dear cost.

Two lions roared, then more as a group, as if challenging one another. Perhaps it was a night of passages for them as well. They continued much of the night. I wiggled closer to Schalk once I knew he was asleep. I gasped when the roars were loudest, but my heart beat so hard it threatened to bruise my ribs when the time between roars lengthened.

I grew light-headed gulping air scented by the old bones in the cold soil. I stared so hard at the fire that I was certain none had ever been brighter. I pulled my wool blanket close: it was abrasive to the point of pain. I strained to hear every sound in the clamoring night. But it was more than just listening; I was so alert it was as if I could *feel* the sounds. I was intoxicated by it all and was no longer bothered that I could not sleep.

Ah . . . so this is fear.

A RED DAWN PALED to pink when we began stalking. I was exhausted from the sleepless night, but I worked to step in the exact footsteps of Schalk as he inched through the bush. I had never been so concerned with the direction of the wind nor so fretted over the snap of a single branch. With each of my impatient mutters, Vader and Schalk both squinted threats; this was serious. They expected it to be their last chance for game before they would be hunting foreign invaders.

Bored, bloodied by thornbushes, and asleep on my feet, I finally picked a flat spot and sat. I plucked stickers from my legs and watched the hunters' strategic gestures to each other and the way they disappeared so gradually it was as if the bush had time to grow up around them.

I picked a cochineal beetle off a prickly pear and squeezed the bright red dye out of it as Schalk had shown me; it could stain your fingers for days. I used it to put my initials on a big rock. I watched the sky and imagined animal figures in the clouds. I finally leaned back and slept. The shot woke me and I ran a jagged path through bush, ducking branches as I could. The men stood at the edge of a clearing, looking down at an animal nearly the size of Vader's horse. Vader and Schalk removed their hats and said a prayer of thanks and then a prayer in praise of the animal.

Stalk it. Kill it. Pray for it.

They both set about the gutting, reaching elbow-deep into its cavity, steam rising from within. From the tangled gore, Schalk carved out a purple organ and held it in my direction.

"Liver . . . take a bite," he said. Blood traced a thick path down his arm.

"No . . . Schalk . . . please . . . no."

He savaged a bite with exaggerated enjoyment, blood painting his chin. He handed it to Vader, who also bit and then twisted his head to rip loose a piece of raw meat. He held it toward me, the scallops of their bite marks at the edge.

"No." I turned away, stomach rising.

The cleaning and quartering took most of the morning. Vader led the loaded pack mule at a slow pace, leaving Schalk and me in a private tandem ahead, riding together as we had on many afternoons. Schalk always filled the outings with his veld lore. He showed me the annoy-ing gray lourie, the goaway bird, which would screech a warning to the prey he might have stalked for an hour. He often fished for barbel, which were giant fish that could, he claimed, wiggle up out of the water and travel on land for miles if they sensed the stream they were in was going dry.

I loved riding together, the way we moved with the horses' stride and how the tall grasses reached our stirrups and spread like a wake in a golden ocean. The springboks pronked in front of us, giving off a honey-musk scent from the white fin of fur on their backs. We often spent the time sharing and confiding. He surprised me once with the story of his misguided courting of Mijnie de Bruyn.

"I rode Kroon in circles outside their house until her mother finally came out and asked me if I wanted to come in for dessert."

"Then what?"

"I went in and sat down . . ."

"And . . ."

"We ate."

"Did they know why you were there?"

"Of course."

"What did you say?"

"They were clearing the table and I asked if I could sit up with Mijnie. And everybody disappeared. They didn't even finish with the table. Just vanished."

"Oh, Schalk."

"And they lit the candle . . ."

"Oh, Schalk."

"It was the biggest candle you've ever seen. And Mijnie started talk-ing about how her sister Rosina got married after sitting up through only one candle with Fredrick Coetzee, and they had a baby within a year."

"What did you say?"

"I just kept looking at the candle—it seemed to be burning fast . . . and hot."

"Did you kiss her?"

"No . . . couldn't if I wanted. She never stopped talking . . . about her sister . . . how much she wanted to be the next one to get married . . . how much she wanted a family . . . babies. . . . She kept talking about babies. And living with her family."

"Did you say anything?"

"Finally . . ."

"What?"

"Thanks for dessert."

"Thanks for the dessert?"

"That's all I could think of."

"And then what?"

"I don't know. . . . I just remember jumping onto Kroon and kicking him hard for home."

6

December 1900, Concentration Camp

Warm weather made it easy to escape the crowded tent and walk during the day. Moeder accepted my absences when I told her of having stopped to help someone with the burden of heavy laundry or trouble harnessing a wild child. She warned me against "borrowing sorrow," but I convinced her that it was God's work. And truly, I was excited to meet so many new people.

At first I felt the energy created by the nearness of so many. But I was a plague of curiosity, introducing myself to all who passed, asking their names, how they were, and where they lived and then telling them about my family. Everyone backed away with suspicious looks. Several times, women just interrupted with, "What is it that you want?"

I expected that we would feel an us-against-the-world togetherness, that we'd be united by the bond of our shared condition. But the bulk of those I passed seemed to prefer staying at arm's length rather than linking arm in arm against our fate. After a few weeks, though, I was walking with my head down like the rest, eager to hear no more stories of sad displacement and loss. Soon I could tell which people were new to camp when I recognized in them the unwelcomed openness I had once shown.

I was not less sympathetic, just more practical. I started focusing on one of my books to keep me from assessing the needs of each person I passed. I had read it through several times by then, so I did not have to concentrate, nor did I have to hurry. My walking was rarely with intent or direction, just going row to row, tracing a grid at a pace barely above stationary. I considered it ambling, *amble* being one of my new words.

The sack Oom Sarel had tossed to me when he confronted my mother in our tent contained a small *Chambers's Dictionary*. Tante Hannah had written a note on the first page: "To help your writing."

I was already very comfortable with English, but I decided I would put the time in camp to good effect by learning every word in the book, start to finish. So many were not practical, though, particularly the long ones that others did not understand. I decided that going around using big words would seem supercilious.

But I loved the short ones that captured the perfect meaning with just a syllable or two. *Deft. Adept. Dank* became a favorite, as it exactly described the air inside a crowded canvas tent after days of rainfall. I wrote the words on scrap paper and then committed them to memory. Each time I smelled wet canvas, I mentioned to someone that it certainly was dank. Sometimes they gave me long looks, impressed by my intelligence, I assumed. So on this day, I ambled, and if anyone asked, I would edify them.

I learned to glance over the edge of the book to be sure I was not about to collide with someone or trip on a tent rope. I was startled back into the moment by what sounded like a barnyard of warring hens. More than a dozen women were at the fence line between our side of the camp and the Hands-Uppers and Joiners on the other side.

Two guards sought to bring order to a pack of women straining to reach a small clutch on the other side. Some of the insults were so profane I'd never heard words combined with such hateful imagination. I did not write them down but committed them to memory in case I ever needed a vile condemnation. We take our lessons where we may.

Several of those on our side spat comets of fluid at the other women's faces. A woman on our side reached through the fence and grasped the dress of a struggling woman and pulled her tight against the wire. That made it easier for others to claw at her, too. They tore at her dress, shouting each time they came away with a piece of ripped fabric, waving it about like a trophy of war.

The taller of two guards pried women from the fence with the butt of his rifle, and when he broke their grip, he shoved them backward. The shorter guard contributed nothing by holding his arms extended, since the women merely ducked beneath.

An old woman fell and dragged down several others. In a tangle, they screamed even louder and tumbled in their attempts to rise. A rifle fired, freezing the women as if in a photograph. By the time the echo faded, the women on the other side had retreated. The last of the group to get away was the woman with the shredded dress, the back of her white underskirt showing like a flag of surrender.

Even in victory, our women remained agitated, and the taller guard kept his rifle readied. The shorter one tried to help them to their feet, although each shrugged him off, and several slapped his face. One of the women scrambled up despite another's standing on her skirt, ripping her hem, but she did not seem to notice. She was one of the spitters, and she unleashed a full charge at the tall guard, who slapped her before wiping his face. It was Mevrou Prinsloo, the quiet woman from the wagon that had brought us to camp.

The shorter guard intervened and sorted through the fallen women, who cursed his existence and the fertility of his mother. Those near me aligned their clothing, shouted their contempt one last time, and dispersed to spread word of their victory.

"Are you all right?" the short guard asked me as I turned away. "I'm sorry about this."

He was not worth the breath it would take to form an answer. Besides, he had red hair, which I had never liked. That night I tried to write about the drama and the looks on the faces of the women. I sorted through the dictionary for better descriptions and came upon the word *ire*. But that didn't capture the savagery of the women on our side, nor the look on the faces of the Joiner women, which was something like fear but more fragile. Maybe no one had yet created words to describe the kind of things seen in places like this.

I THINK I WAS drawn to Janetta Maartens as a friend because I saw myself in her. When we walked past her in our first month in camp, Moeder pointed her out, saying she could be my twin, slender, with wide eyes and light brown hair. Perhaps that made it prideful to see myself in her, but it helped start a friendship.

"Ma . . . ," I complained when she stopped to make Janetta and me stand next to each other to reinforce our similarities. But I was soon delighted that she had, and we were inseparable after the first day. I embraced the idea of having a twin sister, or any sister who wasn't still a child like Cecelia. As much as I loved little Cee-Cee, we could share time but not thoughts. Having a girlfriend my age was one positive to come from being taken into camp, since our farm's remoteness prevented close friendships. It was interesting when we first spoke to learn that Janetta actually did have a twin, her brother Nicolaas, who did not resemble her as much as I did.

When anyone was nearby, Janetta and I talked about our families and the things we missed from home. And when we were by ourselves, we talked about boys to the exclusion of all else. We lowered our voices, looked around to be certain of privacy, and spoke quickly for fear of interruption. Benefiting from the closeness of her brother, Janetta was an expert on boys. It was as if she were fluent in a foreign language or had spent time as a spy in an enemy camp. I confessed that boys confused me.

"They're simple . . . and all the same," she said. "They have no idea who or what we are, and no matter how much noise they make, they are afraid of you."

"They certainly are not afraid of me."

"Oh yes, they are," she said. "They may just be too simple to realize it. You must assume they are three years less mature than a girl their age. That's why girls need to marry boys at least three years older."

From the first day, I could ask her things I never dared ask Moeder, and put my thoughts into words I had never voiced. To my great relief, she felt many of the same things I did. I had been certain the devil himself planted sinful thoughts in me, luring me personally into the fires of hell. It calmed me to discover I was not the only one wrestling with powerful forces. Of all the concerns we had in the camp—thoughts of the war and hunger and health—none ever came close to overtaking the discussion of boys as our most important topic.

I told her about the few boys from the nearest farms at home or those we would see several times a year when we gathered for the Nachtmaal services. Either they weren't the right age for me or I didn't think much of them. She easily decoded their behavior for me. She asked about my brothers, and she wanted to know all about Schalk, but not Willem, of course. She had lived close enough to a town that she went to a schoolhouse, so she knew a number of boys. I begged her to tell me about them so often and in such detail that it came to feel as if I knew them.

She tired of my questions about her twin, Nicolaas. He was one of the few boys in the camp who was my age. I expected he was old enough to be with the men on commando, but he had not been well, she explained, not strong, and her mother would not permit it. I saw no shortcomings in him and was happy he was here, even though he paid me no attention.

"No . . . no . . . he would never be interested in you," Janetta said. "You would remind him too much of me and that would feel strange."

"Strange?"

"We're so close," she said. "We know what the other is thinking."

There were so few boys in camp that we found ourselves debating the attractiveness of the old men, the ones who had been unable to go with the other men and were brought in with the women and children. Most of them scared me; they were so thin, with hollow cheeks and long beards that hung in gray strands or were bunched up like storm clouds. They spoke almost completely in scripture, as if in final preparation for meeting God.

I grew heartsore when I thought how it must feel to be a man unable to fight. It was a reality they had not had to face until the war started. At some moment during their dignified aging they must have recognized they could no longer ride for long periods, or even mount their horse, or sleep on the ground. How it must have wounded them one day to realize they would be left behind with the women.

I thought them lucky to be safe from bullets, at least. But as a woman, I did not understand old men any better than I understood young men or boys. What happened to them, I asked Janetta, when all that they had was taken?

"They are once again young boys, but bent and gray, and a lot less happy."

7

December 1899, Venter Farm

Once the men left, the farm duties were redistributed among the rest of us. But whenever time permitted, Moeder urged Willem and me to go to Tante Hannah's house for schooling. Willem spread his feet and refused.

"What if the British came when I was there? What would Pa say?"

I sensed she was about to retrieve Oupa's *sjambok* to adjust his posture. "Ma . . . please . . . if he doesn't want to be there to learn, he'll just be a distraction."

She stared at me, then at Willem.

"Fine, Aletta, then you'll be responsible for passing along everything to Willem afterward."

"I'd rather chew rocks."

"What did you say?"

"Delighted."

Willem thanked me as I left. "You are without hope, anyway," I told him.

I was not keen on the idea, either, as I wanted to do more things at home with Moeder. Mostly, I wanted to learn to cook. But since the men had left, suppers had become quick gatherings for simple foods: little preparation, no variety, and quiet eating before cleaning up for nightly Bible readings and psalms. I decided that after I learned to cook, I would like to start lessons on the organ so that I could play the way my mother did. But work allowed none of that now.

Willem was saddled and "patrolling" a radius at dawn the morning after the men left. The third time that he charged the house in alarm, certain that British forces were bearing down on us, Moeder forced him to get down and help with the daily chores. The family could not afford a full-time sentry, she said. It was hard to remember that only a few months earlier he had been a little boy who spent his days shaping toy animals from mud.

Before the men left, Moeder schooled us in the late afternoons as Bina started meal preparations. She stressed the importance of our mastering English, with bits of time spent on history and general knowledge. And after supper, Oupa Gideon would conduct Bible studies and quiz us on the smallest things, things we couldn't possibly remember.

I feared Tante Hannah would try to force embroidery on me as she had when I was younger, which I viewed as torture in small stitches. But when I arrived, she had turned her kitchen into a classroom. She made her mother, Ouma Wilhelmina, sit in the parlor or on the porch during our classes, where she smoked her pipe and grumbled to herself. The table was filled with books, and I discovered I could not keep my hands off them. Some had shiny covers with pictures from around the world. I most favored the ones that were weathered, as I imagined how many people had read them before me. I sensed their presence in the smell of the dusty pages.

"We can travel through these books," Tante Hannah said. "I've never been out of the Free State, but I feel like I've seen the world." She opened a book to a picture of Cape Town. "Can you believe how beautiful this is? I have a sister there."

The first day, we "visited" cathedrals in Europe, palaces of India, the beaches of the South Pacific, and the mountains of the American West. When I saw pictures of oceans and sailing ships, I wished Oupa Gideon were home so that I could borrow the book to show him. Instead I wrote descriptions so that I could tell him about the "whitecaps" that rose like menacing teeth from the stormy sea. It would feel as if I were teaching him something for a change.

When my mother instructed us, it was by strict schedule, half an hour of one thing and then half an hour of another, in cycles measured precisely by the mantel clock. With Tante Hannah, one topic led to another, guided by my curiosity.

When I asked Moeder questions about the war, she most often told me to ask Vader and Schalk when they came home. I think she was afraid I would worry too much about them if we talked about it. Better not to think of the possibilities. But Tante Hannah brought newspapers from town, and we read reports from them, even some that contained bits of coverage from British papers. The news was spotty and delayed, but it still made the war seem more real.

"Some are afraid of the news," she said. "I think we should study every bit of it we can get. History is happening in our country. . . . The world is watching our two little republics taking on the mighty British Empire."

"Nobody can say 'British Empire' without the word 'mighty' attached," I said. She brought out a map and showed the span of British influence across the world. "Mighty" seemed an inadequate description.

"The British reporters label us, too, always calling our men the 'wily' Boers," she said.

She read details of early battles as well as editorials. She showed me one English paper that contained rude cartoons portraying the Boers as simpletons led by a froggish President Kruger.

"Do you think they really know much about us?" she asked. "No, so they believe what they're told. So then, ask yourself: How much do we really know about them?"

I had not thought of their view, nor of the British being anything but an army of mindless bullies marching for their frumpy queen. A local paper criticized the British greed for our gold and diamonds. I almost laughed when I heard of "our" gold and diamonds. No one I knew had gold or diamonds.

"The mines are mostly owned by international bankers already," Tante Hannah said. "Many of them are British."

I was confused. Then why the war?

"Because that's what empires do."

News reports explained that the British had "the greatest fighting force on earth" and would overpower us with sheer numbers. But we surprised them with tactics and determination.

We read that the British could sometimes see across great distances by sending men into the skies attached to balloons that rose because they were filled with hot air. One paper had a picture of two men in a wicker basket suspended from a balloon so high it had to feel as if they were flying. Tante Hannah then spent fifteen minutes teaching the "laws of physics" that caused warm air to rise and allowed such a miraculous thing to work. How could we win a war against an enemy that could fly?

Bold headlines read, BLACK WEEK FOR BRITISH: BOERS WIN SUCCESSIVE BATTLES, AND ENTRENCHED BOERS REPEL ADVANCEMENT.

One dispatch from a British reporter praised the commandos: "The individual Boer mounted, in a suitable country, is worth four or five regular soldiers. The only way of treating them is to get men equal in character and intelligence as riflemen, or failing the individual, huge masses of troops."

When we read of our men being taken prisoner and sent to Ceylon or Saint Helena, Tante Hannah pulled out maps to locate those places. The mention of Saint Helena led to research on the island and a discussion of Emperor Napoleon and his exile there. He was undone by his power hunger and arrogance. Did that sound like the British now? she asked. "Shouldn't they have learned from that, and shouldn't we now learn from this so there are no more wars like this a hundred years from now when it's almost the year 2000?"

Even the news accounts of our victories were disturbing. She showed me a clipping in which a British reporter described the Tommy lines after the battle: "Corpses lay here and there, many of the wounds were of a horrible nature. The splinters and fragments of the shells had torn and mutilated them. The shallow trenches were choked with dead and wounded."

I could not believe they would put such things in newspapers. Still, the words came only one at a time, and the reader could absorb them in bits. But this story was illustrated with a photograph, and it rose up and struck me like a mule kick. Men lay like jackstraws in awkward positions in the bottom of a trench, many dozens of them. It showed their faces, their arms and legs twisted like broken dolls.

"I know it's upsetting," she said. "But this is what is happening. People need to know this. No war in history has had such news coverage. Think how much better informed the public is about what is actually going on in battle. We can see the horrors of it. . . . It's not just numbers of dead anymore. . . . It's the actual faces of the dead."

8

January 1901, Concentration Camp

J anetta and I often held hands when we walked; the same size, the same clothes and *kappies* . . . we must have looked like the dolls cut from folded paper that I used to make for my little sister, Cecelia.

"Sisters taking a stroll?"

A Tommy guard leaned against a post in front of us, watching people pass, nodding and offering comments as they did, most drawing no response or chilled looks. It was the shorter guard from the skirmish between the ladies at the fence. The one who'd tried to talk to me.

"Friends," Janetta said.

I had ignored guards for the several months we'd been in camp, turning at the sight of them or grunting at their existence, resentment my only weapon.

"Do you have names?"

"Janetta," she said. "And this is Aletta." I stepped back, ready to leave. I would not be seen talking to one of the guards. When she tried to pull me forward, I wrestled against her.

He was not much taller than either of us. He pushed back the brim of his helmet. He was freckled and pink, unequipped for our sun, and probably not much older than Schalk. He was literally a *rooinek*, as Moeder called them . . . their red necks burned by our relentless sun. The uniform and rifle seemed just a costume.

"Did you know each other before camp?"

"We met here. We're the same age." Janetta backed up a step to stand beside me, in the same posture, to emphasize our similarities.

"It must be nice to have a friend here."

"I have a twin brother . . . but he's a boy . . . of course."

Dear God, our Heavenly Host, what is she doing?

"My brother was born just before midnight on a Friday night, and I was born only minutes later, but on Saturday. So we're twins with different birthdays."

I had not known that, and as I stored that unique fact, the guard turned to me.

"Well . . . how about you? When's your birthday?"

I would not waste a single word on him, but then I thought of Bina's telling me how words can be stones. I would practice; I would see whether I could wound him with words.

"None of your business."

"No," he laughed. "Fine, I'll cancel the celebration. What family do you have here?"

"That's not your business, either," I said.

"I understand. . . . Your mother would not like you talking to a guard . . ."

"It has nothing to do with *her* not liking it. I don't like it. . . . I don't like you. . . . I don't like this camp. . . . I don't like the British. And you can stand me in front of a firing squad, but I won't tell you my birthday."

He stepped back and put his hands up, laughing as he pretended to surrender.

"And you don't like being friendly, either?"

I pointed to the rifle slung over his shoulder. I raised arms to both sides and gestured to the enclosure. How dense can the British be?

"*Dolt.*" I projected the word as much like a stone as I could. "Noun, meaning a dull or stupid fellow."

He looked at the rifle as if he had forgotten it was there. "Oh, they make me carry it . . . for appearances."

"The last Tommy I talked to put a rifle in my face and threatened to kill me. . . . He killed our animals and burned our house . . . burned my things . . ."

"I'm sorry," he said. "I *am* sorry."

His apology disrupted the series of comments I was readying.

"What's your name?" Janetta asked. I could not believe her, but since she knew more about boys, I assumed she was positioning him for an insult or had devised a way to use him to our benefit.

"Thomas," he said. "But they call me Tommy."

Janetta laughed. I stared her down.

"The humor?" he asked.

"We call all the British soldiers Tommy . . . or Khakis," Janetta said.

I tugged at her hand, pulling her halfway around.

"Yes . . . the mythical Tommy Atkins . . . but I'm the real Tommy Maples."

"Maples?"

"Yes . . . like the tree."

There was no excuse for this. I pulled hard enough to get Janetta turned.

She struggled against me but relented rather than let me create a scene. She punished me with a lecture as we walked away.

"We should have asked how old he is," she said. "Not much older than us, I don't think. He's just a boy, really. A man . . . but a boy. I like his eyes. What color would you say those are? Green? Green blue?"

"Janetta, I didn't notice his eyes. . . . I saw his red hair," I said. "Is there anything worse? He's so . . . pink . . . pale."

"His hair looks good with his skin," she said.

"What is wrong with you? He is just another of the devils who burned our houses."

"It wasn't him doing the burning," she said. "He's in here, too, just guarding fences."

"How do you know?"

"I looked at the men who burned our house. . . . I don't recognize him."

"The devils all look alike."

"I don't think he's the devil at all."

"He's hideous. . . . He's spotted and his teeth are . . . askew."

"Askew?"

"*Ja* . . ."

"You mean, what . . . crooked?"

"*Ja, askew*, one of my new words."

"Lettie . . . think about it. . . . You saw his teeth because he smiled at us," she said. "How many other men are smiling at us in here?"

9

===

October 1899, Venter Farm

As she had since discovering I could not say the word she used for a greeting, Bina always said "peace" when she saw me approach. I liked it. This morning, she had finished collecting the oxhide *riempies* that Vader had hung over a tree branch to stretch into flexible strands to be woven into banding for chairs and furniture.

"Can I help?" I asked.

"I'm done; maize next."

I knew others thought me a pest with my questions, but Bina said she didn't mind because I was the only one who asked her things. She would sometimes use just a few wise words to respond to a story I might have taken many minutes to tell. I often wrote down the sayings she shared.

She told me once that a person's face tells everything about them, and I had an "open" face. Another time she said that my wide eyes and long lashes reminded her of an ostrich. She held the back of her hands to her eyes and waved her fingers like long-lashed blinks. I liked it best when she said that I was as smart as a grown-up "but still made of soft clay."

The one thing she did better than anyone else was this: listen. When I spoke, she looked in my eyes and listened until I was finished. I thanked her for it once, and she said it was a sign of respect, one I always should show others.

"We are who we are through others," she said, and then she repeated it while looking straight into my eyes.

I wrote that down later, and I thought at the time that Oupa Gideon would have objected, as he always said we were created and driven by God's will. Other people have nothing to do with who we are, and even we can't change God's will for us. The path he has charted is already writ, Oupa said.

I came to believe that the things Bina said were closer to whatever might be the real truth than most grown-ups told me. I asked her about her parents. They had been apprentices for farmers, but she did not explain.

I asked about her daughter, Tombi, and Bina told me that she was a happy girl and smart. Tall. A woman now, and gone to live with her husband, taking with her a piece of Bina's heart. When Tombi was born, she said, the men in the village poured water over Tuma as a lesson that a daughter must learn to change shapes, like water. I asked what they do if the baby is a boy. "They beat the father with sticks, as a reminder that boys are of war."

Bina hoisted the basket of maize to the top of her head to carry it to the chairs beneath the blue gum tree at the side of the house.

Sometimes when she sang, it sounded like shouting; other times, it was a soft chant. It was almost always repetitive, and in rhythm with the physical motion of her chore.

"My name means 'to sing,'" she told me. "When I'm happy, I sing. When I work, I sing. When I cook, I sing. My mother said I sang when she carried me at her back."

I tried mimicking the words. It made no sense and it made her laugh, but the sound was nice. I was probably saying something stupid in her language, but that was fine with her, as nothing seemed so serious when we sang. "Did you look up into the branches before you sat down here?" Bina asked.

"Yes . . . every time."

"You were too young to remember."

"Only the stories. How long was the snake?"

Bina held her hands at least four feet apart.

"Really?"

"Maybe bigger . . . green and black . . . nearly fell on top of you when you were crawling . . . a boomslang . . . would have killed you with one strike . . . and you were laughing like you had a new plaything."

"And you saved me?"

"I was there with the big knife, snatched it by the tail . . . cut its head off."

"I'm sorry you had to kill it."

"I'm glad it didn't kill you."

She sang another song. It rose and fell like gentle waves and was soothing.

"What's the song about?"

"About a boy who kills a lion to become a man and marry the chief's daughter."

"Did Tuma kill a lion to get you to marry him?"

"Gave my father ten goats," she said.

"Ten?"

"If you don't pay for something," she said, "you don't know its value."

I would write that down.

"He wanted you more than anything?"

"He was young."

Bina stopped her song and looked into my eyes so deeply that it felt as if she entered my mind.

"Your time is coming," she said. "We celebrate it . . . not hide it."

As with many of her comments, I didn't understand but nodded and smiled as if I did.

"I don't think my father had to pay for my mother . . . not goats or anything. . . . He said God brought her to him."

Bina started to sing again.

"They don't say much in front of us . . . but they don't get cross, not like Oom Sarel and Tante Hannah."

She pulled more maize from the basket.

"Do you think Oom Sarel gave goats for Tante Hannah?"

She shrugged.

"They almost never talk to each other."

"Words can be stones."

I tried to picture Tante and Oom throwing rock-hard words at each other, and each ducking as they neared.

"Tante Hannah is nice to me, but I don't think she likes Moeder."

Bina resumed her song.

"Do you think she does?"

Bina sang for another moment and then answered the question with one of her sayings.

"Some women—your mother—can make it rain."

I imagined that her next line would have been that Tante Hannah was dry, but it went unsaid.

"I made a doll . . . for under her pillow . . . woman's *muti* . . . to help with babies," Bina said. "Oom Sarel threw it in the fire."

"Oom Sarel threw away a doll you made?" He had better never throw away my doll, I thought.

"Do you fight with Tuma?" I asked.

"No."

"Never?"

"A little, before Tombi."

"What made you stop . . . do you remember?"

"His mother."

Cicadas hummed so hard it added to the heat of the day, and sweat seeped into my skirts. I waited for more explanation from her. I checked the tree limbs above me again. Sometimes she gave in when I waited.

"Threatened us with the marriage tree. . . . Stops fights."

I loved her stories of these strange practices. I passed them on to no one else but always remembered them.

"How?"

"They tie you under a kind of tree with special fruit."

"How long?"

"Until you're done fighting."

"No food or water?"

"Just fruit, if it falls," Bina said. "Baboons love the fruit. . . . It sours in the sun. . . . They eat it and get drunk. Elephants, too."

"And they leave you tied to the tree? With drunken baboons? Drunken elephants."

"Hmm. They say."

"What if a lion comes to chase the baboons? Or scorpions crawl on you?"

"Yes . . . yes . . . better not to go there. My mother told me . . . be like the river," Bina said, dragging a hand slowly in front of her to show gentle waves.

I looked up in the tree again.

"You were brave. . . . You saved me," I said.

"You won't forget."

"No . . . never."

"Do you know why you'll remember?"

I was alert for pending wisdom.

"Deeds live," she said.

I turned those two words over to look at all sides of them. They applied whether the deed was good or bad; people were affected by it, and they didn't forget. It helped me understand the saying about how we are the person that others see. I was all at once Mother's helper, Father's little girl, Schalk's little sister, Oupa's star-watching friend. I was a bright light to Cee-Cee but a bother to Willem. And at least as far as Bina saw it, the things I did would be remembered. I know her deeds lived with me. So did her words.

10

February 1901, Concentration Camp

In an otherwise ordinary conversation, Janetta voiced a thunder-clap sentence: "The first boy I kissed smelled of the cold meat he'd eaten for lunch."

I should have acted as if such a comment were common and natural, so I wouldn't seem such a backcountry cousin, but she could not have shocked me more if she'd said she had tea with the queen of England. Before I completely turned into stone, I must have made some kind of sound that caused her to look at me as if I were a sad little girl.

Janetta was more than a friend: she was my mirror. Our images matched, but we were reversed in many ways. She had been exposed to towns and people and . . . life. I grew up in the middle of an ocean of scrubby grass. I'm sure she saw the innocence in my eyes and heard it in my stories.

"What kind of meat?" I asked. I was so uncomfortable even saying the word "kiss" that I asked about the meat. Who was the dolt, now?

"I don't know," she said. "I couldn't actually taste it. The kiss was just on his cheek."

When I could shape words again, I began the interrogation.

"Who was it?"

"Koos du Toit."

"What did he look like?"

"Like a frightened boy."

"Why did you pick him?"

"I wanted to try it and he was there."

"Did you like him, at least?"

"Maybe . . . not really."

"How did you make your lips go?"

"You've never kissed a boy?"

"No . . . almost," I lied. "How do you make your lips go?"

"Like you're about to whistle."

I whistled.

"Like you're *about* to whistle . . . not actually whistling."

I tried it again and couldn't do it without going ahead and whistling. Fool. I would need to practice.

"What did he do?"

"He was just standing there."

"Then after . . . what did he do after?"

"He ran away."

"Really . . . he ran?"

"Like his hair was afire."

I felt embarrassed for her.

"What about your eyes?"

"Closed . . . you're supposed to do that."

I thought that was terrible advice. . . . You might miss . . . or go too slowly or too fast. Wouldn't seeing it be part of the experience?

"Like this . . ." She leaned toward me, eyes closed. Her breath touched me first, and her lips settled lightly on the apple of my cheek.

"Now you," she said.

I stared at her cheek, estimating the range before closing my eyes and easing in. I felt softness and warmth, and tiny pale hairs against my lips.

"That's right," she said. "But soft, and keep your eyes closed."

I leaned in again, softer.

"Like that," she said. "Good."

"Jan . . ." I stopped.

"What . . . say it."

"I am just surprised."

"That I've kissed a boy?"

I nodded.

"Aletta, there are girls from my town who get married at fifteen or sixteen. . . . That's not unusual at all," she said. She was right. I hadn't thought of it that way. "And we'll both be fourteen soon."

We went back to her tent because it was less crowded and her mother and brother were often out. At the time, they had no other family sharing their tent.

"Praise God we're in this camp," she said.

I had never heard that comment before. "What?"

"It is much better than the one we were in before," she said. "I've seen problems here, but not cruelty. I haven't seen that here. Not yet. Not like the other place."

"You're serious?"

"Yes. The first one was in a bog, never dried out, so there was malaria and typhus," she said. "The pumps didn't work, so water had to be brought in by wagons, so there was never enough to drink . . . so forget laundry or washing."

"What did everyone do?"

"Got angry . . . a lot of them," she said. "Women would fight . . . pull hair . . ."

"Against Joiner women?"

"Our women, against each other," she said. "It was horrible . . . bloody fights. Lettie, some would steal your rations. . . . Some would report others to guards to try to gain favor."

I shook my head, disgusted but doubting.

"Worse . . . our commandant beat my mother."

Another shock. "Beat her . . . physically?"

"*Ja*, we were allowed outside the camp to collect sticks we might burn. We'd spent the whole afternoon, and when we got back, the commandant struck Moeder with his *sjambok* and took the sticks from us for his own fire."

"Struck your mother?"

"*Ja*, and then joked that he'd have to pay for it on Judgment Day," she said. "He joked about it, but I hope he does pay for it, in hell. There won't be a shortage of fuel for him there."

I had not heard of such a thing in our camp, although I did not discount it.

"How could they get away with that?" I asked.

Janetta laughed at me. "How old are you?" she asked. I was embarrassed by the tone of her question and felt as if I were shrinking in her eyes. She knew how old I was.

"How did you get sent here?" I asked.

"Ma had a few gold sovereigns sewn into the hem of her skirt," Janetta said. "She found somebody who could get us out of there and she bribed him."

"How lucky she had that."

"Smart, not lucky. Here's what Moeder says: You can only count on what you have and what you carry."

"All I brought was my book and some clothes."

"Not just what you can actually carry in your arms, but what you have, your brains, your backbone."

I was frightened and so confused I could not stand still. I needed to go back to our tent.

"I forgot to tell you," she said. "I talked to the guard—Tommy Maples—he asked about you."

She had seen him when I wasn't around? Had she gone without me on purpose? What could they have talked about?

"Lettie . . . did you hear me? I saw the guard and he asked about you, told me to tell you hello."

"I don't care," I said.

"Oh, really?"

"Fine, what did he say?"

"I told you . . . he said to tell you hello."

"That's all he had to say?"

"Thought you didn't care . . ."

I WAS OF TWO minds when Mother first asked that I take over as "teacher" to Willem and Cee-Cee.

"Teach Willem?"

"Yes."

"Could I scrub the latrines instead?"

"Aletta Marie Venter."

"I will try." I sincerely did. I stayed patient and calm. I knew that none of us needed more stress in the tent. But Willem was impossible. My choices were to find a solution or strangle him lifeless. The solution came from my notebook, where I'd reread Bina's wisdom about living through others. I decided that the problem with Willem was my shortcomings as a teacher rather than his as a pupil. This was a matter of communication: I had to speak a language he understood.

He would stare me down as if in front of a firing squad if I gave him mathematics problems, but he would lean close and focus if I framed the question properly: "If the British had fifteen pieces of artillery and the commandos capture five, what percentage remains from the original amount?"

"Oh, God, don't talk about the war," Mevrou Huiseveldt interrupted. "Don't bring that war into this tent."

"Think hard, Willem, this could be important if you're called up to fight," I said, ignoring the woman and noticing that Klaas had suddenly drawn close and become attentive. Men are so easily manipulated.

Cecelia was a dream to teach, as she had been in every other way. I spent our time with letters and songs, and she took it all in so quickly that I believed she might catch up to Willem. And I still made up stories for her at night, which gave me a closeness I felt nowhere else. One night I told her a story about a little girl who looked like a lamb; Cee-Cee wanted to hear it again and again. I began adding chapters to it—the adventures of a little girl living on an imaginary farm. As the story went, the little girl had a beautiful big sister who always came to her rescue whenever her life became troublesome.

"That's you," Cecelia would say when I mentioned the big sister.

At times, the big sister would take the little girl sailing on trips to the great cities around the world. If Cee-Cee asked questions about the war, I left her open to imagine that a heroic big sister would arrive at the moment of greatest danger and save them all. I fashioned a false but powerful image of myself, discovering the beauty of fiction.

11

December 1899, Sarel Venter Farm

I declare an armistice from war," Tante Hannah announced as I arrived at her farmhouse for another afternoon of study. I was reasonably certain she did not have the power to cause the war to halt, even temporarily.

"No talk of war today."

The usual array of sweet treats was on the table. I no longer needed them as incentive to visit, but I did not think she had to be told. My mother had not baked much since the men had left, and I missed the smell of it in the house. Beside the cakes was a package in bright wrapping paper.

"This is for you."

I tore into it to find two notebooks and a book.

"You need to read more," she said. "And to start keeping a journal."

I scanned the cover: *The Story of an African Farm.*

"An African farm?"

"On the Great Karoo," she said. "Written by a woman named Schreiner."

A woman wrote this book? From the Great Karoo? I thought the Karoo was the most desolate place in the world, in the *gramadoelas*, as Oupa Gideon used to say—near to nothing, far from everything. There was nothing there but prickly pear cactus and empty horizons.

"What kind of a story does somebody tell about living on the Karoo?"

"Read it and see."

"Have you read it?"

"Yes."

"What did you think?"

"I don't want to say. I want you to form your own opinion."

"Is it like . . . real?"

"It's about people, fictional people, but real in their way."

"A woman wrote this?"

"Yes, Aletta, a woman . . . a woman from South Africa who may have been a lot like you at your age. I thought you'd enjoy it, and it might give you ideas."

I turned the book over, front to back, and then opened to the first page. "Ideas for what?"

"Writing."

"Me?"

"I've heard stories you tell Cee-Cee, and they're wonderful. And I've never known anyone more curious. That's a start. Write about your life."

All I knew about was my family and our life on our farm. My story had characters but didn't seem to have a plot.

"I don't see how I could make a story."

Tante Hannah's mother, Ouma Wilhelmina, came into the kitchen, and Tante Hannah quieted.

"Let's walk," Tante said, leading me to the path in front of the house.

"If nothing else, you should keep a journal . . . the things that you see and do. . . . Memories change too much otherwise."

I kicked an egg-shaped rock off the path with the tip of my shoe.

"I wouldn't know where to start."

"Like your stories for Cecelia, you let your imagination take over. I know you have great imagination."

And she had no idea the things that came to my mind when I dreamed. "Tell me how."

"I don't have your imagination, but you can start anywhere." She pointed at the rock I had kicked.

"Do what you naturally do. . . . Ask questions. How did that rock get here? Whose hands have touched that rock? Maybe a man centuries ago stalked an animal to this spot. He picked up that rock."

I saw the man, frightened, wearing just a cloth.

"What was going through his mind in that moment, the most dangerous moment of his life, not knowing if he would kill the animal or the animal would kill him?"

"What happened?" I wanted to know: Did he live or die? I was already interested in his fate.

"You decide."

"I decide?"

"Yes, you."

"That seems like . . . power." I had no other power that I could think of. I suddenly embraced the idea.

"Yes, you control it all."

"Would anybody care?"

"Maybe. Think about the man this way: Is what he's feeling so different from someone poor and hungry in a city somewhere today? Or, in that moment, what he feels might be what a soldier feels before battle. In his case, hunger made him braver than he ever thought possible. It drove him to take chances."

"Or maybe the animal ate him," I challenged. I started thinking of all the directions his story might go, feeling the power of creation.

"The story is up to you, and even if the story is about something else, it's really about you. Look inside and then tell people what you see."

"I don't know what's in there."

"Keeping a journal will help you find out."

Being a writer seemed a more practical goal than becoming a ship captain. I devoured the book Tante Hannah had given me. The characters were young people in my country, and the author opened up their minds for me to look inside. The characters were all so serious, though, and some questioned God's dominion. But it fascinated me, and I began thinking of people as characters, and I worked to observe them and capture their traits.

I thought of my mother. In the house, she was so presentable and prepared for the day, with hair and clothing in proper order. She was a different woman in the fields after the men left, covered in dust and chaff, sweating like a native. It made her real nature only more visible. "Unbowed," I wrote of her. Father was easy: "Indestructible."

I thought of Tante Hannah and her too-eager embraces offset by her kind teaching. I could not write anything too warm because my mother might someday see my journal, and I could write nothing cruel because Tante Hannah might someday see my writings.

Of Hannah's mother, Ouma Wilhelmina, I wrote "filled with emptiness." The words seemed an illogical pairing, yet perfect for her. I imagined tapping her on the shoulder and hearing an angry echo as from a hollow gourd.

I tended to write more about Bina than about anyone else. She was unique in my life. I did not understand all she said, but I wrote down her sayings to study later. I wondered whether anyone had ever written a story about a native woman, because I did not think that Bina could write one for herself. I thought that someday I might invite her to tell me about her life and all the truths she hadn't shared.

Before filling half of the first notebook, I turned the pages back. So much had changed that the early words already seemed like someone else's life. But the writing helped me gather my thoughts. Writing was like prying a cactus sticker from beneath my skin. Sometimes the process was painful, but it felt better once it came out, and only then could the healing start.

12

March 1901, Concentration Camp

Janetta's twin, Nicolaas, was fevered with a rash. Measles, surely. Moeder insisted I tell them to put a bottle of hot water on his chest and another on his back directly between the shoulder blades. But they would not allow entry, so I relayed the message to Janetta through the tent flap. I fretted for her health and then for her brother's. And after a moment's thought, I worried for mine as well. I'd been very close to her recently, touched her, taken in her breath. And now she was swallowed up by her tent.

Two days earlier, Nicolaas had acknowledged my existence for the first time, saying hello when I came to gather Janetta. This, I thought, was the start of something. I spent the next day going through possibilities that included Janetta's being family. But that might have to wait now. It seemed absurd that, as far as I knew, my brother at war was still healthy, while hers, in this camp, was ill abed.

I had to fill my time without her. Looking to free more pages of rules that had been tacked on posts around camp, I found a message for a hymn meeting for young people to be held in the large tent. Moeder denied permission after having heard the word "measles." I pointed out that if I had been infected by Janetta, I would have had the rash by now.

"But a gathering of many children . . . in the same tent?"

"Singing hymns, Ma, singing his praises. I'll pray for us all. What better use of time?"

She called as I stepped from the tent. I peeked back in. "Do you think they have an organ?" She moved her fingers as if playing an invisible keyboard. I hadn't thought how much she must miss playing, having done so almost every night at home.

I was early but was soon joined by many dozens of others who entered behind me. They were so thin and dirty. Who were they all? They looked like shrunken adults, with worn faces, appearing twice their actual age. And were there no boys at all?

"*Welkom*, boys and girls," the *dominee* said. I hated being considered a little girl. "So nice to see you here. This will be an evening of rejoicing and song."

"Rejoicing" was not a word I had heard in camp.

As if he had read my mind, he said: "Yes, rejoicing. . . . Your families may be sundered by war, but your men are protected by the hand of God, and we have all been given this day through his Holy Providence."

I looked across the tent. There were no guards, so it seemed safe for the preacher to talk about our men being guided by God, a comment that probably violated some rule. The *dominee* started a tune on his autoharp and encouraged us to clap. We failed to catch the rhythm at first.

"Psalm one forty-six," the *dominee* said. When he started singing, I found I had to clear my throat and focus on the process. I always sang so poorly that it drew nasty comments. So I sang only to amuse Cee-Cee and most often at home in the barn, and those were children's songs about chicks and pigs and the like. It took several scratchy lines to find the rhythm, but then I felt a joy of stretching muscles that had gone unused. I decided I would sing in the tent. It would remind me of better times, and, of course, it would annoy Mevrou Huiseveldt. So rarely is an activity rewarding in two important ways.

After the psalm, the *dominee* repeated lines he wanted to stress.

"Recite after me," he said. "He upholds the cause of the oppressed and gives food to the hungry . . ."

Gives food to the hungry?

"The Lord sets prisoners free, gives sight to the blind . . ."

Sets prisoners free?

"The Lord lifts up those who are bowed down, and loves the righteous . . ."

The words made me worry again about those stubborn thoughts that were less than righteous. Was this psalm written specifically for me?

"You praise God with your voices," the *dominee* said. "And know that he hears you. He hears and sees everything. And we are here by his will. Know that, if you are tempted to doubt."

I doubted. I doubted every day. I was doubting at the very moment the *dominee* told us not to doubt. God had sent his warning to me through the preacher. Moeder never doubted. Oupa Gideon never doubted. It must get easier with age, I thought, although surely it must be more difficult.

The *dominee* plucked a few notes on his autoharp again and then put it aside to tell the story of Zacchaeus, the crooked tax collector. Zacchaeus had been judged evil, but Jesus could see through the faults to the good that was inside the man. I worried that if Jesus could see the good inside Zacchaëus, he could see the doubts and sinful thoughts I sheltered. When Jesus visited, Zacchaeus changed his ways and became righteous. I could be righteous again. *Save from wrath and make me pure.*

I looked at the faces around me. I spotted a boy. I smoothed my hair and a few strands fell out. When I looked harder, I realized the boy was only Willem's age, but tall enough to fool me at first. Too young, but he had caught my attention. Was shedding hair my punishment for having had sinful thoughts in the house of the Lord? Wait, does this qualify as a house of the Lord? A tent? Be righteous again, I told myself. And be rewarded.

The *dominee* finished by reading Psalm 27. I studied his face. He was old, but not terribly old, I thought, and he had a deep, pleasant voice. He was not one of those who spit damnation with each breath. He may have realized we were dealing with enough fearful moments.

"Take these words with you tonight," he said. He spoke this psalm slowly with no music or singing.

"When evildoers assail me to eat up my flesh . . . it is they who stumble and fall. . . . Though an army encamp against me, my heart shall not fear . . . though war arise against me, yet I will be confident."

I tried to memorize the words he'd chosen, as they were perfect for us. But they did not take root, and I began to think I was not as sharp as when Tante Hannah was schooling me at home, when every fact found a welcoming home in my mind.

"The Lord will hide me in his shelter in the day of trouble; he will conceal me under the cover of his tent . . ."

The *dominee* swept his right hand above him with the mention of a tent. God will conceal us . . . but I knew the tent would not conceal my thoughts from him.

The preacher picked up his autoharp and played a livelier tune. We clapped louder. Those who had been silent when they entered left the tent humming or singing or chatting. I talked to a few girls on the way back to our tent. . . . Maybe I could meet with them at the next gathering. I wanted to tell Janetta all about it, to share it with her, but their tent was silent when I walked past.

SOMEONE SQUEEZED A SAD requiem from a concertina in a nearby tent that night. I felt the slow rhythm of music, and it invited restfulness. When the tune ended, the player added a dozen or so quick-tempo notes that caused me to look at my mother. Her eyes closed, her head swayed.

"What is that, Ma?"

"Shhhh."

She looked at me only when it stopped.

"That's for a *tickey-draai* . . . a dance . . . the music that played when I met your father."

What? Wait. What? Moeder. Dance? Young girl? Dance with Father? A flutter of unconsidered images flashed in my mind. Her existence did not start when we were born? She had a life before she was a mother? How could it be possible that she had been a girl at one time?

"Tell us about it, you've never said anything . . . please."

She looked at Mevrou Huiseveldt, who could be expected to protest. A story like this might make her head *actually* explode.

"Please, Ma, I've never heard."

"Not now . . . not here."

I was not about to allow the dour looks from Mevrou Huiseveldt to deny me this story. The only thing Moeder ever shared with me of her youth related to her mother's brush set and how she used it. But never anything about dances and certainly not her meeting Vader. How many other things had she been hiding about her life?

"Ma . . . what else do I . . . do we . . . have? We've never heard this."

"Not now."

I threatened: "I'll start singing."

She sat straight and smoothed her skirts. Willem pulled up his little *riempie* stool to join us.

"I was seventeen," she said, shaking her head, understanding that we could not picture such a thing. "The dance was in town, and I'd practiced the steps with my sisters."

I stared at her face, mentally erasing the toll of time, to see a fresh-faced young lady.

"I was waiting for Piet van Niekirk to show up, but your father's brother came up and took my hand to dance."

"Oom?" Willem shouted. "You danced with . . . ?"

She would not allow the use of Oom Sarel's name. I could not picture him asking Moeder to dance, much less her agreeing to it. Willem and I looked at each other at this family revelation.

"Once," she said. "Just once. . . . Shush if you want me to tell you."

"Wait . . . wait . . .," I insisted.

"Aletta . . ."

"Moeder . . . you danced with Oom Sarel?"

"Piet did not arrive . . . and . . . your father's brother asked. He was about my age. . . . I had practiced the dances. . . . I wanted to dance."

"Just once?"

"Once . . . yes," she said.

"Was there something wrong?" I asked.

"That was enough. I turned away and went back with friends."

"And then you saw Vader and wanted to dance with him," Willem said. Cee-Cee and Klaas and Rachel quieted and turned to follow her story as well. The adults never conducted story times.

"No, I didn't even know of your father. . . . He was a little older. . . . I had never spoken with him. I don't know that I'd ever seen him. This was probably the first time."

"So he asked you to dance?"

"Not until I was about to go home," she said. "I was walking toward the door. He came to me just as the music was starting. I wanted to dance a *tickey-draai* and he was standing there with his hand out. I took it and we began spinning. That's what a *tickey-draai* is, turning in tight circles, as if around a threepenny piece."

She held her finger and thumb apart the breadth of the tiny coin.

"Teach me, Ma, I want to learn," I said.

"No . . . let me finish."

"Vader danced?" Willem asked.

"You don't really have to be a very good dancer with a *tickey-draai,*" she said.

"But he was handsome?" I asked.

"Mmm . . . not to make you stop to look."

"So?"

"We danced that one and the next one, and he never said a word. Very shy. He just kept looking away . . . or at my neck."

She touched the empty collar of her dress.

"Your neck?"

"My *ouma*'s cameo brooch," she said. "She let me wear it that night for the first time."

"Do you still have it, Moeder?" I asked. "Please tell me you brought it from home."

"It's safe in my bag," she said. "Maybe it will be yours someday."

Willem punched my shoulder, but it didn't bother me, as I was stunned to hear that I would someday wear that brooch. It was beautiful and I wanted it immediately.

"You should wear it," I said.

"Not here . . . no." She squinted me quiet. It wasn't fair to Willem.

"What happened . . . with Pa . . . he didn't talk at all?" Willem asked.

"Well, not much. . . . I talked a little bit to him, but he mostly just kept staring at the brooch. So I asked him if he liked it."

"And?"

"He smiled."

"That's all?" I was sad that Vader had not done better. "He didn't say anything?"

"He did . . . but not much."

"What?"

She turned to the attentive Mevrou Huiseveldt and then leaned toward us so that she might not hear.

"He said: 'It would be better if they had carved your face on it.'"

"That's all he said?" I asked.

She nodded. "It was enough."

BARELY AFTER SUNRISE, TWO Tommy guards shoved back the tent flap, a gust of wind dramatically blowing as a small officer in a tailored tunic walked inside.

"Go through their things," he said, pointing with a *sjambok*. One pulled the blanket out from under Willem, causing him to tumble into Mother's cot.

"What gives you the right?" Moeder asked.

"I'm the commandant. . . . That gives me the right . . . and the duty."

The men shook the rest of our bedding to see if anything fell out, and then they rustled through our few belongings. Moeder grabbed the arm of the one who pulled open her bag; the other twisted her away, ripping the sleeve of her dress.

"What are you looking for?"

"Whatever we can find," the commandant said, with his gloved hands sorting through Moeder's things, which were now scattered across the cot. He picked up her brooch and held it to her neck.

"Here we are," a guard shouted when he unrolled my bedding. He handed the paper to the commandant.

"What are you doing with this copy of the rules?" he asked me.

"It had fallen off a post and I brought it home so I could study them," I said. I opened my eyes wide and looked up at him through my lashes.

"What's this, then?" a guard asked, holding my notebook by the spine and fluttering the pages to see if anything would fall out. I lunged at it; I couldn't allow anyone to read that. He lifted it above his head, and I leaped but could not reach it.

"Give me that." I jumped like a springbok, time and again, but came nowhere near it. He laughed at my effort. "Give me that. That's private. . . . That's mine."

He handed it to the commandant, who flipped Moeder's brooch back onto the cot. "What's in this . . . notes on the camp?" The commandant skimmed through, reading a page or two. I was glad my handwriting was poor and I'd written everything so small to conserve space. I doubted anyone but me could read it.

"Just my journal . . . little-girl thoughts," I said to the commandant.

He tossed it back at me.

They looked inside the teapot, under folded clothes, in our shoes.

Moeder tried to elbow into their small group every time they pawed through our few belongings.

"Looka this," one guard said, having found more paper near Willem.

The commandant looked through several scraps.

"Here it is," he said, holding it up to Moeder. "Troop deployment . . . artillery. . . . Take them."

The Tommies closed in around Moeder, who asked, "Where would we see troops and artillery here? All we see are your guards and that fence. There's nothing else in sight."

I came from behind the commandant and snatched the paper. I thought I could eat the paper and swallow it, to destroy any evidence of whatever Willem had been doing.

The commandant grabbed at me but could reach only my hair. I could feel the roots surrender their hold. As I put the notes up to my mouth, I could see the writing. It was Willem's math work. I yanked myself from his grasp, leaving the commandant with a thatch of my hair.

"It's my brother's studies . . . arithmetic. . . . That's the only way he'll do problems . . . adding and subtracting rifles and troops."

I handed it back to him. "Look at the numbers, the writing. . . . It's a little boy learning math," I said, turning to Willem. "Tell him, Willem. . . . What portion of twenty is five?"

I tried to send the answer through my eyes by concentrating so hard on it that it had no choice but to arrive in his mind.

"Well, boy?" the commandant yelled.

"Twenty-five percent," Willem said. "One-fourth."

My mother and I let out a cheer and clapped our hands. Willem grinned as if he'd won the war. The commandant looked at the childish markings on the paper and tossed it back to him. He released the guards with a head tilt and stood in front of Moeder. He was no taller than Moeder, but he stood with feet wide and shoulders back.

"We were told by sources that letters to commandos have been coming from this tent."

"What?"

"Messages to the enemy."

"Who?"

"One of you."

"Who was the source?"

"You don't think I'll tell you that, do you?"

Moeder stared.

"An informant," he said.

"Someone is lying to you," Moeder said.

"That has happened with your people before," he said. "But if you're up to something, we will catch you, you know?"

"And do what to us?"

"Do what?" His shout seemed to push back the tent canvas. "Anything I want to do. We're at war, have you forgotten?"

"I am . . . aware," Moeder said.

"Good," the commandant said. "We're watching you." He backed up and stepped toward the tent flap, turning cold eyes to me. "And I'm watching you especially."

13

October 1899, Venter Farm

When the call-up notice arrived for the men, they cheered so hard that Cecelia covered her ears. They were told that each man was responsible for his own mount and weapons and two weeks of supplies. Bina's husband, Tuma, would attend the men as an "after-rider," taking care of the horses and cooking.

The men objected when my mother mentioned that the issue might be resolved without war. "These are white Christians we're fighting," Oupa said. "And they're driven by a hunger for gold. But it shouldn't take long for them to see that we will not just turn and run. And then it won't be worth their cost. Can you imagine the expense of sending an army to the other end of the world?"

My most troubling worries came from an unexpected source: Ouma Wilhelmina, Tante Hannah's mother. As the men made their final preparations in the barn, I was watching Cee-Cee in the parlor. My mother peeked in and summoned me to the kitchen. "You can pack the things for Schalk to take."

"Really?"

"It will be special for him."

It felt like a promotion to adulthood. The kitchen smelled of food and burlap, and a mound of many dozen rusks rose like a *kopje* in the middle of the table. Dry and crunchy, resistant to spoilage, rusks were perfect for a hunting trip or the like. Moeder also prepared a pouch of necessities for each of the men: extra bootlaces, a tin of salve against sunburn, a few common medicines, a needle and thread.

Moeder and Tante Hannah, at opposite ends of the table, packed for their husbands. Ouma Wilhelmina prepared Gideon's things, even though their relationship was only a suspicious sharing of time at family gatherings. I took my place at the middle of the long table and readied to pack for my brother.

Bina cinched the tops of the rusk sacks once they were filled and piled them near the door. Then she hefted a large sugar bag to the center of the table.

"Coffee then," mother said. "Salt, tobacco . . ."

"Biltong?" I asked. I knew they would expect biltong.

"Oupa will handle that," Mother said. Oupa guarded his secrets for seasoning and curing the biltong, and he would distribute the dried, spicy meat when he was ready, in portions he deemed appropriate.

Across the table, Ouma Wilhelmina pulled her pipe from the pocket of her skirt. "I've done this before, you know," she said. "Packed for war."

"Moeder," Tante Hannah tried to interrupt. "We have so much to do . . ."

"I should be packing for my own man, but this is all that's left," Wilhelmina said, raising the pipe in front of her and then toward each of us around the table. "Did you know that, Aletta? This is what I got back after my husband went to fight: his pipe."

She slid it back to the corner of her mouth, into the indentation formed by years of smoking.

"A pipe . . . that's all," she said. "I never even learned where they buried him. They wouldn't tell me where. . . . They were so afraid that I'd go out there and get myself killed. He went with the other men to save us from the thieving devils. We had to fight off the raiders who kept stealing our stock. Had to stop them before they took everything. My Izak killed half a dozen of them himself."

Wilhelmina held the pipe out for further examination, fingers on the bowl, pointing with the mouthpiece, which had been gnawed ragged. "Made of a bone from an ostrich foot. He carved it himself . . . not another like it."

We rarely saw her without it, and the teeth on that side of her mouth looked rusted.

"Had it in his mouth when he took wounds from three of the kaffirs' assegais," she said. "Three of them. Three. He kept firing when the first spear went through the meat of his side. Another went in his leg . . ."

"Moeder!" Tante Hannah raised her voice, but Ouma Wilhelmina kept looking at me as she pointed with her pipe to parts of her body to illustrate her Izak's wounds.

"The first two spears didn't stop him. He didn't even try to pull them out. Just kept shooting. He killed another one before they threw the spear that went right through the front of his throat."

She removed the pipe and pointed at the hollow place between the cords rising at the front of her neck.

"They said it drove him back, and the spear stuck into the ground . . . pinned him there . . . pipe still in his mouth."

"Moeder . . ."

Packing stopped.

"Nothing but his pipe came home. . . . Think about that."

THE FIRST SOUND WAS the stamping of impatient horses, and Oupa's drumbeat instructions to Tuma. They were leaving for war, and nobody woke me. They'd already had breakfast and coffee, and no one noticed that I wasn't there? People moved so quickly in the kitchen that they bounced off one another. Tante Hannah carried Cee-Cee on her hip. Bina cleared breakfast as Tuma backed out the door with supply bags in each hand.

Moeder directed it all from the table, crossing items from her list. Her hair was pinned up and she wore her brooch at the neck of her Sunday dress.

I had barely cleared my head of night fog when everyone emptied onto the *stoep*.

I heard the call of the *piet-my-vrou*. Oupa mimicked the bird's three-note call. "Almost time to plant," he said to Moeder. "If we're not home soon, put Bina to the plow."

The men wore their felt hats and suit coats, ammunition belts across their chests like sashes, the cartridges longer than my fingers, aligned in perfect military order. The four of them were mounted in a line, the stages of man: Oupa with his thick gray beard, Vader's beard brown and waved, Sarel's beard lighter, and Schalk's with its wisps descending only at the jawline and invisible above his mouth. The first burst of sunlight caused them all to stand out in silhouette.

"Every man a hero," Oom Sarel said.

"No heroes," Gideon said. "Just proud Boers."

"I mean . . . his divine favor will guide our steps," Sarel said.

"Amen," Vader added.

I thought of Ouma Wilhelmina's stories and worried over their leaving.

"We have been chosen for his purpose," Oupa said. "Lord, redeem me from the oppression of men that I may obey your precepts."

Bina lifted her eyes to Tuma.

"Psalm twenty-five." Oupa removed his hat and recited the verses from memory.

"To you, oh Lord, I lift up my soul. . . . Oh my God, let me not be put to shame; let not my enemies exult over me."

The horses mouthed their bits as if trying to recite the psalm. Cecelia cried. Vader opened his eyes at the sound and nodded to Moeder rather than to me. Moeder took her to her hip and bounced her. She stepped between the horses of Vader and Schalk. Vader reached down to run his hand through the little girl's woolly hair and put his palm on the side of my mother's head. She leaned into his leg.

"God's grace," she said.

She leaned toward Schalk and squeezed his knee.

The men clucked and the horses backed away. I tried to catch Schalk's eyes, but his hat was pulled low.

My throat swelled shut. Moeder squinted into the sun to follow their path. She was already making plans. I loved that she was strong for us, for me and Willem and Cee-Cee. We watched until the dust from the horses faded.

"Lettie . . . take Cecelia," she said, turning toward the house. "We have work to do."

14

March 1901, Concentration Camp

J anetta was so tightly quarantined that I rarely even got responses when I called at the tent door. I used a low voice so as not to disturb Nicolaas in case he was able to rest. I bent near the flap and spoke at intervals with pauses.

"Janetta . . . it's Lettie." Nothing.

"Can I do anything to help?" Nothing.

"Can I get you anything?" Nothing.

It was probably for my own good that they did not invite me in. I pictured her inside, tending her brother, hearing my voice but sitting in silence. I considered just walking in, perhaps taking a bucket of water in for them. I thought of writing a note of warm thoughts and well-wishes for Nicolaas. But I had no idea what was the right thing to do. Was there a book somewhere that told you how to act in these times? I looked at others passing in the row; perhaps they knew the family and could tell me how Nicolaas was doing. No one lifted a head to notice me.

"It's Lettie. . . . Can I be of any help?" I tried again.

"Go away." It was the voice of a woman, a woman impatient with my questions.

And that was all. Janetta said nothing. I left and did not go back, hoping that she would reappear one day during my walk and we would be close. I wanted to tell her of the commandant and his threats, and how I now feared we'd been targeted by some informant in camp. Her experiences at the other camp might help us now. But I would have to wait.

Without my companion, I went back to my pattern of read-walking, idling along the camp perimeter with my face in my book or my dictionary. It was a way to occupy my mind. During my walks, the space beside me felt empty, and sometimes I would start to say something as if Janetta were there. I worried about her as I would my own sister. I suppose that drove me deeper into my books, so much so that I almost never looked up from them when I walked.

I came across guards a time or two with each trip around the camp. "Away from the fence," they would say, and I would veer a few steps until I was out of sight. I sometimes saw the guards who stormed through our tent with the commandant. I avoided their eyes but sensed menace in their nearness. I thought of Schalk's stories of how the animals could sense threats, and I tried to grow alert to those who might be watching or following as I walked. I passed the latrines, the hospital tent, the reservoir, each with its own sounds and smells so that I could identify my position without looking up. It was most quiet along the eastern fence line, especially in the afternoon, so it was there that I felt the safest. Until . . .

"What have you got there?"

The pink-faced guard occupied my path.

"Aletta, right? What's your book?" The guard knew my name. How? Was he looking through British paperwork? Keeping files on us? Snooping . . . monitoring?

"How do you know who I am?"

"Your friend told me, remember?" he said. "You were standing right in front of me. You were so angry you made your face look like a fist. Remember?"

I hoped it would bother him that I could dismiss the memory of him so quickly. I did not even shake my head in response.

"Where's your friend?"

I tried walking past.

"What are you reading?"

"Are books outlawed here?" I adopted the tone Oupa Gideon sometimes used with Tuma.

"Just curious what you're reading. . . . Must be good, you almost ran into me."

"Who are you?" I asked without looking at his face.

"Tommy Maples . . . I told you. . . . Let me see."

I held it away from him so he could see the title but not touch the book.

"*Chambers's Dictionary*," he said.

"You can read," I said, acting surprised.

"Yes, the queen taught me."

I kept my focus on the pages, skimming for a full definition of the word *fence*.

"*Fence*, noun, a wall or hedge for enclosing animals or for protecting land," I read, and then I said, "Enclosing animals . . . yes . . . the proper use for a fence. It doesn't say anything about enclosing humans."

He ignored my comment. "Do you have any books to help me find gold or diamonds?"

"You haven't taken enough?"

"Haven't found any. . . . Recruiters promised us we'd be trippin' over nuggets and gems," he said. "Have you ever found any?"

I turned around to get away from him, but he continued beside me.

"You should have seen the men when we'd set up a camp, they'd start pawin' at the dirt," he said. "They told us about a gent who just bent over and picked up a diamond that was one hundred seventy-five carats."

I had no idea how big that was. I turned again, but he stubbornly followed.

"Something like that had to be the size of a cricket ball," he said. "Men find more snakes than nuggets. Nobody told us about the black mambas that rear up and drop you with one bite. They'll crawl into your bedding at night to stay warm and then you roll over on them and wake up dead. Scare the life out of me."

I had dealt with snakes all my life and had not been bitten . . . thanks to Bina. I considered telling him that story but clamped my jaws. Who was he to come into our country and then complain about our snakes? But his fears seemed a strategic opening. Who knows how I might disrupt the British plans if I started a rumor that spread to their troops in the field?

"We have spent years training our snakes to kill you British in your sleep," I said. "Thousands of them, at our command: they're coming for you. An army of them. Crawling into your bedding. No fence can stop them, you know." I pointed to the fence and made a wiggling motion with my hand, showing how a serpent could slither through.

"You've taught them well, then," he said, adding a shiver. "They're everywhere. . . . Hate the bleeders."

It was worth a try; if it kept some of them awake at night, they might be sluggish in battle. But he was not as simple as I had hoped.

"You should go home, then." I pointed to the north.

"Right . . . yes, I'm all in favor of that. I asked about that very thing, but it turns out they won't let me. I still have more than four years to go. I thought it might be a few months here and then some soft duty somewhere else."

I sneered.

"They had some bad times before I got here, I guess, Spion Kop and the like. But when we marched into Pretoria, everybody had a big party, and they stood up there and told us that the war was over. Major said exactly that . . . said we'd accomplished our mission in South Africa."

He bobbed his head so that it caused his helmet to slide down on his brow.

"Did you know that I saw you before I met you with your friend . . . that day with all the crazy women at the fence? I didn't want to go near them."

I stopped walking to make a point: "You had to protect your dirty helpers on the other side."

"We hate them the most," he said. "If they turn on their own, they'll surely turn on us. That's the first thing the officers told us; they could be spies working against us from the inside. If we see anything out of line at all, we're under orders to shoot 'em down. Or put together a firing squad."

"My *oom* Sarel is on the other side." I pointed to the far side of camp. "He's a traitor, but I miss my *tante* Hannah . . . his wife."

"Members of your own family?"

"A traitor's heart cannot be trusted," I said. It was one of Moeder's opinions.

"True, but they may end up benefiting," he said.

"Did Judas benefit?"

"I don't know. You tell me."

"For a very short time," I said.

"Well . . . maybe that's the case with them," he said. "At least your uncle is safe. He won't be anybody's favorite, but he'll be alive and able to start over."

"Not after we win."

The guard tilted his head. "Could happen."

"You don't know my father and grandfather," I said, pointing a finger at his chest. "They'll never quit."

"Bitter-Enders?"

"To the finish."

"Wish them well," he said. "Just hope we can all go home soon."

"Keep your wishes and take them home with you," I said.

He pulled something shiny from his tunic, a tin box, red and gold and blue.

"Queen sent it to me. . . . Got her likeness right here on top, with her signature." He held it out for me to see.

"Igghh . . . she looks like Kruger without the beard."

"Speak well of the dead."

He was right; that was unchristian.

"She sent a hundred thousand of these boxes, filled with chocolate."

"There are a hundred thousand of you here?" Was he planting information on troop strength?

"Oh . . . that was just at the start. . . . More now . . . many more . . . five times that now, probably."

He opened the container, and a delicate smell overcame me. I'm sure it had been empty for months, but I could still smell the chocolate. It angered me.

"You kill our men and burn our farms, and the queen sends you chocolates?"

"Yes, she did. . . . Generous, I thought. Some men sent them right home to their girls or family, but it would have cost five shillings and I decided I could use it more than my mum."

The box was beautiful.

"Here, smell," he said.

"Put that away."

"Just a smell . . ."

"No." I yelled this time. But did not back away.

He held it closer to my face. My mouth flooded.

"No."

At the edge of the crinkled inner wrapper was the smallest sliver of candy that had broken off, smaller than a flower petal, a smudge. I touched it, and it cleaved to my finger. I brought it to my nose and it was chocolate, the slightest essence, or maybe it was just a memory of chocolate. I touched my finger to my tongue. And there was a taste, or the memory of a taste, and it lasted for days.

I WAS ACCUSTOMED TO jarring sounds when I slept at home, since nightbirds would call at certain times of the year, and animals' lives came to noisy ends in the thick darkness. But the shrill, one-note whistles in the camp at night were foreign to nature and impossible to attribute to memory or dream. It sparked fears of phantoms whistling their threats. I twisted in my small nest, blanketed between my sister and the tent wall, Moeder's cot at my head, Mevrou Huiseveldt's at my feet.

The commandant's intrusion had made us realize nothing in the tent was safe or private, and Moeder made us go through our belongings to be certain we were not in jeopardy if the guards visited again.

She took us aside when the commandant was gone to ask whether we had any idea what had caused their suspicions. Had either of us tried to send letters out of camp? No, Ma. Did we have any idea who might have tried to inform on us? No, Ma, do you? She tilted her head side to side a few times and then up and down slowly. As if the motion itself had shaken loose the thought, she whispered, "Oom."

Moeder could not even bear to say the given name: Sarel. Her conclusion made sense: if he could turn on his country, he could turn on his family. Moeder might have frightened him so badly when he came to our tent that he was striking back with lies to the commandant. Not that anyone in the camp could be trusted, but it felt a relief to think it was Oom Sarel and not . . . yes . . . I had thought it . . . Maples.

I thought of him again during my restless sleep. With each body shift, I adjusted my "pillow," which was the rolled-up pinafore I had never worn in camp. It had seemed too dressy at a time when I decided it was wiser not to call attention to myself. The first night, I had needed something for my head when sleeping on the ground, and the pinafore was soft and could be balled up. Since then, it had faded to the color of the tent floor.

The pillow added small comfort, since the ground felt harder now, and it seemed to pull harder at me, so that I woke up sore. Sometimes it was easier just to get up and fetch water or stand in line for rations early. Or just lie awake and think about the plans for the day and plot which direction I might walk. My path might lead me past the red-haired guard again. I thought about the guard's schedule and where he stood at different times on different days. What would I wear today? As if I had options. Well, yes, I did.

When the others awoke, I asked Moeder if I could start helping with the laundry. She focused on the small black dots in the very middle of my eyes.

"I could wash my things so you wouldn't have to," I said. "Really, Ma, I should help. At least do my own."

"What do you want washed?"

"I just want to help."

"Aletta . . ."

I held up my filthy pinafore.

"Soap is dear, Lettie," she said. "Why now?"

"It would protect my skirts; it's really just an apron."

Sound logic.

"If I get it white, then I can wear it if I go for psalms and hymns, and it will look nicer than these skirts and be more respectful of the service."

Moeder unrolled it and held it up to my shoulders.

"I'll be grown out of it if I don't wear it soon."

She could see that. "You're taller now . . . more mature."

I helped carry the basket to the reservoir.

"Ma, did you hear whistles last night?"

"Mmmm."

"Are they birds?"

"Perhaps . . ."

"What kind?"

"Try to sleep through them."

We went to the far end of the small dam, keeping a distance from others. Doing laundry was difficult and a constant chore because of the dust and mud and the other filth tracked around camp. When the white clay soap could not be had, some no longer bothered, but many still washed as they could, agitating the items in the shallow water.

Chatting as they scrubbed and rinsed, women bobbed like animals drinking at the edge of a water hole at sunset. They passed on what news they heard of the war or home, or rumors and camp gossip. The common complaints circled endlessly. How could the commandant consider soap and candles "articles of luxury"? Did you hear they put things in the food to make us sick? At the edge of this muddy pond, the women placed the blame for all the bad things in our lives on the Hands-Uppers and Joiners, even more than on the Tommies. This talk kept their hatred fresh and whipped to a froth.

Moeder liked to stay away from the knot of women, whom she said came to the reservoir to "wash with their tears." They dragged one another to greater depths. "Sharing your sorrow does not diminish your own," Moeder said.

That morning on the crowded bank, I strained to overhear the women's gossip, catching only phrases amid the splashing water and the prattle of the mindless.

". . . boy in the next tent passed . . ."

". . . the coffee was so . . ."

". . . measles, I . . ."

". . . no soap since . . ."

". . . pity the family . . ."

". . . one of twins . . ."

". . . fourteen . . ."

". . . should have . . . commando . . ."

". . . safer there . . ."

". . . pity . . ."

It had to be Nicolaas. Janetta's brother Nicolaas. That beautiful boy.

"Moeder . . . did you hear?"

She was focused on the wash.

"I think I heard that Janetta's brother died. . . . Can I go?"

She looked at the basket.

"Of course. . . . Keep your distance."

I had not seen Janetta for several weeks. I hated that I hadn't been there to help her. It felt wrong not to support my best friend. I had tried her tent almost every day, at least at first. The tent, now, was cinched, their crying muted by canvas. I stood and waited, fingers touching the door flap, waiting for clearance to enter that was never granted.

The death of a brother would carry such pain, but how much more was the loss of a twin? She had to feel the death of a part of herself. They shared a connection I could never hope to understand. Would she be harnessed to guilt for having been the one to survive?

I listened harder and waited. I hoped that she had stayed healthy and that her sorrows would fade enough that we could be close again. She did not answer when I called. I went back a time or two, to no effect, until one afternoon I could see the tent flap open as I approached. I pulled up my skirts and ran. All is better. Nicolaas had been healed, the talk had been of some other boy, and Janetta was now free to join me again. Praise God.

"Janetta . . ."

Three women and an old man sat on blankets in a circle. They startled and the man rose as if to fight me off.

"Where's Janetta?"

"Who?"

"Janetta, my friend . . ."

The man stepped closer to me. "No Janetta," he said.

She was gone. Her family was gone. No good-bye. No explanation. I wondered whether it had been another product of her mother's ingenuity. My pulse had gone from racing to a cold stop. Friendships in camp were suddenly not worth the investment. I had told her everything. She felt like my twin, and she was gone. Maybe she had died, too. For a moment I welcomed that explanation; it made her disappearance less of a personal rejection. I knew then that I needed to be closer to Cee-Cee and connect better with Willem. We have only our family, they said, and that had to be enough. We'd been tight as a sheaf, and there was such strength in the collection of us. And when I thought of us pulled tight against whatever might challenge us, it was no longer Oupa Gideon or Vader I pictured at the center of it all. It was Moeder who was the family heartwood and, in her way, the strongest of us all.

15

December 1899, Venter Farm

Bina swept the scythe so smoothly the tall oats seemed to lie down willingly, as if bowing to her. Her hips, rounded like the quarters of a draft horse, tilted and then rolled with each sweep. Smooth and tireless, smooth and powerful, her rhythm made work a dance.

Hard lives had grown harder with the men gone, but I think we wanted it that way. It felt as if we were sharing the sacrifice, working toward a victory ourselves. I came to appreciate the farm as I never had when I did such little outside work. I saw this as proof of Bina's saying that you can't know the value of something until you pay for it. And we all were paying with our labors, now. For the first month or so after the men left, Bina had been able to do many of the outside chores herself, but the oat harvest brought Moeder and me to the fields.

It was left to Moeder to guess at the timing of the harvest. All things were drying now and the clumps of weeping love grass were encroaching on the field. We had to pay attention to such things. Moeder tested the firmness of the grain head and judged the color of the stalk. When the morning winds told her there would be several days of dryness, we began.

At dawn, dew reflected rainbows off the stalks, and the oats smelled of musk. Moeder followed Bina to rake and stack the sheaves she had reaped and I tied each around the middle with dry stalks that cinched it all like a tight belt.

Bina sang for us all. Moeder said they were such noisy people, with their drumming and chanting. But Bina's songs moved the work along, easing it through time, the sweep of the scythe and the rhythm of the song paring the day into tolerable pieces.

Moeder's plan was that we reap the few morgen of oats in several days. Oupa Gideon suggested she bring the *sjambok* into the field in case incentive was required. Vader told us that Oupa had been generous with his stick on his sons when they were young, particularly Oom Sarel. But I hadn't seen him strike Bina, and Tuma only a few times. He cuffed Schalk on the back of the head or across the cheek a number of times when he was younger and had spoken to the adults with a tone Oupa deemed disrespectful. He cited scripture to justify the discipline in all cases. But Bina needed no reminders; she worked at such a steady pace that she did not even appear to tire. I wondered again at the girth that strained her robes, and at her curious pairing with the reed-thin Tuma, who could not have measured one-third her span.

Toward midday, the drying stalks took on the smell of dusty silage, and Moeder announced that we needed to be more efficient. She would take up a sickle of her own and start clearing a row at a slight distance, and I would rake and stack sheaves for both her and Bina. I could see from the start that she tried to emulate Bina's hip sway. She was stiff, though, and the stalks grabbed the blade and turned it in her hands. She looked so slight compared to Bina. Slender and light haired, she more closely resembled the oat stalks than she did her fellow reaper. She stopped, listened to Bina's song, and began swinging the scythe in time.

I raced between the two rows. I know I missed some and was not as tidy as Moeder had been, but I tried to keep up with them both. Swipe, step, swipe, step, to the sound of Bina's song. A dark line of sweat spread down the back of Moeder's dress. The bending and bunching lit a flame in my lower back. When I returned to Moeder's row in the late afternoon, I could see she had torn cloth from the hem of her apron and wrapped it around her hands.

The day passed: Bina sang, curious birds flew near, and the heat pressed in from all directions. My heart fluttered each time I heard the scales of fleeing snakes scrape against nearby oat stalks. By quitting time, blood had soaked through Moeder's hand wrap and dripped down the scythe handle in spiral patterns. Our sweat was powerful and our bodies smelled of yeast. Chaff and straw cleaved to our clothes and gathered in whatever folds of skin were exposed. When we told Bina it was time to stop and she straightened and lifted her head, the sweat-caked chaff aligned like tribal neck rings. She was the color of field dust except in the streaks where sweat had channeled down the rills of her face.

"Enough," Moeder said to Bina. "Start potatoes and onions for supper." I followed Moeder to see how I could help. She was still unbent but moved so slowly toward the barn that her small steps were unseen inside the radius of her skirts.

"Ma?"

"Go in the house."

"I can help."

"Then look through the cans for turpentine."

"Another job before supper?"

"*Ja*," she said.

She sat on a bale, turned her hands up, and blew across her bloody palms.

I remembered the time Oupa nearly severed his thumb with a saw. He poured turpentine on it and bound it tightly with a cloth. But when it festered several days later, he had Vader slaughter a goat, and Oupa sat for hours with his hand in the still-warm stomach cavity. He soon pronounced it healed, and it was never addressed thereafter. I saw the wedge where flesh had been gouged from the base of his thumb almost every time he gestured while telling a story or pointed to the stars on our secret nights together.

I found the turpentine on a shelf, but the cap was so tight I strained to break the seal. The smell of it cleared my head. Moeder lifted her hands, skin worn raw, the palms seeping blood, red meat showing in angry rows. Only a few months earlier I had seen her rubbing mutton fat on her hands each night to keep them soft and womanly.

"Pour," she said.

"Ma?"

"Pour."

She stretched her fingers wide and opened the palm beyond flat, breaking open anything that had started to heal.

The turpentine splashed and mixed with the blood and ran between her fingers. Moeder opened her hands wider still. The smell burned so deep it brought tears. I could not imagine the feel of it on blistered, open wounds.

"Pour," she said again.

She had set her jaw and was biting hard enough that muscles flexed on the side of her face. Pale with dust, she sat motionless until she could regain her breath. She inhaled in small gulps and blew on her hands and then waved them in the air to speed the drying.

"Do you want me to kill a goat now?" I asked.

She looked up, curious, but did not ask for an explanation.

"Put the can away. . . . Let's go."

When we reached the house, we heard laughing in the kitchen. Tante Hannah was on the floor on all fours, with Cecelia on her back, riding her like a horse, kicking and giggling. Tante made horse noises, fluttering her lips, tossing her head.

"What is this?" Moeder surprised me with her tone.

Tante startled at her question and sat upright, bucking Cecelia to the floor. Cee-Cee laughed again, as if it were part of the game.

"I was going to get supper started for you all, but I got distracted playing with Cee-Cee instead," Hannah said.

"Aletta, watch your sister." I led Cee-Cee to the table by the hand. My back had stiffened so that I could not bend to pick her up.

"Willem," Moeder called. He would pay for having left Cee-Cee with Tante Hannah.

Moeder washed the field off herself and splashed water on her face. But touching her hands to her face brought the scent of turpentine into her eyes. She straightened again, stretched her neck from side to side and back to front, allowing a small groan to escape.

"Bina . . . potatoes."

"White woman with a black shadow doing the work," Hannah mumbled.

Moeder looked at her sister-in-law without expression. "There are more of us," Moeder said.

"*Ja*, I know . . . all your children to tend," Tante Hannah said. "If you have work to do . . . you and Bina . . . the children could come to our place so you wouldn't have to worry about them. I would take them. I would . . . they would enjoy it."

"Who does your work?"

"I get it done. We get it done. There's not that much."

"How do I value a gift that most satisfies the giver?" Moeder asked. "We're fine. Your schooling Aletta is enough."

Cecelia chattered at her doll.

"Set the table, Lettie," Moeder said.

"Right away . . . then I'll make tea," I said. "Tante Hannah . . . tea?"

"That would be nice," she answered, easing into a smile for me.

The family ate, but Moeder kept her hands to her side until Tante Hannah went home and the little ones had gone into the parlor. Bina knew Moeder was hiding her hands, and held her own palms open as an invitation to see Moeder's.

"I've got *muti* for that," she said.

"Later," Moeder answered. "Bible reading now."

Cee-Cee asked for her to play "The Eagle Hymn," the name she had given to a piece that contained the line *On eagles' wings we soar.* It always made me imagine floating on the warm winds above the veld. I wanted to hear that, too. Moeder told Cee-Cee it was too late for the organ, but I knew the truth was that she would have been unable to stretch her fingers to the keys.

When she came to get me in the morning, her hands were still pinched into claws, but she had already made breakfast and we were off to the field again before the sun cleared the horizon.

16

March–April 1901, Concentration Camp

I f Moeder caught me slipping out deep in the night, or the newly watchful guards snatched me up, I had an excuse prepared: latrine. Who could argue the timing of nature's demands? To make my ventures less of a falsehood, I always stopped first at the latrines before I wandered farther. The appalling place was less trafficked in the middle of the night, and I preferred it that way. Many kept buckets outside their tents, since some refused to walk all the way to the pits, especially in the cold or rain. But I never mastered the use of the bucket, which was tricky as well as humiliating.

The night made it more private, but rarely completely so. Thinking I was alone one night, I jumped when a woman dealing with diarrhea groaned near me. In the way that so many feelings now clustered in surprising combinations, sympathy and disgust collided. I was very sorry for her but delighted it wasn't me. I pitied her condition while hating her nearness.

During my daylight walks, I discovered a favorite spot at the most distant edge of the camp, where I could turn my back on all the tents and all the people and all their problems. Except for a few *kopjes* rising in the distance, the land was featureless for miles. Most of the year it was nothing but lion-pelt colors from tan to brown, unchanging all the way to the indistinct horizon. There was terrain, but it was mostly internal, carved by streams into *dongas* and *spruits* that split and converged like wrinkles in old skin.

The sky, though, was endlessly active, showing white hot to lucid blue, or raging black with storms, or spotted with clouds that gave shape to the shifting winds. At times, the winds pitted your skin with grit, or carried rain and hail in extravagant amounts. But the sunsets that bled in layers across the horizon were God's reminder that only he could brighten such a desolate pit with infinite beauty.

Being at the fence line was a freedom by degrees. But even an illusion of freedom was welcomed, and I think that's why Moeder was patient with my absences. Besides, it wasn't as if I could wander off and get lost. But every move now carried a risk. Not just to me, but to the rest of the family, too, if the commandant was to be believed.

There were physical costs, too. I found myself breathing heavily and wearing down when I walked to the edge of the camp. Time seemed thicker, now, as if it had weight. It did not just pass on its own but had to be pushed through, shoved aside, like wading against a current or walking uphill, and all directions now felt uphill.

It seemed more of an escape in the darkness, when the sky came alive with stars. Sometimes the moon fattened and brightened and drew nearer, always facing the earth, always watching. On those nights when the sky dipped closer, it seemed like the ceiling of a shrinking room. The storms or lightning arrived to set off vibrations I could feel rising up from the ground. Excitement and fear—two other newly inseparable senses—sparked with every splintered bolt, causing me to flinch and gasp and pray for safety, and then pray that another might strike soon.

On this cold night, vapor rose in a small cloud in front of my face with each breath as I labored toward the far fence. I needed to risk a walk after dark to think about Nicolaas and to pray for his soul. He was the first person I actually knew who had died, and he had been my age. When I told Moeder, she shook her head, squeezed her lips for a moment, and said, "Shame." What else to say? I knew others were dying. But this was the first one whose face I could still remember, and I was forced to realize that I would never see that face again. I needed quiet time to find a spot for that in my mind.

The stars helped. Patches of clouds skimmed past, veiling the stars for a moment, but I liked to study them, too, to scan their layers and texture and depth and see in them the shapes of animals or angels or spooks. Between the clouds, the sky was streaked with light. Others called them shooting stars, but Oupa taught me that they were meteors, pieces of broken stars. From the horizon, a comet flared, brighter and larger than all the meteors combined. I'd never seen such a display. It had a split tail . . . a double-tailed comet.

"Look," I said, pointing at the comet. It was a reflex. I knew Oupa could see it perfectly from the veld. It would be the first thing I'd ask when this was over: Oupa, did you see the double-tailed comet? It was something I would write in my notebook in the morning. I would describe it precisely so that I could tell my grandchildren about it . . . maybe on a porch some night when I would sneak them out to have coffee and rusks.

A thought of the future was so rare now that it felt as if I'd been ambushed by it. Surviving from one day to the next took such focus that there was little room for seeing beyond a blank wall of time. But the comet, that brilliant flash of light, made the camp seem so temporary, so small. Finite. I expected that by the time another comet like this passed, this camp would be gone and the ground would have healed up over the memories. It was a reminder that there were things bigger than this camp, things that were bright and natural and gave off light, things that could fly over this insignificant cage in the time it took to blink. I actually felt myself smiling for a moment . . . until I heard sounds that made me certain I was being followed.

MEMORIES OF NICOLAAS PLAGUED me every time we went to the reservoir, the place where I heard of his death. Would every daily chore for the rest of my life carry attachments to this time? I saw the value in Moeder's advice to stay as far as possible from the other women. Their conversations produced little truth and less good news, and in their own way, they spread a kind of illness.

Our laundry became more burdensome, but Moeder and I continued to go even though there was no longer any soap available. We would each hold a basket handle and walk in time like a yoked team. I measured myself against her when she wouldn't notice. The top of my head had reached the level of her chin. I felt taller, but maybe she did not stand quite as straight anymore, making my growth another illusion.

Walking back with the silence of an ox team, we heard a call from the inner fence.

"Susanna."

"Tante Hannah," I answered, happy to hear her voice.

Moeder turned and stood. Silent.

"Susanna . . . God keep you."

Moeder walked slowly, now, directly at Tante Hannah.

I squeezed the basket handle with both hands.

"Susanna . . . I've prayed every day for you," she said, frantic to get the words out before Moeder had a chance to start a fight. "I've tried to catch you near the fence or send you letters. I know you're angry, but I—"

"Go back to your traitor husband."

"Ma . . . please." I just wished to calm her, to take her away from this.

"I'm so sorry," Tante Hannah said, palms open, trying to give her apology like a present. "I just wanted to tell you how—"

"How what? How you can live with that man? How you can live with yourself?"

Moeder pulled us nearer the fence.

"You don't understand," Hannah said. "He was hurt and needed care. He can hardly move his arm. . . . He can't sleep . . . night terrors."

"He can't sleep because of his conscience."

"He had no choice."

"We heard his lies already," Moeder said. "Did you know that?"

"No." Her shoulders dipped.

"He came to see us . . . to get me to write to Matthys to ask him to surrender in the same cowardly way he did."

"He didn't say. . . . I didn't know. . . . I'm . . ."

"You tell him I won't forget . . . ever . . ."

"Susanna . . ."

"No . . . Hannah . . . no . . . what would your father think? Your dead father?"

"My father would be alive now if he hadn't gone to war."

"See . . . Sarel has infected you."

"Sarel wants this all to end. . . . If this were over, we'd all go home . . ."

"Ahhhhh . . ."

"They all say we can't win. . . . There's no chance. . . . What's the reward if everyone dies?"

I knew she would not budge Moeder, but I could not interfere.

"If it lasts another year, we still lose," Tante said, "and what about the children?"

Moeder's jaws ground.

"You know nothing of children."

Tante Hannah was struck by a series of coughs and raised a white handkerchief from her sleeve to her face.

"Susanna . . . please . . . I had . . . ," Hannah said, gripped by coughing again. "More reason for us all to cherish the ones . . ."

"No, you don't understand. . . . That traitor has infected you. . . . You have caught his cowardice."

"He is my husband . . . by God's Holy Word. . . . Susanna, you know that. I honor the vow. And his heart is . . ."

Moeder stepped even closer to the fence and whispered. Hannah mirrored her move and leaned in.

"Don't try to get in my way if I come after him," Moeder said with clarity, if not full control.

She pulled me around again, with the basket handle, and we almost raced toward the tent.

"Susanna . . . Susanna . . . ," Tante called after us. "Don't keep Lettie from me . . . please."

"You put yourself over there," Moeder yelled without turning. I could scarcely keep up, my legs aching from the lengthy strides. She turned sideways so that we could slip into the tent.

"Ma, can we . . . ohh!" I shouted at the sight of her and dropped my side of the basket. Her face was puffy, and one of her eyes was completely red where it should have been white. She had ruptured vessels in her rage.

MOEDER APPEARED TO HAVE calmed, but her anger still occupied space in the tent. She understood when I told her I needed to take air. I could not look at her for the dread of seeing that frightening eye. Neither Willem nor Cee-Cee noticed, somehow. I walked the eastern fence line in the afternoon again. It was a Tuesday but it felt like Sunday. So I didn't even bring a book, just prayed as I walked, and hummed psalms that came to mind. At intervals, I turned quickly to see whether someone was following me.

"That's pretty," the guard said, surprising me just as I turned to look forward once again. He pointed at my pinafore.

"Just an apron," I said.

"Nice . . . new?"

I did not answer. The garment wasn't even dry from washing it that morning.

"How are you?"

"Me?" It was the first question about my well-being that I'd heard in some time. Certainly the first from a stranger.

"I haven't escaped yet," I said. "But it's early."

"I've got something for you." He leaned his rifle against the fence, fidgeted with a button on his tunic, reached inside, and produced a book.

"I saw that you like to read," he said. "I'm finished with this. . . . Thought maybe you'd like to take it on."

"Dickens?" I asked, before I could see the cover. What else would a Brit be reading?

"Dickens . . . right . . . *Copperfield.*"

"*David Copperfield*?"

"Heard of Dickens?"

"Yes, but haven't read any. My *tante* Hannah . . . my aunt on the Joiner side, has told me of Dickens. She loves him. She told me I should try to write myself."

"Have you seen your aunt?" he asked.

"Just once. . . . She used to teach me. . . . We used to talk . . ."

"About Dickens?"

"Sometimes."

"Well, he's my favorite," he said. "They love him at home. He sold his books bits at a time . . . in the papers. . . . People would queue up all night to be there when the next chapter came out. You can have this."

"Have it?"

"I've read it. . . . You can keep it. . . . Just taking up space in my tent."

"This is for me?"

It was my second book. Third, counting the dictionary. It was three times as long as my other book. I held it with both hands and felt the heft of it.

"Ample," I said. Then I immediately thought myself a fool for abusing my newest English words. "I mean . . . it's long."

"You probably have time to read, though, eh?"

I opened the book and skimmed the first sentence. I could not imagine anything so completely capturing my thoughts. I read the sentence aloud as if it could make the fences fall and the war subside: "Whether I shall turn out to be the hero of my own life . . . these pages must show."

"I wondered the same thing when I was young," the guard said. "Where will it all take me? Will it be ordinary or something more? It's already been something . . . being in Africa. You'll see. . . . Little David gets by in hard times. . . . Inspiring, I thought."

That one sentence, written decades earlier, somehow created the same response when read by a British soldier as it did when read by a young woman in Africa. That's what Tante Hannah talked about and I hadn't been able to understand. I wanted to race away and bury myself in the story. It would be a good way for me to learn about England and British culture. I might want to travel there someday, so this was educational. Tante Hannah would be proud of me. If Moeder ever let me speak to her again. Oh . . . Moeder . . .

"I can't take this."

"Yes, it's yours now."

"No, take your book. I can't have it."

"I'm finished with it."

"No." I shoved it back toward him, but he balled up his hands in his pockets.

"No one has to know."

"I'll know. I can't even be talking to you. You might tell the commandant."

"I probably dislike the commandant more than you do," he said. "How's this: you can borrow it to read. . . . It won't be a gift from the enemy that way."

That made sense. But not enough to those who might ask questions.

"No." But I couldn't help starting to read again. It was glorious. It was Dickens.

I started walking again; I needed to be away from the guard. But he kept talking, anyway.

"I worked in a mill until I got sacked, so I joined to serve . . . steady work . . . improve my station. Thought it would be an adventure."

"Adventure?"

"Nobody said much about it being a war . . . not like the Crimea or such," he said. "A month cruise and then a few months seeing Africa, and it would all be over. Came as a surprise your folks had much of an army. Been interesting, though, and beautiful . . . from the first day. Steamed into Table Bay at night and there were dozens of ships at anchor waiting to off-load troops and cargo. . . . The sight of all their lights reflecting off the water . . . I'll never forget."

"You were in Cape Town?"

"Two days. . . . Rode the electric trams, went up to that big, flat mountain," he said. "Most amazing city I've ever seen. Truly. Every kind of people in that city."

I was jealous. This British soldier had seen more of my country than I had.

"I'm a man of the world now," he said, tipping his hat like a proper gentleman. "I hadn't even been on a train until I joined. I've been on too many of them now . . . mostly hopin' they didn't get blown up."

I turned, but he followed me again.

"Saw the giant smoking chimneys of the gold mines on the Rand," he said. "You should see them at night. Like lit-up castles. The Golden Reef, they called it. Beautiful. The whole country, really, so bright, so vivid."

I had not yet worked that far back in the dictionary, so I would skip ahead to *vivid* that afternoon. I finally broke away from him and was eight pages into the Dickens book by the time I entered our tent.

"Where did you get that?" Moeder asked.

"Janetta . . . she gave it to me before she left." The lie came so easily.

"Wash your hands after you read it," she warned. "You don't want it to infect you."

17

Mid-December 1899, Venter Farm

Schalk often told stories of my father's uncanny horsemanship. But Vader never put on showy displays in front of us. It left me stunned, then, when the men came home from war the first time and Vader dismounted at a gallop and hit the ground like a springboard that thrust him onto the *stoep* for an embrace with Moeder. It was so speedy that it took several moments for the dust from his horse to arrive and envelop them in a cloud of privacy.

The men all wore the same clothes as they had the day they left, and they were cloaked in filth. Vader released Moeder and tossed his hat to the hovering Willem, who replaced his own with our father's and could hardly see from beneath the brim. When Vader reached down to lift Cecelia, his jacket stretched tight across his back. He looked strong. Lean, but well. War suited him.

He reached me, then, and lifted me as he had when I was smaller. It was something he had not done in several years. He smelled of leather and dried sweat and things I couldn't know.

"Missed you, Pa," I said, sorry then to be placed back on my own feet and have to occupy any space that wasn't in his arms.

"Have you been good for your mother?"

Ja.

Schalk applied a hug, the first I could recall that was not accompanied by teasing or wrestling. His neck and throat were sunburned, but his face was still pale where it had been sheltered by the protective brim of his hat. I expected him to look older, even though it had been only a few months, but he was like the same boy straining to grow whiskers. He smelled of campfire and tobacco.

"You smell," I said.

"And you've grown."

"No."

"Then I've gotten shorter . . . must be from all that ducking behind rocks." He pulled his shoulders up toward his ears like a frightened tortoise.

Oupa tapped me on the shoulder, and when I turned, he scooped me up with one arm under my knees and another behind my back. He rubbed his whiskers on my cheek, and I squealed. He would be disappointed if I did not.

"Did you see Taurus, the Bull?" Oupa asked me. "It was so bright."

"And the Seven Sisters at his shoulder," I said. "Almost like they were riding him."

"Almost," Oupa said with another whisker rub before putting me down and moving to Moeder.

"Too many oat heads scattered in the field. . . . You waited too long to harvest," he said. "They fall off if they're overripe."

Moeder turned toward Bina, but she was helping Tuma offsaddle the horses.

"Gideon, welcome back to our home," Moeder said.

"Thought we'd be back sooner," he said. "They called an armistice for Dingaan's Day."

"Blessings to God," she said. "We'll celebrate the covenant together."

"I thought you'd have killed all the Tommies by now, Oupa," Willem said, carrying his grandfather's rifle, the ammunition belts slung over his shoulders now dragging on the stairs.

"We're trying . . . would have if it were up to your father. If it goes long enough, he'll be an officer," Oupa said. "And all the time we thought he was just a farmer."

If this goes long enough? Moeder and I looked at Vader. He smiled at his father's comments, as if a longer war appealed to him.

"Tell us," Willem begged.

"Nothing to tell," Vader said. "That's Oupa talking. . . . He and Oom Sarel can tell you all about it."

"Sarel go straight home?" Moeder asked. Vader tipped his head in that direction.

"You seem well," he said to her.

"Are you eating enough?" she asked him.

"Enough to keep us going," he said. "Don't have much time for it. Some of the men say our greatest strength as an army is that we starve well."

Moeder spent the afternoon cooking mutton and cakes. Bina helped, too, and the fields were allowed to rest. As soon as Moeder pulled the table netting off the meal, Vader and Schalk attacked the food.

"Wait. . . . Give thanks." Gideon spread both arms over the table.

His grace was shorter than was customary, and the men set upon the food with the fervor of those who had been long denied. I held back, watching, fixing the memory—home again, together.

Having dragged bread over his plate in small circles to soak up the meat juices, Oupa Gideon lit his pipe and pushed back his chair to begin telling stories. I helped clear the table and clean but was eager to hear his experiences. Different weapons had their own sounds as Oupa brought the war to our parlor: the *boo-ahhh* of the big naval guns (arms flailing upward from the blast), the *dat-dat-dat* of the Maxims. When he told of shooting at Tommies, he held his left arm crooked and sighted in an invisible rifle, punctuating the story with a *dok* sound and a recoil of his shoulder.

"God and the Mauser," Oupa said. "That's how we will prevail. Two things the Brits don't have."

Willem wanted to hear Schalk's version of their efforts, but Schalk disappointed him, telling only how well his horse, Kroon, handled the days of riding without water or rest, and how much better suited he was to their needs than the giant, slow chargers the Tommies rode. He made it sound as if the horses were doing the fighting.

"It's like they're trying to chase a leopard with an ox," Schalk said. "It's almost unfair."

Most of Oupa's stories furthered common themes: the British were poorly disciplined and inadequately prepared, and their leaders were completely *dof*. In his stories, our men were never harmed, only Tommies.

After our meal, Vader brought his boots into the kitchen to repair a few holes where the soles met the uppers. He held one up and put his fingers through the gap and wiggled them at me.

"How has Miss Aletta behaved?" he asked Moeder so that I could hear.

"She is helping with the chores when she can get away from her reading and studies," she said. "Her mind works so hard you can watch it from the outside."

"I know that look," Vader said. "Sometimes a dozen questions and then silence." He mocked me with a look of wide, blank eyes.

"I don't look like that . . ."

Moeder gave me the same look with a slight head tilt.

"She's been taking care our *lammetjie*," she said. "A good little helper with her little sister."

Vader reached over to Cecelia and ran his fingers over the tight, white curls that had caused me to start calling her "our little lamb."

"Willem?"

"Willem is a boy . . . practicing to be you. Always testing me. Sometimes with his mouth, sometimes just with his eyes."

"Cee-Cee?"

"Lettie's little girl . . . always repeating the things she hears from her all day. She has God's spirit."

"The farm?"

"Keeping to the schedule. . . . The plowshare broke and it cost three shillings to get fixed and sharpened, and a half a day waiting for it," she said. "The apricots are fat and almost ready. We'll put them up for when you come home next time."

"Pumpkins and potatoes to plant soon," he said.

"Lettie . . . write that down, would you?"

"And watch for sheep lice," Vader added.

Another note.

"We may be back before you need to do any of this," my father said.

I studied my parents, seeing how they behaved after this separation. These were the things they would talk of . . . the farm schedule? I suspected the personal things would take place in private, at night. Or maybe they each knew the other well enough that they did not have to put thought to word. They were man and wife, sharing the yoke. I wanted to know the secrets, but they allowed so little to be seen.

The moment Gideon finished the Bible reading that evening, Vader announced his fatigue and readiness for bed. He reached out for Moeder's hand to help her from her seat. She looked at his hand and rose without taking it, putting her own in her skirt pockets. He kept his hand out, palm up. She followed him into their bedroom. I could not recall Vader offering a hand that way. I'm sure he didn't know why she rejected it. I suspected he'd find out about the scabs on her hands soon enough.

OUPA GIDEON DOMINATED OUR Dingaan's Day remembrances, filling the parlor with a story of treachery, murder, and the miracle of the Holy Covenant.

"We were the children of God led into the wilderness," he started, patting his leather-bound Bible like an instrument, "off to find our own land, away from British tyranny, where we could honor our Holy Father."

Oupa's passion heated the still air.

"There were more than ten thousand of us on our Great Trek . . . following different trails . . . fighting savages, hunger, illness . . . tsetse flies killing our stock," he said. "We traveled for months in jawbone wagons, over the Dragon Mountains through narrow passes . . . wagons falling over cliffs, dragging down a dozen oxen with each."

Ouma Wilhelmina nodded, smoke threads rising in a loose braid above her pipe.

"Whole families drowned at river fords . . . but we followed God's will. When our party reached Natal, our leaders sought a treaty with King Dingaan—the Vulture—who lured them into his kraal for a celebration of peace. As they raised their cups, the Zulus slaughtered seventy men, crushing their skulls with knobkerries . . ."

"And when they found the body of Piet Retief, he had the treaty of peace from the savages still in his pouch," Wilhelmina interrupted. "The last time we shall respect promises not our own."

Oupa paused to allow his impatience with her to register. This was his presentation. She interrupted every year.

"The Zulus then attacked one of our laagers, killing hundreds of women and children while they were asleep," he said. "My family survived, but we lived for almost a year in hunger and in fear that the same fate would be ours."

"Except for God's great Providence," Wilhelmina interjected again. He paused.

"We prayed to God and vowed that if he would grant us victory, we would build a church on that spot and forever consecrate the memory of the day. And then the savages came, unaware that our vow to God had steeled us in our cause."

He raised the Bible to his lips with eyes closed.

"There were twelve thousand of them against only five hundred of us in a circle of wagons beside the river," he said.

"Four hundred seventy," Wilhelmina said.

"Outnumbered twenty to one."

"Twenty-five," she corrected.

"My mother and sisters loaded the rifles for my father," he said, beginning a rapid-fire description.

"The muzzles were so hot they burned their fingers loading them . . ."

He mimed the fast action of loading a hot rifle. Bible in his left hand, he sighted targets over it.

"So many shots were being fired that the sky was cloudy from the powder . . ."

He squinted.

"They surged in for hours . . . hours. . . . Screams filled the air . . . piteous moans . . . God's great wrath upon them."

I closed my eyes and tried not to hear death moans.

"And in the heat, the bodies of thousands of Zulus lifted a stench to the heavens. . . . Yet all but three of our men still stood . . . witnesses of God's great blessing upon us . . ."

I felt that heat and had to lift Cee-Cee off my lap, the room was so tight and air so precious. I wheezed as if I had been smoking Ouma's pipe, my head grown light.

"God's will," Oom Sarel said. "How else could four hundred burghers defeat the Vulture except for the Providence of God? The British are nothing to us compared to that. We should make another covenant, now, to defeat the British."

I opened my eyes and inhaled thick air. The idea of a vow sounded so out of place in our time. The first was so long ago it seemed like a biblical tale. I wondered if God would be interested in causes purchased with the promises of men he created to be flawed and weak in the first place.

Oupa ignored Sarel.

"And that is why this day is holy . . . and why we must revere this solemn vow . . . and why those who forsake our covenant should be delivered to hell."

18

========

May 1901, Concentration Camp

Willem and Klaas created private space beneath a blanket on the far side of the tent, perhaps imagining it a fort from which to fight their imaginary foes. At times we all pulled into small spaces of our own creation, which at first seemed another level of confinement: a cocoon inside an enclosure within an encampment.

I focused on my writing, having discovered the ability to wall out distractions almost regardless of the commotion. In time, the pressure of all the nearness seemed to squeeze words from me. But even with as many pages of rules as I could rip down, paper was dear. Instead of putting every meteor flash of thought to paper, I made them take form before they reached the page. The act of writing gave them substance, and they occupied space, and that made them real. I decided I should always write as if pencil and paper and light were scarce. When each word is valuable, you spend them with care.

Some things that went on were impossible to ignore. It wasn't more than twelve feet across the tent, and in the right conditions, the sounds of even whispered conversations bounced off the canvas and arrived without distortion on the other side. The discussions between those high-pitched little-boy voices came across clearly, and when I heard Klaas mention my name, I listened.

It turned out that Klaas had taken a liking to me, an admission that sickened Willem and did me very little good. When Klaas returned to the matter, saying he would somehow come to my rescue and be my hero one day, Willem threatened to leave and never speak to him.

They talked of the war, cataloging the stories they had heard—atrocities by the Brits, bravery by our men, and the most gruesome descriptions of war wounds; men being shot in the eye while looking through field glasses, men being shelled while in the latrine, several men standing in a row being shot through with the same bullet.

Both decided they were ready to break out of the camp and join the men on commando. They were old enough and could ride and shoot better than the Tommies. Willem reported having killed a duiker as evidence.

"They're fast and very tasty," Willem said.

"You have to be fast if you're tasty," Klaas said, countering Willem's duiker with his own claim of a bushbuck. After volleying tales of manly acts, they agreed they were both fit for duty.

"Won't the Tommies punish our families if we escape?" Willem asked.

"Glory has its cost."

"How do we get to the commandos with no horses?"

Reasonable foresight—rare for them—spoiled this plan.

"Then we'll just have to start killing guards in camp," Willem said.

"*Ja . . . ja.*"

As the plan took shape, they would look for a lone guard. Klaas would distract him by falling down as if stricken, and when the guard bent to offer help, Willem would steal his rifle and shoot him. They would run back to the tent as if nothing had happened.

"But what if the guard doesn't try to help me?"

"Then you get up and we look for another guard," Willem said. "They won't suspect us."

"But what if the guard tells on us?"

"He won't know it was a plot if it doesn't work . . . and if it does work, he'll be dead and he can't tell anybody."

"And we can keep doing it until they're all dead and the camp will be set free," Klaas said.

"And we'll be heroes."

"Legends."

They sealed their agreement on the plan by alternating punches on the shoulders, each harder than the last, until Willem admitted pain.

Maples certainly would fall for the trick. I was suddenly angry at the boys.

And if it failed? "We'll still be heroes," Klaas said. "At least for a while."

Yes, I thought, until they were hanged.

"Japie would have been good at this, " Willem said.

"*Ja*," Klaas said, offering a brief eulogy for a boy they knew who had died of wasting sickness the previous week.

"Bad way to pass," Willem said.

"Oh, typhoid is worse," Klaas argued, triggering another grim debate as the two boys, in whispers, weighed the drawbacks of various deaths. After listing symptoms and miming effects, they arrived at the best way to die in camp: being shot by a guard. Quicker, less suffering, greater dignity.

"Or," Klaas suggested, "if you can tell you are getting really sick, then it would make sense to just attack a guard and hope he shoots you. That would save time . . ."

"And suffering. I was almost shot by a Tommy firing squad," Willem bragged.

"No, you weren't." Klaas rejected Willem's claim so eagerly that he raised his voice loud enough for everyone to notice.

"I was. Six of them . . . all lined up . . . wanted to shoot me as a spy."

"They did not."

"Lettie," Willem called to me. I looked up as if lost in thought. Both boys stared at me, blanket pulled back to their shoulders. "Firing squad . . . me?"

I looked at Klaas and nodded my head.

Suddenly, Willem was his hero. I started to write notes on this exchange but thought of another invasion by the commandant and knew the consequences. Still, I was saddened that boys not yet ten spent time considering their deaths and plotting the deaths of others. I was further saddened that their arguments made so much sense.

DAVID COPPERFIELD WALKED WITH me most days; I carried his unending struggles in my hands. When it rained, I pulled my scarf over my head and shoulders and leaned forward like an old woman to make a lee to protect my book. When it was too foul to be outside, I burrowed beneath my blanket to make a tent inside the tent, and my shrouded place became England in the last century. I left space alongside the tent wall to let in enough light to read by, but it felt dark and misty, exactly the atmosphere I wanted for my time in England with David.

Within a few pages, Dickens convinced me I was right there living beside the young English boy. I liked David and felt . . . what? Akin. That's the word. And I was, in a way, since Moeder's grandfather had been born there.

I had pictured England as a place of palaces and wealth. So to hear of David's difficult life came as a surprise. Our lives on the farm were hard in many ways. But not like David's. And he seemed such a good-hearted little boy, doing his best, trying to see the good in people. I did not see how David could be an enemy of my country. But his stepfather felt like an enemy to anyone with a sense of humanity; he abused and bullied David in the way some of the Brits treated those of us in camp.

I was so happy that I yelled aloud when David passed his threshold of tolerance with his stepfather's beatings and bit him on the hand. I wanted to be like David. After teaching Willem and Cee-Cee one day, I asked them if they wanted me to read Dickens to them. Willem was gone before I had finished the sentence.

"Can I come with you under the blanket?" Cee-Cee asked.

"Of course."

Cee-Cee liked when David was called Master Davy. Sometimes I read for hours, my throat so sore and lips so dry that it was hard to go on. She would point at words and ask what they were. That was how I started to teach her to read. It would be my gift to her. I hoped she would always remember that I taught her, and she would think of me when she was old enough to read to her children. After a while she would just fall asleep in our little nest.

Sometimes when she dozed, I'd hold the book to my face and smell it, thinking that it had been in Maples's tunic, next to his chest. He'd held the cover and touched every page.

Rachel Huiseveldt asked several times whether she could crawl under the blanket with us and hear the story. I looked at Cee-Cee for her opinion. She squinted. I told Rachel there wasn't room. "Master Davy is for us," Cee-Cee whispered once we were covered. And he was. It wasn't the same as having Janetta to walk with and share womanly things. But it was warm and familiar and it was nice to hold Cee-Cee as we read how someone else's strength carried him through a difficult life in a hostile place.

But when I held her now, she felt barely there.

19

March 1900, Venter Farm

Moeder and I must have been a sight, colliding in a scramble from our bedrooms in our nightclothes, her with the rifle in her hands and I with a lantern. A shout came from the darkness: "It's us." Vader cut loose a high whistle from between his teeth. It had been a few months since their first visit, and the horses' ribs stood out in a row of shadows along their flanks.

"I was ready to shoot," Moeder said when Vader climbed the stairs. He hugged her, and she winced as his bandoliers dug into her chest.

"You wouldn't have hurt us with that thing," he said, pointing to her small rifle. "How are you?"

"Later . . . I've got some good news for you."

Moeder turned for the kitchen and had a fire going under the coffeepot and buttermilk on the table by the time the men got the horses settled.

Schalk was the first in the kitchen.

"Did we scare you?"

"We were ready," Moeder said, still in her nightdress.

Oupa Gideon lifted his glass and did not place it back on the table until it was empty. "You would not confuse us with a column of Tommies," Oupa said.

He studied Moeder. "Putting on weight?" he asked. "Lazing about?"

"We are here to witness, not to judge, Gideon," she said.

"More likely you're taking it easy on the girl."

"Bina's a good hand," she said. "We couldn't do it without her."

"I could help if we were going to be here long enough," Schalk said.

"We won't," Gideon said. "Gone tomorrow."

Schalk had removed his hat, yet his matted hair continued to show its shape. He was different, more a man, just slightly smaller than the others. He lifted his bandolier over his head, cartridges now scant, like the smile of an old man missing teeth.

Willem awoke and stepped into the kitchen, curious about the commotion, eyes like pinholes.

"Our sentry," I said.

Oupa took his pipe onto the *stoep*, and Willem followed.

"Would you like some *koekies*?" Moeder asked.

Schalk nodded without interrupting his gulp of buttermilk. She retrieved the pastry and sat between Schalk and Vader.

When Vader reached for one, a dark mark on his forearm peeked from his sleeve. Moeder pulled back his cuff. The scar was half the length of his forearm and jagged. I could not tell whether the wound had been deep or serious, but the coloring looked a sickly green. The stitches were uneven, the skin was pinched and puckered, and the wound was seeping in spots.

"What happened?" she asked.

"What?"

"There."

"Where?"

"There . . . right there. . . . I'm looking right at it."

Vader looked down.

"Oh, got it caught on something. . . . Didn't really have time to stop and get untangled."

Moeder examined his face. He responded by chewing his cake with greater enthusiasm. We looked closer. The fading stitches were made with the green thread she had packed in his kit.

"Who stitched this?" Moeder asked.

"He did," Schalk answered, pointing at Vader and laughing.

"You did it yourself?" Moeder leaned toward it.

"*Ja*, not bad." Vader pulled his sleeve back down to cover it.

She touched his arm, then his hand. "I'll mix a poultice," she said.

"He didn't call me until he needed the knot tied," Schalk said. "He stitched it with one hand but couldn't tie the knot by himself."

Willem interrupted with shooting noises as he acted out one of Oupa's stories.

"Does Gideon ever tire?" Moeder asked.

"Never."

"We'll be hearing these stories for ages, won't we?"

"In some form," Vader said, heading outside for his pipe. "They're getting more dramatic already."

Moeder brought more milk for Schalk.

"How are you, Moeder?"

"Well. Learning about farming. And stock. Doing some things I haven't done on the farm since I was young, and some things I never did. Everybody is helping."

"I mean, how are you?"

"Well."

"You feel well?"

"Yes . . . well . . . why?"

Schalk stared at her and then sat back from the table and packed a pipe. It looked strange, as if he were pretending to be an adult. It was a perfect chance to make fun of him, but he'd been gone so long I couldn't. I hoped Willem didn't see the pipe; he'd be asking for one next.

Schalk took another bite of the cake and combed crumbs from his feathery beard, retrieving and eating those that fell onto the table.

"This is so good," he said.

We heard more sounds of mock battles from the porch.

"Tell us . . . something about it, Schalk," I said. "Anything."

He chewed longer than was necessary, nodding to bide time.

"Schalk?"

"Some of the men are going home and not coming back," he said, shaking his head. "The British promise they'll be left alone."

"Anybody we know?" Moeder asked.

"Not yet."

"What else?"

"That's it."

He closed in on another bite.

"Schalk," Moeder said, pressing him. "Your father?"

"Fine . . . the best. Oupa is brave but thinks he's still a young man," Schalk said. "He is not."

"Sarel?"

"Oupa is hard on him. Never lets up. Doesn't seem to matter what he does."

"And you?"

"Watching and learning . . . staying safe."

The war he and Vader presented was not the one I had seen in the reports in the newspapers at Tante Hannah's.

Moeder tried to stroke his hair into place, but it was stubborn. I expected him to complain, but he allowed it.

"Is it close to over?" I asked.

"Moeder," Schalk interrupted, "will you play something?"

She questioned him with a look that brought no answers.

"Come," she said, moving into the parlor.

By the time Moeder struck a few notes, the family had gathered.

> Be still, my soul, though dearest friends depart
> And all is darkened in the vale of tears;
> Then shalt thou better know his love, his heart,
> Who comes to soothe thy sorrow and thy fears.

The sight of the men, who looked worn but mostly healthy, soothed my fears—at least the worst of them. And as we all sat in the parlor, Moeder playing softly, I wanted to think of it as another of our quiet evenings before the war. But we had all changed. Moeder looked at Vader and asked, "Is there something you'd like to hear?"

It surprised Vader. He thought about his options. "Sarie Marais," he said.

She played it at a lively tempo, and the men sang. "*There by the maize, by the green thorn tree, there my Sarie lives.*" She held the final note, and as long as she pumped the pedal, it continued to resonate. She leaned close to the keys so that her stomach touched the organ.

Vader stood behind her and surprised us all by lifting her to her feet with a hug.

For the first time since they had left months ago, Oupa came in to get me in the night.

"Very quiet," he whispered. On the way through the parlor, I could see the slim dash of lamplight under my parents' door; they were still awake. That was never the case. We walked so slowly that my eyes adjusted and I was surprised that a sliver of light could illuminate so much.

Oupa and I did not risk even whispers on the *stoep* but still pointed at the constellations and smiled at each other. And when we returned, my parents' lamp was doused. I hoped they had not heard us. I didn't want to give away our secret.

They had time only to load supplies and inhale a standing breakfast before leaving in the morning.

"God's grace, Susanna," Vader said.

"His grace, Matthys."

They used each other's given names so seldom I had almost forgotten them. We watched the men turn and go, but it felt different this time. We could no longer pretend it was a glorified hunting trip. The visit upset me, bringing the war nearer. When their dust trail faded, Moeder went to the side of the house. I watched her, in case she needed my help with her next work project. She leaned with one arm against the blue gum tree and then slipped around the other side. She returned only after I'd gone inside, looking pale and unwell.

PART II

Chosen Vessels

PART II

20

June 1901, Concentration Camp

The words floated out in rippling waves, the way old women with trembling voices try to reach difficult notes in hymns. She must have been new to the tent across the row from ours because I'd never heard singing from that space. Since the evening when we had gathered for hymns, I'd tried to sing a bit but had been shouted down each day. Cee-Cee liked it, Moeder just gained distance, but the rest gave off a howling like jackals over a carcass. To hear the neighbor woman singing—poorly, at that—encouraged me. If I sang in her tent, I might be considered gifted.

A little one ran from the tent and almost struck me as I tried to peek inside.

"Marthinus, come."

I put a hand on the little boy's shoulder and led him back into the tent.

"*Dankie*," the woman said.

"I'm Aletta." I pointed to our tent.

"Marghretta van Zyl," she said.

"I heard you singing."

"Trying to calm things as I can. . . . It doesn't seem to work."

The woman, with three children now arranged around her, was too old to be their mother. I guessed ages and tried to decipher their relationship.

"I'm their *ouma*," she explained. "My daughter passed when we were taken."

I nodded with the sad, knowing look I assumed after I realized the futility of saying "I'm so sorry" to every person I met. It was easier now to mirror our frowns and share head nods without the burden of details. The children were all younger than Willem. Three at seven and under, I guessed.

Another child, the middle in size, crawled behind me and ran from the tent.

"Could you?"

I chased the child, again leading the little one back inside the tent with a hand on her shoulder.

"Agile," I said.

"Especially compared to me." Her spine curved forward at the midpoint, leaving her eye to eye with me. I imagined the challenge of her duties, getting water and rations, scraping together meals, laundry . . . all the while trying to keep three little ones from tearing across the camp.

While the children were occupied in a game they created with a string and two twigs, the woman pulled me toward the tent door.

"I should explain; she was killed, actually," the woman said. "My daughter. She didn't just pass."

"British?"

She nodded. I nodded. And we each pinched our lips tight.

"We saw smoke from the next farm over and tried to get away," she said. "We had the wagon packed and were heading out for some caves we knew of. A few of them came after us. . . . My daughter tried to get the wagon down a *spruit* to hide in the willows and brush."

The oldest boy pushed down the youngest, and all three tangled on the ground.

"Pffffffffftttttt," I said, pointing a finger at them. They turned and sat in place, perhaps unaccustomed to correction from a stranger.

The woman looked surprised.

"Powerful," I said, looking at the tip of my finger. "Their mother?"

"They couldn't even see who we were," she said. "They just started shooting. . . . Missed the children, praise God. . . . Got Emma through the stomach."

I put a hand on the woman's shoulder.

"Took two days for her to die," she said. "The British kept giving her water, which was the worst thing, but it didn't matter. The main Tommy kept saying he was sorry, that he had no way of knowing we weren't commandos."

"They didn't know who it was, so they decided the best thing to do was just shoot into the trees?"

"That's what he said . . . and then he blamed it on us," she said.

"On you?"

"He said, 'You Hollanders are to blame for us being here,' and, 'We wouldn't have to shoot you if you didn't run.' As if they would convince us her death was our fault."

"The children?"

"Well, they had a chance to say good-bye to her . . . but I hope they will lose the memory of those days."

"At least you were there for them."

"I wish it had been me."

She was so sincere, her sigh an apology for having lived instead of her daughter.

I asked Moeder later if she knew the woman across the way.

"I see her doing laundry sometimes . . . trying to keep three little ones from falling in."

"Did you know what happened to the mother . . . to the children's mother?"

"Just talk, nothing from her."

"The British shot her," I said. "They were trying to get away and the soldiers shot . . . just fired wildly at their wagon."

"They didn't see who it was?"

"Didn't care . . . two women and three children."

"I'm sure she wished they'd shot her instead," Moeder said, echoing the instinct expressed by Ouma van Zyl. It made me think: What if it had been we who ran? What if it had been Moeder who had been shot by the British? How different one bullet fired into the brush could have made life for all of us. We would be here by ourselves, just the three children. I would have to be the mother of our little family, for now and forever, every one of us changed by one pull of the trigger. It seemed so real I felt a weight of responsibility.

"That woman needs help, Ma," I said.

"*Ja*," she said. "You should, Lettie."

"Water . . . rations . . ."

"*Ja* . . . however you can help . . . poor woman."

The next afternoon I introduced Willem to the Van Zyl children, and he and Klaas ran with the oldest boy while I took the two younger children for a walk to give the woman a rest. She asked that I call her Ouma. When it was too cold or rainy, I sat with them in the tent and told them the stories I had made up for Cecelia back on the farm, the ones about pirates and travel and adventure and the big sister who was always there to come to the rescue whenever danger lurked. I thought they could use some fairy tales.

I TRIED TO SPOT Maples from a distance, peering up from my book every paragraph. If another guard was nearby, I turned and walked down a different row and worked my way back a while later when he might be alone. It was natural to look aimless.

Sometimes it seemed as if Maples was watching for me, or maybe it was just his job to look in all directions. If Maples had given me the Dickens book so that he could later say that I stole it from him, it had been several weeks and he surely would have sprung his trap before now. It had been a gift, not a trick. Yet I had to be careful if others were watching. I might approach him, but I never spoke first. If watchers took note, it would always be a matter of my speaking only when spoken to by a uniformed representative of the Crown.

His head was down. He was reading a letter. I needed to just walk past this time. He might be luring me into a trap that could put our whole family in danger. I veered away and noticed his rifle propped against the fence as he read. The war would have been over by now if all Tommies were this lax. He probably thought no woman would rush up and take his rifle. I stored that thought in case we ever needed a weapon to break out or protect ourselves.

Walk past without a word, Lettie. If he doesn't speak first, he's not even here, just keep reading.

"Wait . . . Aletta."

I looked up, surprised to see him. I looked at his unattended rifle. He saw me notice it. Maybe this was his trap.

"Oh, please, you could nick it right now . . . and shoot me in the foot or the leg, too, please. I could say I was hit by a sniper from outside the camp, and they might send me home . . . with a medal, even. Or maybe you could take this thing and trade it for one of the Mausers your men use . . . much better."

I looked into his eyes, the way Mother did when she searched for reflections of falsehood.

"I hate the thing. . . . It's so heavy," he said. "Never shot one until I joined."

It was easier to see him as something other than a soldier when his rifle was not in hand. He was just a young man in a uniform and did not seem comfortable in it at that.

"At least I don't have to do anything with it except carry it around in here," he said.

He hadn't mentioned being in actual battle, in the line of fire, shooting at our men. But that's what he now implied.

"You were out there?"

"For a while, fighting the 'wily' Boers—that's what the officers called them," he said. "Always something up their sleeves."

"Oh?"

"We followed some up to a farmhouse, but they disappeared. We asked the old man there where the Boers were hiding. In the queen's English, he said he was from a British family and would be happy to help us find the bleedin' Boers. He wanted us to do away with the lot of 'em. He told us to go one way and follow some dingus or dongus or some nonsense, and we'd find their camp."

"And?"

"We rode down a little stream channel and they jumped us. . . . The old man sent us into an ambush. . . . We were all lined up in a row nice and neat for them to pick us off."

"Ah . . . *uitoorlê*," I said. "That's our word for 'outfoxed.'"

"Rude, don't you think?"

"What, someone being ungentlemanly in war?"

"Oh, we learned that," he said. "Some would wave the white flag, and when a column came up to get 'em, they pulled down and shot 'em up."

"I don't believe that," I said, but then I thought of some who were capable of it.

"There were times when we'd bivouac in tall grass and the Boers would set fire to it all, and we'd suddenly be running for our lives and get confused by all the smoke, and bullets would just come ripping in at all angles, not caring a bit what they hit," he said. "I found a low spot and flattened out inside it. I was in there cozy when an officer jumped in, too. Couldn't believe they were just firing into the smoke. Officer said something I'll never forget: 'Nothing blind as a bullet.'"

These were not the stories I heard from our men. It sounded like the experience of Ouma van Zyl, except these blind bullets were being fired by the other side. I soured at the topic and it must have shown. I started walking.

"Wait," he said. "It's not all like that." This soldier, this boy, seemed aching to talk, as if he had no one else in the whole British army who would listen to him.

"We heard of one of your men who was so sad about killing one of ours, he was on his knees praying so hard for him that we just walked up and took him prisoner. We saw others risk their lives to save their friends. Unbelievably brave . . . racing through open fire to rescue a wounded man. Some helped wounded Tommies . . . sheltered a man from the sun, or gave him their last canteen of water. There's some fine men . . . and there's scoundrels . . . like our army."

"Like the ones who called us spies?"

"Who is that?"

"Your commandant . . ." I stopped in case Maples might be in league with the commandant.

I could not imagine Maples among those setting fire to our house. Most of the time, he didn't seem to know a war was being conducted. His talk this day was the first that caused me to imagine him involved in anything more dangerous than breaking up a hen fight among caged women. But each time I readied to tear into him, he deprived me of the pleasure by agreeing with me.

"You say our rifles are better?"

"By a sight . . . magazine load . . . smokeless powder," he said. "You can't see where the bullets are coming from. . . . Just start flying past. You don't need to hear about all this. It's not good for you . . . or anybody."

"Maybe I'll write about it someday."

"You can ask your men about it."

"That's just one side of it."

He smiled a bit; I think he liked for a moment to think of himself as more than just the guardian of the eastern fence line.

"This little bit, then. Your men never miss. . . . Make every cartridge count. They hide in those trenches and just start plucking us when we ride up. Officers had never seen such a thing, troops popping up from the ground with no warning."

"The warthog backs into its hole so it can come out fighting," I said. "My brother Schalk told me that."

"Well, it works. Our officers said we underestimated your men . . . especially the way they know the land. One captain said that as your numbers go down, the quality of the men fighting goes up, and as our numbers go up, the quality of our soldiers goes down."

I thought of Oom Sarel coming to camp while Oupa, Vader, and Schalk were still fighting. It proved Maples's theory.

"The prisoners I saw were very solemn . . . never a curse word or threat," he said. "They weren't all very bright, and they smelled like rotting meat, but they were very pious . . . praying every night and singing hymns. One night . . ."

"What?"

"Sure . . . here's a story for you to write about," he said. "Sometimes one side or the other would call for an armistice to collect the wounded . . . or what have you . . . and we'd just rest in our camps with a holiday from war. We did that one afternoon and then the evening cooled and the moon came up full, making everything silver. Across the valley, in their camp, the Boers started singing. We couldn't believe we could hear them so clearly."

"They always sing," I said. "Usually hymns."

"That was it . . . and we recognized the hymn right off . . . 'Old Hundredth' . . . like a church choir on the other side of the clearing. Some of our men then joined in, too. Then all of us. We were all singing together; they could hear us and we could hear them. It was beautiful. I'll never forget that afternoon and evening."

"Then what?"

"When the clock ticked over to the end of the armistice, we could hear the breech bolts of Mausers start clicking. . . . Time to go back to work."

"Right then?"

"In the morning . . . but I kept thinking about that time." He sang in a timid voice:

> You faithful servants of the Lord,
> Sing out his praise with one accord,
> While serving him with all your might
> And keeping vigil through the night.

I tried to picture the scene, two armies so close that they could harmonize, yet knowing what the next day might bring. Danger did not seem so near in this camp. It was not easy for us, but we did not have to consider the flight of so many stray bullets.

"Faithful servants of the Lord," I repeated.

"You know it?"

"Of course."

"Of course you do," he said. "That's all we ever heard from the men we captured. God and duty. God will protect us . . . God's will. A minute wouldn't pass without thanking God and quoting scripture. Not a one could fight without a Bible in his pocket."

"Our way."

"But God offers a lot of different advice."

I tilted my head.

"The Joiners in here . . . God told them to surrender; God told them it was the best thing." He lifted both arms and looked to the sky. "God tells some to fight and some not to fight. Has anybody in this country ever done anything that God didn't have a say in?"

"Just because your army is godless . . ."

"We are not godless. . . . It's just that you are so . . . so bloody Godful."

"A coward will cling to any excuse," I said.

He nodded. I nodded. I looked at the sky; he looked at the ground. I was ready to move on.

21

May 1900, Venter Farm

We considered ourselves capable farmers in the absence of the men. Our only real problem arose when Moeder injured her back when we tried to rid the sheep of lice. The sheep had been clustering like clouds in a storm front, rubbing against one another, almost sparking from friction. Moeder parted a clear space on the back of one, and blue lice raced from the light to the safety of the thick wool. With a small growling noise, she announced that we would have to send them through the dipping tank.

The men had complained of the sheep for years at the time of dipping. Neither Oupa nor Vader cursed nor blasphemed, but their screams at the sheep made their frustration obvious. "Stupidest animals alive," Vader yelled one time. "Sent by God to vex us."

We found a bottle that bore a simple label in Vader's hand: "Sheep." There were no instructions for mixing. They had never foreseen anyone else's having to take over when lice invaded. Bina and I filled the dipping pool with water, and Moeder poured in the dip mixture. Willem rounded the sheep up and drove them down the thornbush chute into the tank. The men were right: they were stupid. And stubborn in the chute. They shook and balked and protested in their crying-child voices. And they came up coughing after Moeder forced their heads under.

A fat ewe particularly objected and tried to back out the chute, getting hind legs caught in the thornbush wall. It panicked further and twisted against the binding branches. The ewe screamed in pure, ignorant fear as Moeder pulled it by the front legs. It kicked at her, crying like death into her face, its eyes flashing desperate white, and then it loosed a piteous wail.

Moeder reached farther to grasp the wool at its rump. The ewe twisted and raged, burying the thorns deeper in its hocks. Moeder bent lower, nearer the shanks, and lifted. Nothing. Lower, harder, with her back and shoulders and legs. When she screamed, it shocked the sheep into silence. She released the ewe and fell backward. When she opened her eyes, she gasped sips of air, teeth clenched. I jumped into the chute and pried the animal free from the other side with Willem's help.

"Breathe, now, breathe," Bina said, leaning over Moeder, trying to block the sun from her eyes. She inhaled with a catch and panted again, arms crossed tight at her stomach. She looked flushed and gave off heat.

"Oh, dear God . . . Matthys . . . ," she yelled with more panic than pain.

"He's not here," I said.

"She knows," Bina said. "Be still."

She lifted Moeder's head into her lap and spoke softly. "Are you carrying . . . is that your worry?"

Moeder nodded toward Willem and me. "I don't want them to see."

"Be still," Bina said. "Then we get you to bed."

Bina hummed low. The sound filled space and pushed away distraction, as when Moeder pumped the organ bellows with just one finger on a key. It steadied Moeder's breathing.

"Take Willem and the little one and go to Tante's," Bina told me. "Spend the night. Your mother needs quiet. She hurt her back; she'll be all right. Stay a full day. I've got *muti* for this."

I wanted to stay and help. But I trusted Bina, and my duty would be to the little ones. Tante Hannah welcomed us and began telling us all the things we could do. I had to interrupt her to say that Moeder had hurt her back and we were sent to spend the night.

"Delightful," she said.

The next morning I helped Tante Hannah make breakfast, and later she accompanied us home. It took Moeder two days to get back in the field, and she was slower, more deliberate, and very quiet.

22

June 1901, Concentration Camp

Water grew heavier, the buckets stretching my arms and fingers. I fetched for our family, for Ouma van Zyl most days, and now for the Huiseveldts, since Klaas had taken a cough.

The line formed before dawn. The cold reached down and chilled me from the inside, so that I could feel the exact shape of my lungs. I thought of the men on commando, wherever they were, and I hoped they had fires and blankets and a safe place to spend each night. I pictured them still with the coffee and rusks and biltong we had packed for them when they left, but I knew that was impossible.

The pump wheezed a three-note groan, up-down-up, coaxing the stubborn water upward when everything in its nature told it to go the other way. Some women brought pitchers; others, enamel basins. We had a bucket, and so did the Huiseveldts. I studied the water each day, admiring the way it adapted to its container, caring nothing about shape, only direction. Some days I could see through the water to the silver metal at the bottom of the bucket, and at the right angle, I could see my reflected image. Other days, especially after a storm, it was brown as a puddle in an ox path.

This day, it was near freezing, and my knuckles stung from the weight of the buckets. Maples leaned against the fence post and looked out to the east. Three women walked toward me. I put my water buckets down and retied my boots until the women turned up a row.

"Morning," he said.

"Morning . . ."

"Hallo . . . isn't that what you usually say?"

"Bina, our native girl, says 'peace' . . . her tribal word for peace, at least. . . . That's how they greet each other."

"Peace?"

"Yes, the first thing she says when she sees me."

"Peace," he said.

"Right."

"You're wearing your apron again," Maples said.

"Pinafore."

"I'll have to tell Betty."

"Betty?"

"Betty . . . my girl back home," he said.

"A servant?"

"No, my sweetie."

"You . . ."

"Sure . . . haven't I told you? I've told you how much I miss her. . . . That's why I call this Betty." He pointed to his rifle. "Whenever I hold her, I think about holding Betty."

He pulled his rifle to his chest and petted the barrel as if he were about to dance with a slim, rigid girl.

"We write letters almost every day," he said. "I've mentioned her to you."

"I have to get the water to my family," I said, walking on.

"I'm sure I told you about her . . . haven't I?"

He stepped alongside me.

"We were seeing each other for half a year before I left," he said. "I'm worried she'll tire of waiting."

Shame.

"I told her she should go and complain to the minister of war. If she yells at him the way she has at me sometimes, they'll probably call the whole thing off and bring everybody home."

Wonderful, his girlfriend is connected to government officials. "Does she know him?"

"That was in jest," he said. "She works at the Provincial Laundries with a hundred other girls. She stirs steaming pots all day. She comes home exhausted. She wears an apron like yours, and it gets stained from bleach every day."

"Must look a fright."

"But she cleans up. Takes forever . . . all the skirts and layers of things . . . like the queen . . . rest in peace. She wraps her hair up around on top of her head and holds it up with a hundred pins."

"What color?"

"Color?"

"Hair."

"Brown, shiny brown . . . and thick. It goes to her waist when she lets it down."

"Do they wear *kappies*?"

"The bonnets like yours? When it's sunny . . . so not much. They wear hats . . . some with feathers and flowers, the size of a platter. She asked me to pick up some ostrich feathers and bring them home. I've got a bundle of them for her, and porcupine quills—they were everywhere out there—and some shells from a beach near where we landed."

"You're taking much of our country back to her."

"That will have to do until I pick up some diamonds," he said. "I thought about sending my chocolate back to her, but I needed it more than she did."

The last time he'd said he considered sending it home to his mother. That proved he was a liar and couldn't be trusted.

"I mentioned you in a letter to Betty."

"Oh . . ."

"Told her that you are a little Boer girl reading Dickens—she sent me the book—and that you're trying to learn things about us and the war because you want to be a writer."

"Little girl?"

"Right . . . about twelve, right? . . . That's what I told her."

"Twelve?"

"Right . . . and you remind me of my little sister, Annie . . . she's eleven."

Little sister? Twelve?

"I'm fourteen," I said, raising my voice without intending to.

I walked away resolved never to speak to him again. When I neared the tent, Moeder was out in front looking for me.

"Put the buckets down," she said. "What took so long?"

"Long line," I said.

"Willem, get out here," she said toward the tent. She pulled him to her side. "Lettie, have you been bothered by any guards?"

"Me? No. What is it?"

"A guard swept up Willem and took him in for questioning," she said.

"I said nothing to them," Willem said.

"What did they want?"

"They asked him if he was plotting against the British," Moeder said.

"He's nine, Ma," I said.

"I know. . . . Has anyone talked to you? Followed you? Asked you about our family?"

"No, Ma, nobody." I squinted sincerely, hoping to mask the lie.

"Lettie, be careful," she said. "Trust no one. For some reason they think we're up to something. . . . They thought Willem was making plans to kill guards."

23

June 1900, Venter Farm

I demanded privacy when I stripped down to bathe at home. I convinced myself I was more womanly each time. Maybe I didn't look it, but I felt it. And I worried about even taking time to consider the matter after Oupa Gideon had planted in me the gift of guilt. In a sermon not long before the men left, he railed against the sin of pride. "All is vanity and a striving after the wind," he said. I was only curious about my growth, and I had never heard curiosity listed among the many sins on his list.

Moeder voiced her "amen" the evening of that sermon but then took me to her room and showed me how she held her silver hand mirror with one hand and shaped her hair with the brush in the other hand. The brush set had belonged to her mother, who taught her to pinch her cheeks for color and to brush her hair in certain ways. Moeder taught me those things that night. She unpinned her hair, still spiraled from the day in braided coils, it fell thick past her shoulders. She swayed so that it fell to one side where she could brush it. I memorized the move and tried it when she handed me the brush and mirror.

"Taking care of yourself is merely tending God's gifts, and it honors him when you are at your best," Moeder said. That would also be my interpretation from that moment forward, and as much as we appreciated the Gospel that Oupa preached to us, Moeder and I shared the belief that he knew nothing of women.

I could see that the work and chores in the field had made me stronger, with veins branching just beneath the skin of my leaner hands. My face was no longer as round and childlike. Bina noticed. She told me one day that my face was starting to tell a different story. She smiled and said she needed to start singing a different kind of song for me. The song was lively, and she slapped her hands on a woven basket to add a rhythm. I liked it.

This night was cold, and when I pulled the pelt quilt up so that the fur warmed my chin, I seemed to melt into sleep more than fall into it. And in my dream, Oupa came to get me and pressed his finger to my lips again so I would not alarm anyone. I smiled. His finger smelled of his tobacco and of dirt and campfire. He whispered, "We're home."

Fighting through a depth of sleep, I forced open my eyes. It really was Oupa.

"Go wake your mother. I don't want to frighten her."

"Oup—" I started to shout in excitement, but he stopped me.

I opened her door and whispered. She awoke at once.

"They're home."

"I didn't hear . . ."

"We sneaked in, Susanna," Oupa said as she entered the still-dark parlor.

"Light a lamp," she said.

"Just one . . . in the kitchen," he said.

"Where's Matthys . . . with the horses?"

"Not here," he said.

"What?"

"No . . . be calm. . . . He's fine," Oupa said. "He went with another unit. We were told we could break off for a day."

"I thought you stayed together."

"He helped plan a mission and they needed him," Schalk said, squeezing in the front door and closing it quietly. "He wouldn't let me go with him. I tried."

"Could he have come home?" Moeder asked. "I need to tell him—"

"They needed him," Oupa said. "They follow him. . . . They don't follow just anybody."

"But I—" Moeder started.

"Settle, woman," Oupa said. "This is important. . . . He's important. . . . If it wasn't, he'd be here."

"Did Sarel go?"

"They didn't need him. Do you have supplies ready? We can't stay."

"Bags are there," she said, tilting her head toward the false wall. "But smaller."

"Did Tuma go with him, at least?" she asked.

"No, went straight home."

Oupa did not ask about us.

"Help me." Schalk pulled at my elbow, and I went outside as he tended Kroon and walked him to the barn. Schalk smelled, and his shoes made sounds when he walked, the soles tearing free from the top leather.

"Tell me . . . is Vader all right?"

"He's fine; the *veldkornet* asked for him and he went. Be proud of him."

"I am. . . . We miss him."

"How's Moeder?"

"She hurt her back, but she didn't act like it. She wanted to tell Vader about it, but . . ."

We gathered in the kitchen for cold meats. Gideon asked the blessing and talked briefly about stock and crops. There were no war stories. He went to the *stoep* with Willem in his footsteps. Moeder sat between Schalk and me. . . . Cee-Cee never awakened.

"How are you, *seun*?"

"Well . . . and you?"

"Well."

They looked at each other, and Moeder turned away.

"Is his arm healed?" I asked.

"His arm?"

"Where he stitched it."

"Oh . . . I think so. . . . It must be. . . . That was a long time ago."

"There have been other things since then?" I asked.

"There are always other things. . . . Don't worry."

"Don't worry?" Moeder opened her hands.

Schalk startled.

"It just . . . does no good," he said. "Not about Vader."

She knew that better than any of us.

Their stay was so different, almost silent. So few words were exchanged. Even Oupa had no stories to tell. And Moeder said very little even to Schalk. A short night, a quick breakfast, and they were gone at dawn.

When we neared the finish of the next day, Moeder urged me to go to Tante Hannah's for a class. I could hear an argument inside by the time I reached her stairs. I knew I should turn and go home, and even tried to step away, but my curiosity froze me and then drew me closer. Tante Hannah said only a few words at a time, and it wasn't until I stood near the door that I could hear Ouma Wilhelmina.

". . . weakness . . . mistake . . ."

I listened closer.

Tante Hannah coughed and cleared her voice. "Wives must submit to their husbands as they submit to the Lord," she said.

"Stitch that," Wilhelmina shouted, "on a pillow."

A noisy wind crossed the *stoep* and muted all but the words that were stressed.

". . . vow . . ."

". . . a man . . ."

The house vibrated. I looked away. With the windblown dust, the blank veld blended into the gray sky. I had to go. But if I left, they might hear me, and it would be obvious I'd been listening. I knocked. As the argument paused, I entered, acting out of breath, as if I'd just hurried to the door.

"Lettie . . . hallo. . . . Go into the kitchen, and I'll be there in a minute," Tante Hannah said. "Have a rusk."

Ouma Wilhelmina, now eye to eye with me, followed.

"Good-bye, Aletta . . . I'm leaving . . ."

"Leeee-ving?" I stretched the word. No one in our family had ever just left. I hadn't known it was possible.

"Cape Town, to live with my daughter Grieta and her husband . . . a good man."

"I'd like to go to Cape Town," I said. "I'm dying to see the ocean."

"Come along," she said.

"I can't," I said. Moeder would not allow that.

"You should come, you all should come. Hannah should come," she said. "Get away from here."

I could barely bite through the crunchy rusk. I studied the pattern on the plate, the delicate flowers on the edge. I ran a finger across them as I tried to be quiet.

"I'll smoke all I want," she continued in fragments. "He shouted at me . . . disrespect. . . . It's not his tobacco. . . . He can bully her, but not me. No more."

It was not my business.

"I'm packing," Ouma said, spinning toward her room as if she could not tolerate another minute.

Tante Hannah set out the old newspapers she had collected in town.

"Thank you for the food," I said.

She smiled.

"They don't get along. . . . You know that," she said. "The visit last night did not go well. Oom Sarel was upset . . . the war. And she . . . she's always upset."

"Schalk and Oupa did not talk much. . . . Vader didn't come home at all."

"Is he all right?"

I'd been lectured so often to say nothing about their condition and location that I hesitated.

"Lettie . . . is he all right?"

"They needed him on a mission."

"Your *oom* said nothing about it. What did Oupa say?"

"Oupa said they asked especially for Vader . . ."

"Didn't ask for Sarel?"

"Vader helped plan it, they said."

Hannah took a moment.

"Did they say anything else?"

"No . . . very little. Did Oom Sarel?"

"Yes . . . and we should talk about it today . . . as a lesson."

She handed me a paper but summarized it before I could read.

"The Tommies walked in and took over both capitals without a fight."

This seemed impossible. "Does that mean the war is over? . . . They won?"

"No, it's not over," she said. "It was a strategy by our men. . . . We just walked away. . . . Better to fight them out on the veld instead of around the cities."

"I can't imagine our men backing from a fight."

"The papers are calling them 'guerrilla' tactics," she said. "It means 'little war' . . . picking their places to fight small battles. The Tommies want to fight like pieces set in place on the chess board, to benefit from their power. The commandos want to hit and run so that they benefit from their mobility and knowledge of the country."

I could see Vader and Schalk stalking game in the bush. They could make themselves invisible. I thought of an entire army creeping about the country in silence.

"So we can win that way?"

She gestured with uncertainty.

"The British are using new tactics in response," she said, explaining a plan by Lord Kitchener for dealing with the commandos.

"Since it's not the way they're used to fighting, they're calling us all spies, just for giving support," she said.

"Spies? Us?"

"They want to try to stop the men from getting supplies from their homes and farms," she said.

"How?"

"They're burning them."

"Burning them? Burning what?"

She nodded. "Yes, homes and farms."

"Where?"

"Here."

"What are we supposed to do?"

"I don't know."

24

June 1901, Concentration Camp

Maples concentrated on stitching a button on his tunic while still wearing it. It allowed me to look at him again, longer. He was better looking from a distance, and he was always more attractive in my thoughts than he was in my presence. I vowed at night not to risk talking to him, yet when I set out, it was in his direction. Half the time I would turn back toward the tent, only to retrace my steps toward his post. After Willem had been snatched up and threatened, I needed to be more vigilant. But here I was.

"Can you give me a hand?" he asked. "I was hoping to see you today."

I looked down the fence line and toward the tents. I closed Mr. Dickens but walked on. "I shouldn't."

"Good thing I've got my *hussif*," he said.

"Your what?"

"Housewife," he said more clearly. "My sewing kit. That's what we call it, our things for mending. I keep my needles and thread and extra buttons in my empty chocolate tin now."

"Oh." I had stopped and rooted at the mentioned of a housewife. "I thought . . ."

"I hope Betty will have me when I get back. . . . We haven't had that talk. Her father scares the wits from me. He's a butcher, with forearms like a stevedore. Huge mitts. I think he just pulls the meat apart with his hands. He almost crushed my fingers when I came to get Betty for our first night out."

"Have you sat with her?"

"Sat?"

"Here, the custom is to sit together, with the candle burning."

"Never heard about this."

I turned and backed toward the fence so that I could scan for anyone who might be watching. I explained our *opsitkers* tradition—the parents lighting a candle and leaving the room to give the boy and girl privacy until the candle burned out.

"They just leave 'em be in the parlor? By themselves?"

"*Ja.*"

"How big are those candles?"

"Depends on how well they like you."

"Have you done this?"

"Schalk, my brother, has."

"How old was he?"

"Almost sixteen . . . then."

"So young."

"I'm almost old enough, but there are no boys here . . . and few candles."

No boys. No boys until the war was over. The words made it real. Would there ever be boys? Would I be too old? Would they all be taken? I looked at Maples again. He was not so homely. I asked the Lord's forgiveness for sinful thoughts. But asking to forgive the thoughts made me rethink those thoughts. I tried to shake my head quickly, and hard, in hopes that the physical action would stop the cycle.

"Are you all right?" he asked. Oh, dear God, he noticed. He must think me daft. Thoughts returned. I asked for forgiveness. The cycle spun in my mind like a dust devil.

"Is there something wrong?" he asked.

I shook again. Forgive me, dear God.

"Aletta?"

"What? How did you know what I was thinking?"

"I don't. . . . What happened . . . I mean, with your brother?"

"Nothing, he got frightened and rode off," I told him. "Only time he's admitted to being afraid."

"Just left her there?"

"When he got home, he was shaking. A month later the war started."

"Well, then going to war was better for him than getting locked up with a gal too young; he might have ended up cursing that candle," Maples said. "She might look better to him now. He's had some long, cold nights to think about her. If he can't wait to get back to her, he's in love. The way I am with Betty."

"Do you long for her?"

"Do I *long* for her? Where did you hear that?"

"My book."

"I didn't see that."

"Not *Copperfield* . . . the other one . . . from our country. One of the characters said she felt an 'unutterable longing.' *Unutterable* means she couldn't even talk about it."

He laughed and my face went hot.

"Well, you can't know what it's like from a book. You know it when you feel it. When you're older."

"How old are you?"

"Nineteen," he said.

Nineteen. Schalk is seventeen, I thought.

"I'm almost seventeen."

"You are not."

"Almost . . ."

"You are not. You told me you were fourteen."

I'd lied so often I was losing track.

"You'll know when you're older. . . . You sometimes feel so empty."

I usually felt the opposite, so filled with feelings that I did not have room for them all, and that caused them to wrestle in a small space. I decided I had heard all I would need from Private Maples. I would walk on the other side of camp; I would not risk getting caught talking to him by my mother or anyone else. As I stepped back to turn from him for the last time, Maples put his hand out to me—his right hand, offered as if to lead me onto a dance floor. He didn't want me to leave. He wanted me to stop. The gesture implied more: Come closer. My fingers fluttered as I held my palm toward his for this first touch. I wished I had known it was coming; I could have prepared, at least washed my hands. I looked at my nails, jagged from biting, surrounded by a U of dirt. His fingers closed lightly around mine, his palm rough.

"This is for you," he said, so softly I could scarcely hear. "Read it. . . . Destroy it. . . . Don't let anyone see it."

He squeezed my hand harder so that I could feel that there was something cupped in his palm. I circled a fist around it as I withdrew. He tilted his head toward the tents, shooing me away. I settled my left hand in the pocket of my pinafore, but I didn't walk toward the tent, where there would be no privacy. I dared not look down when others were around. It felt like paper: a folded note. I moved my fingers across it to try to sense the words within. A love note? He was one of those boys who could not say the things he felt, so he wrote them instead. I liked that quality. *Coy* was the word for it.

For the first time since being in camp, I went to the latrines when it was not a necessity, and I felt none of the usual nausea. Seated at the far end, I unfolded the note slowly, like a present.

It wasn't from Maples. But I wasn't disappointed. It was from someone very important to me, someone I'd missed but didn't know how much until I read the note. And the reconnection with this person would make it impossible to stay away from Private Maples as I had just decided I must.

Dear Lettie,

I hope this gets to you. The messenger sought me out after you told him I was on this side of camp. He said you told him that you missed me, and that was the best news I've had since I've been here. He told me you were well and said he could get a note to you from time to time. I won't say much this time in case our messenger is not reliable. I know we could all be punished, but he seemed genuine. I wonder whether his interest is to help us or to trap us. But I thought it worth the risk.

I hope you will feel comfortable writing back so that we

can catch up with each other. If not, I will understand. You are my closest family. I have no one else. But I know how your mother feels, and I understand that, too. I don't want to pressure you or make it awkward with your mother.

I will only say in this note that Tuma was captured by the British. The after-riders were taken when a column of Tommies came up behind them. Sarel said it was likely they were taken to one of the camps that have been set up for the natives. Before he was taken, Tuma heard that the British found Bina in a cave with others. She was put to work in one of the camps. I know how important Bina is to you, so I will say prayers for her well-being, just as I do every day for you and our loved ones.

Love,

Tante Hannah

I craved liver. My body was changing so much that I was at times a stranger to myself. Liver had always tasted like rusty metal to me, and the slightest thought of it had caused my stomach to clench. I was so revolted by the way Schalk would bite into it like a predator, and he enjoyed it all the more because he knew it disturbed me.

Yet I found myself growing obsessed with it to the point that I believed I could have eaten it raw, as the men did, still warm from a fresh kill. Who was this person that used to be me? I mentioned it to Moeder, who claimed the urge was my body's telling me I needed whatever it was that liver best provided.

"Sometimes you must listen to your body," she said. "And sometimes you must ignore your body."

This was a riddle I understood only later.

"I remember when you wouldn't touch it . . . almost cried at the sight of it," she said. "You were spoiled. Now you're a woman."

She had never said such a thing to me. That single comment made me feel the duty to behave like one, to do womanly things, to prepare to do womanly things with the dedication with which Willem thought of hunting and fighting and being a man.

"Would you teach me how to cook?" I blurted to Moeder.

She didn't hear me or at least did not stop what she was doing.

I asked again.

"Lettie, we have nothing to cook."

I thought of my favorite meals and could almost smell her springbok pie. She would shred the deep red meat of the leg roasts and bake them in pastry. She put so many things in there, in a certain order, with special spices; it seemed impossibly complex. I remembered its being sweetened with apricot jam. I moved my tongue around when I thought the words *apricot jam.* I tried to remember the smell, but I was losing that memory, if not the sense itself. I tried to think of the ingredients and had trouble with the names of some of them. There had been no need to speak of vegetables or fruit since we'd come to the camp, and the words for them had faded with disuse. I worked to remember them. Potatoes, beans, onions—oh, praise God—onions. But when I fell asleep, it was to thoughts of liver.

When I rolled over in the night, it felt as if the tent had tightened around us like a hungry stomach. I had to walk. The door flaps of the tents were cinched, since most families were sleeping, but muffled noise seeped from some of the tents. I could interpret the sounds of illnesses and veered away from certain tents. Some sounds were indecipherable. Through the canvas veil, I could not tell whether crying was coming from a mother or a child, from an elderly grandmother or an infant. Was it coughing or sobbing? Was it calm talk or prayers?

The stars were blocked by low clouds, and the light rain angered into a storm as I was about to turn back to the tent. A jagged note, loud and distinct, rang nearby. It was certainly not a birdcall. I turned to its source and traced a path toward a tent that glowed with inner light. A Tommy guard stood by the tent flap and blew his whistle again, one long blast that knifed through the quickening rain. I popped behind the next tent to keep from being seen.

His back to me, he shifted from leg to leg and bent over to protect his match as he lit a cigarette. He waved his hand and gave a soft whistle with just his breath this time. I thought of Janetta's kiss. A pair of men pulled a two-wheeled cart toward him, each holding one of the wagon tongues, heads down, shuffling together like weary bullocks. They passed the door flap and then turned so that they could back the wagon toward the opening. Light escaped the tent and gilded the cart. A collection of bones in old man's clothes was stretched still, light reflecting off the hollow face and papery skin. His eyes were deep sockets that held small puddles of rain. His lips were tightened into a ghastly smile.

"Put something over him," the guard said. They shrugged and pointed at the cart. They had nothing for cover.

The three entered the tent, and a wailing escaped, the lower pitch of a mother, perhaps, and the higher tone of some children in chorus. The men emerged with a small body. I could not tell whether it was a boy or a girl. One of the men had to hold it in both arms while the other tugged at the body of the old man to make room for the new passenger. When they moved him, the rainwater ran from his hollowed eyes like a burst of tears. They aligned the child head to toe with the old man for a better fit. The guard signaled to the men to leave, and he moved off in the other direction. I could see that it was a girl on the cart, younger than I.

The two men repositioned themselves at the front and hefted the cart shafts, pulling it down the muddy row toward the morgue tent. Within a few strides, the girl's light body slid toward the back edge of the cart bed, her head bobbing off the back.

I ran. . . . "Wait . . . wait . . ." The little body looked ready to fall into the mud. "She's falling."

The men stopped and were back toward the girl by the time I got there.

"Aletta?" one said.

This man was stooped. And he was trying to lift the body with just one arm.

Praise God . . . Oom Sarel.

"Aletta?"

I stepped back, startled, having been focused on the falling girl. I didn't want her body to fall, but I didn't want to touch her, either. And now this. Answer him? Ignore him? I stared. Rain sluiced off the brim of his hat. He did not look like the devil; he looked pathetic . . . a sad man soaked to the skin.

He waited for a reply, studying me. I stared, blinking the rain from my lashes.

"Lettie? Is that you?"

He knew it was me. We looked into each other's eyes, each squinting against the rain. But I could not speak. Oom Sarel had reached out, and I shunned him. I did not even open my mouth. Oupa would have stoned him. Moeder might have attacked him. But I ignored him. I was ashamed to be that small.

He gave up, turned, and helped place the child this time near the head of the cart, where she would be less likely to slide off. The old man, mouth fallen open—agape—had made room for his new companion, but now his right arm hung partially off the cart. I watched it to keep from looking at the little girl. And with each step the men took, it caused the man's arm to bounce, and his limp hand to wave. I could not decide whether it was a farewell or an invitation to follow.

25

July 1901, Concentration Camp

Dear Tante Hannah,

I have to write small and be precise to get it all on the back of this sheet of rules. After we saw you that day, Moeder was very upset. It seemed there was more than a fence between us, as if the ground had opened and spread apart. I think now that our messenger can be a bridge.

The news about Bina struck me cold. I think of her every day, and her sayings, and her songs. I worry about the men, especially Schalk, but I know how well they can take care of themselves. But I truly owe Bina my life, and if I could repay that somehow, I would. Maybe Tuma will be taken to the same place and they can be together.

I have to thank you for the two books. I lose myself in

them every day. If I am a refugee, as they call us, the place I
find real refuge is in those books. Thank you, dear Tante.
You will be happy to learn that I have another book, too.
Copperfield! Yes, please write when you can and I'll do the
same. I will be certain to check with the messenger often.
It's good to know it is safe to do so.

Your Lettie

Klaas's cough grew jagged and persistent before he gave in to crying.
He turned his head toward the canvas so that Willem would not see
him. I prayed for his health, and also for the Lord's patience, as the
tent filled with a fretful commotion. I could do nothing to help Klaas
other than maintain a respectful distance and not intrude. But every
spoken word was heard. So I could not help being party to the things
that Mevrou Huiseveldt said to try to calm him. I doubted she had slept
for several days, tending Klaas through the nights. These were the first
days I could recall that she did not spend time complaining about her
own health.

Crazed by fever, Klaas cried that he wanted to see his father.

"The British have him far away," she told him again and again.

He persisted. "I want to go see him." Mevrou Huiseveldt looked at
the rest of us. We had no answers. His voice was so much like Willem's
that I often checked to be sure it wasn't. What if it had been Willem
instead of Klaas with pneumonia? They lived in the same tent, exposed
to the same elements and illnesses. Was sickness as random as those
bullets flying through the smoke of battle?

Willem now stayed as far away from Klaas as he could, and the
space we gave the Huiseveldts caused us to back into a tighter cluster.
As Klaas faded, Willem hardly spoke to him, as if Klaas had betrayed

him with his illness. I began taking Willem outside as often as I could, and at times I sent him on errands I thought might feel "manly" to him . . . anything to keep him occupied. I started calling him "our little soldier," thinking he would like it and it would encourage discipline and strength.

I worried so much that I opened up to him and told him a story that I feared would be used against me later. At times when I felt weak, I said, I remembered him in front of the line of Tommies, their rifles pointed at him. I would never forget the look on his face. It was the bravest thing I'd ever seen—brave as anything Oupa or Vader or Schalk could do. "You inspired me to be strong," I said. And he liked to hear that. The first time, at least. The second time I told him this, he saw it as manipulation and resented it.

Moeder asked us to pray for the sick boy's well-being after our Bible readings, and I silently prayed that Mevrou Huiseveldt would take him to the hospital tent so we wouldn't hear his cries. But she was told that mothers were allowed to see children for only five minutes one day a week, and Mevrou Huiseveldt felt better tending Klaas herself.

The crying, hour after hour, through the night, ground away at my tolerance until every nerve was exposed. Mevrou Huiseveldt had given him teas and painted his chest with foul-smelling poultices. Dear God, please make him stop, I thought. Then I corrected my prayer: Dear God, please make him well.

Klaas was worse in the morning. He had changed his repetitive wish slightly. He no longer asked to see his father; he wished that his father could see him, be brought to him, right now, to the bedside. Mevrou Huiseveldt abandoned reason. "We'll see if we can get him here."

I left the tent to fetch water and to search for the *dominee*. I walked past Maples, ignoring his greeting. I came upon a man with a large

camera on a three-legged stand; he had been in camp several days selling photographs of families that they might have after the war for their
men. I thought of Klaas's wish that his father could see him. I urged
the photographer to come to our tent, and we would figure out a way
to pay him for it.

I heard no coughing sounds when I returned to the tent. It had
been only an hour, but he was being cleaned for burial.

"No . . ."

"*Ja* . . . he's gone," Mevrou Huiseveldt said without looking up.

"There is a photographer in camp today," I told her. "I thought he
could get a picture of Klaas that you might send to his father. I got him
here as soon as I could. . . . I'll send him away."

Mevrou Huiseveldt straightened and wiped her face with her skirt
hem.

"Have him wait," she said. We all turned away as she changed
Klaas's clothes.

Moeder helped them carry the boy outside the tent, where the photographer posed them. Standing behind a chair, Mevrou Huiseveldt
held Klaas upright, with a hand on each shoulder, with Rachel on the
other side. She tried to pull open the lids of his eyes for the picture.
After two tries, they stayed open.

Willem and I stood behind the photographer. Willem stared at
Klaas. We flinched together when the flash burst, and the brilliant light
reflected pure white off the boy's empty eyes.

26

1890s, Sarel Venter Farm

Long before Tante Hannah lured me to the world that was hiding inside the covers of books, she tried to share with me her love of needlework. Reading was important to her, she said, because books made her think. But she loved her needlework projects because they made her concentrate, which was a process distinct from thinking, she said.

"When I concentrate," she said, "I don't have to think." I did not understand at the time.

When I was small, she gave me an antique porcelain thimble for my own, with great ceremony, hoping that I would grow to love the work as much as she did. I knew she expected a stronger reaction, but I had to choke back comments and act excited when I was truly bored to tears. She always made sweets as an incentive to continue. It was time spent with Tante, and I should have been eager to learn the womanly craft, but I failed so completely to understand the appeal.

She started with the basic stitches and mechanics. Place the needle precisely, push with the thimble, pull the floss to its natural limit, she preached. Remember, these are made to last; every stitch forever tells the story of the person holding the needle.

In the way Oupa taught me the stars as a connection to family history, Tante Hannah told of her ancestors' working with needles. She had learned needlework at the knee of her *ouma*, who learned from the Dutch matrons who monogrammed their clothing so that it would not be confused with others' when they gathered for laundry at the canals in Holland centuries earlier.

Her grandmother's framed "honeymoon sampler" occupied a parlor wall in Tante Hannah's house. She explained that young brides created these to represent their dreams for the future. Her *ouma's* was simple: A step-gabled house with silken smoke weaving from the chimney, with a garden of bloodred tulip blooms and a windmill in the background. A boy and a girl in oversize wooden shoes stood holding hands in the yard. The scene hardly foretold her grandmother's future in South Africa.

"She told me that you may stitch your wishes, but God has his own pattern for you," Tante Hannah said. "When I started mine, she said I should create scenes I hoped would be God's Providence. Lettie, someday you'll want to make one of your own."

Her own sampler was on the wall of her bedroom. The scene was dominated by a low, red-roofed house with two children and two sheep in the yard, and a tree abundant with colorful fruit. It looked nothing like her life.

At times she leaned over the back of my chair, arms on either side of me, and operated my hands for me as if I were a kind of puppet. I finished it, poorly, and declared myself fully taught and ready to retire my thimble.

Although she hovered over me most times, occasionally she stopped talking and clouded over, her lips pressing so tightly the pink parts disappeared. She would stitch intently, and when she put the cloth away, I could see a white, bloodless line marking the deep imprint of the needle at an angle across her fingers.

Place, press, pull. The stitching, the cloth, the letters—these were her unchanging things. A design crafted with a delicate hand would be beautiful for decades, she said with such emotion I was sad for her. And a scene, or the letters of a name, might go on forever, even though they were only a thread of silk knotted into a piece of linen.

"You can stitch a line in fabric and it will last," she said. "This is not the Holy Scripture, but it is true just the same."

This woman took embroidery far too seriously. But she had so little else.

27

August 1901, Concentration Camp

Dear Lettie,

It appears it is safe to write, but we should be cautious. I've missed you so much and think often of our lessons together. I know you liked them better than the times I tried to teach you to stitch. You should have seen your face! But I'm not giving up on you yet. You might come to like it later. Please tell me of Willem and Cee-Cee as I've heard nothing about their well-being.

I know you don't want to hear about Oom Sarel, but he is having a difficult time, never sleeping, gone at all hours. He seems tormented. He will not speak of your oupa, but I will tell you some of the things I have heard from him about Schalk and your father. He tells of your father having been a loyal brother, and Schalk a peacemaker for them all. None had been harmed when Oom was last with them.

I'm so happy to hear of your *Copperfield* book, and that
you're not holding Dickens responsible for the war. There's
probably no better time than this for reading, or writing.
At least there's that.

Thinking of you always,

Love,
Tante Hannah

Other voices intruded, crowding out my own. The struggles went on
mostly at night and churned like eddies in a stream. I didn't know
whether this meant I was going insane or becoming an adult.

Oupa and Vader appeared, speaking their favorite phrases, repeating their themes, the ones I'd heard for years, the ones I accepted without question. Oupa, clouds billowing from his pipe, proclaimed us
"God's tools of righteousness." I pictured him on a windblown hilltop.

The beauty of these phantom appearances was that I was unafraid
to talk back to them. But if we have no dominion over our lives, Oupa,
why strive to be righteous? If we have no part in our fate, what is the
point?

Vader's voice remained forthright, as if he were standing tall beside
me. The voice itself reflected his strength. It's never wrong to do the
right thing, Lettie . . . and obey your *moeder*. You are a Venter. Yes,
Vader, but so is Oom Sarel.

Most nights, Bina's voice seemed to take over, with her songs and
sayings, and in my sleep I was able to understand them better. A person
is never gone as long as you feel her shadow beside you, she said. And
that explained the sense that Janetta was still with me when I walked.

The voice of Klaas joined in, speaking to me from his seat in front
of the photographer. Lettie, dear Lettie, you finally noticed me. He had

cared for me, and I had given him fewer than a dozen of my words in response. And now he was dead. I tried to push him aside . . . the sound . . . the sad end of it all . . . those eyes. How cold was I that I dreaded the idea that his shadow might follow me? How does one hold some shadows and cut others loose?

At times, everything hurt, and the voices would pop in to explain those problems or revive the memories attached to them. The voices were sometimes consoling, sometimes judgmental. And at times now, they did not always bother to wait until I was asleep to begin their repetitive lectures. They kept me unsettled, on the brink, unsure whether I would be in tears from minute to minute, breath to breath. Look at Moeder, I told myself. But as much as I wanted to be like her, I wanted less to be with her. The tightness in the tent . . . the power of her presence . . . something was pushing me away.

Prayers calmed the voices, if I repeated them, time after time. Other times the voices just became more insistent when I prayed. I added another request to my nightly prayers: Help me to be strong, dear God. I considered the wording for some time, wanting to be concise and to the point. I wanted a small phrase that would cover a variety of situations; I decided the best way to reach God's ears was to be respectful of his time.

One morning, my legs began twitching toward dawn, and I changed positions. Since I had washed my pinafore, I no longer used it as a pillow. I stacked my shoes with toes in opposite directions so the center was level and cradled my head. I slipped back to sleep, and the voices started, all at once, trying to claw their way out of my head this time. I tried to make them stop, but they echoed in there and made my head itch, so that I wakened again as a relief from their chatter. But the itching remained, and I dug at my head with more energy.

"Who's doing that?" Moeder asked.

I paused but couldn't stop.

Moeder struck a match.

"Oh . . ."

"What, Ma?"

She reached into the bag she had taken from home and kept hanging from the back post of her cot. She handed me her mother's fancy mirror. When she lit a match and held it toward me, I saw small trails of blood seeping down my forehead and parting on either side of my nose.

She put down the mirror and used her sleeve to wipe the blood from my face.

"Let me see."

She tilted my head down so that she could get close enough to see. She groaned louder.

"Lice," she said.

"No . . ."

"Yes . . . you scratched yourself bloody."

"No . . ."

I cried and turned to bury my head in my blankets, but I knew there would be more vermin hiding there.

"What?" Willem heard the shouts.

"Lice," Moeder said. "Don't go near her. Feel your hair."

"Ahhhhhh," Willem said. "We'll have to put her in the dipping trench."

Blood on my face and hands, I struck him with both balled-up fists, shouting curses. I had never punched someone and did not know how, so I hit him the way you beat a drum.

Mevrou Huisveldt yelled at me to stop and then urged Rachel to back away from me, as if I carried the worst contagion.

"Probably got them from you in the first place," I yelled at her.

Moeder pulled me off Willem, who had ducked to miss the blows but never struck back in defense.

"We can't do anything until light," Moeder said. "Just sit there by the tent flap . . . and don't scratch."

"I can't stop."

"Sit on your hands. . . . Close your eyes and don't think about it. . . . Pray."

God, make me strong. God, make me strong. God, stop this itching. God, destroy lice. God, make me strong. Don't think about it, Moeder said. Yes, you tell someone to sit in the dark and close her eyes, and you expect her not to think about vermin crawling on her scalp. *You* try not thinking about them. How many are up there? Like an army. I imagined their little pinched faces, marching in formation, each in a little khaki uniform, digging into my flesh with tiny picks and shovels. I couldn't help clawing at them.

"Lettie . . . stop. . . . That only makes it worse. . . . Pray."

God, make me strong. God, bring the daylight. God made two great lights, the greater one to rule the day. And as if accompanied by a chorus of angels, he answered my prayer. A lightness seeped through the tent flap.

"Moeder . . . it's getting light."

"Get up, then."

"What now? Reservoir?"

"Lye soap . . . if we can find any. . . . Let's look, first."

Even though I knew the lice were there, I could not stop scratching, and when I pulled away my hands, the blood was flecked with them. I shivered, looked away, shivered again.

"Lettie . . ."

"What?"

"I need you not to argue about this . . ."

"What?

"The hair has to come off."

"No . . ."

"Has to."

"All of it?"

"All of it . . . now."

Yes. God, help me to be strong . . . right now. I quieted. But my hair? It was the only thing about myself that I liked.

"Are you certain?"

"No other way."

"No other way?"

"No."

Her face was calm.

"Fine . . . do it, Moeder . . . all of it."

She retrieved shears from the tent. In the middle of the row, with women passing in first light, I stood in just my nightclothes . . . exposed to ridicule and to such cold that my lungs burned with each breath.

"What is it?" a woman with a bucket asked.

"Must be lice," her companion answered.

"Ugh."

"She's filthy with them."

"Move on," I said. "I'll be beautiful, anyway. I'm young. . . . It will all grow back. Watch. Watch and see."

The snipping was so loud. Bits of hair caught the breeze and fluttered as they fell, landing like starlings. The women backed away as Moeder tried to pluck the lice and nits from the comb and shears.

I hummed one of Bina's songs: *I am water. . . . I am the river*. My hair will grow back thicker, with more waves, I told myself.

"Willem, stomp on them," Moeder said. "Then wipe your shoes and pull out her bedding. . . . We'll have to be rid of it."

Children pointed at me. I responded with laughs, although sometimes it sounded like crying.

"Still beautiful," I said to Moeder. I was proud; I was strong.

"Good girl . . . yes, you are," Moeder said. "Still beautiful."

Willem took the cue and hid his disgust, but he felt his head with both hands.

Moeder washed my bare head and struck matches to kill the most stubborn. They popped and gave off a stale smell.

"I hate lice, Ma," I said.

"I know, they're gone now."

"I remember when they were on the sheep and you hurt your back that day."

"I hurt my back?"

"When we tried to dip them to kill the lice . . . you hurt your back."

"Yes . . . my back. . . . Willem, get my mirror," she said as if it were urgent. "It's on the cot."

"No, Ma . . . I don't want to see."

"It doesn't look bad. It will grow back."

"Willem, get my mirror, and the brush from my bag, too."

"No . . . Moeder . . ."

Willem handed them to her.

"Lettie, here, take them."

"I don't want to look."

"Then don't. . . . It's not for now. . . . You can have them for when it grows back. It won't take that long. And you can have this to brush every day."

"Mine to keep?"

"Yes . . . to keep. Just keep thinking about them and how beautiful it will be when the hair comes back." Moeder took my face in her hands and looked closely. She leaned in slowly. I had no idea what sort of treatment she was trying now. She kissed me exactly in the middle of my forehead, barely touching, and for the length of a single heartbeat. She then did the same on each cheek. She was so gentle and loving in that moment that I was convinced the lice were worth having.

But it detonated Willem.

"She gets a present for this?" Willem asked.

Moeder, going from silk to steel in an instant, stared with such force it drove him backward. "But . . . ," he said. Moeder closed in on him, and he ran back to the tent.

Cee-Cee watched the commotion without comment or fearful look.

"Well," I asked, "what do you think?"

"I will brush it for you," she said. "When it grows back."

I HOLLOWED OUT A hole in the ground . . . *cleft for me* . . . and climbed inside, pulling the dirt over me like a blanket. Seclusion was impossible in the tent, making solitude a mental exercise. But thinking myself in a trench started to feel like death. A better imaginary escape was submerging myself in water. I could hear sounds, but they were muffled and unclear. Minutes floated past my face, one at a time, drifting to the bottom, where they gathered into hours. When no ripples disturbed my private river for a time, I surfaced to reality. If others were asleep or distracted, I used Moeder's mirror—my new mirror—to reassess my baldness and submerge again.

Sometimes I didn't rise to eat, and no one bothered me. Moeder might ask me a question, but the words were absorbed by the water surrounding me. Once the hours had stacked into days, I crawled out again and studied the crop of stubble that pioneered the white land-scape and darkened over the red blotches. Within two more days, it was thick and softening.

I breathed deeply and tipped my head to Moeder for an examina-tion. She approved. I went first to Ouma van Zyl's out of guilt over not having fetched water for several days. She had heard of my public shearing, so she understood. All three children were sickly. She was worn and smaller still. She looked at my *kappie* pulled down tight but did not comment.

I avoided Maples for another week after my shame, each of those days feeling like three. When I finally saw him on my way for water, he noticed immediately.

"What happened . . . lice?"

I thought having my *kappie* pulled down would hide it. He noticed but didn't seem surprised or even bothered. Shouldn't he be bothered? I reached to shake his hand, with a note cupped inside the palm in the way he'd shown me.

"You should have seen the lice I used to get in my leg wraps. . . . If we camped in one place too long, our kits would be crawling with them. . . . Had to boil the clothes of most of the regiment."

"But did you have to cut off all your hair?"

"Many of the men did . . . all the time. . . . It grows back. It looks fine already."

I asked about his work.

"Extra duties."

"Why?

"Punishment."

"For what?"

"They wanted to remind me they don't care for my attitude."

"That was all?"

"I think they've been watching me," he said.

Praise God, that means they're watching us both.

"I was already on probation."

Praise God, so am I.

"Your probation?"

"From when I was in the field . . . things . . ."

"What things?"

"Too many questions."

I stopped, amazed by my restraint.

"Are you all right?"

"I'm just knackered."

"Better than bald," I said.

"No . . . truly . . . you can hardly tell."

He looked more than tired.

"You don't like it here, either, do you?" I said.

"Better than being under fire, but at least that's . . . what? Manly, I suppose. Marching in the heat . . . being together after a battle. But here, it's different."

"Worse?"

"Different."

"Your friends?"

"Don't have many."

"I don't, either," I said.

"Two of a kind, then?"

"We both have short hair," I said. "What about the other Tommies?"

"Don't always care for their ways," he said. "Things they do, things they say . . . who they are."

He closed his mouth tight, signaling the end of my questions on that topic, too. He backed up a few steps, turned, and walked . . . the first time I could recall that he ended a conversation. Trouble in the field? Things he'd done? I went over each thing he said as I walked back to the tent; I would prepare proper questions before our next meeting. I worried that if he was being watched, it might disrupt his contact with Tante Hannah.

Having buried myself in a hole or hidden underwater for almost two weeks, I was surprised how tired I was, just walking a short distance. I wanted to end the day with the best use of time: cuddling with Cee-Cee, reading to her from the book, or making up more stories of my own that would make her happy. I did not care what Mevrou Huiseveldt or anybody else said: there was magic, or maybe it was *muti*, in that little girl's laugh. I'd spent too much time walking, too much time with Maples, too much time with the Van Zyls, too much time concentrating on books, too much time hiding in my own shell . . . and too little with Cee-Cee.

"Come here, *lammetjie*," I said. "Let's curl up and read some more of the Master Davy book."

She came close and shook her head.

"Too tired," she said.

Dear Tante Hannah,

Thank you for the news about Vader and Schalk. I have been so worried about them, and Oupa, too, of course. You would not recognize me. I had to have my hair cut off. Lice decided I looked like a nice home. I was worried about my appearance, but since I've been shorn, I've seen a number of others in camp with the same style. Willem and Cee-Cee are fine. Tante, I worry we're under a special watch. I don't know what Oom Sarel does with the British, but do you think you could find out why they seem to be watching us? Love you and hope to see you soon.

Your Lettie

Sleep provided escape, too, although it was often so shallow it allowed neither clear dreams nor rational thought, like trying to study the stars through layers of clouds. But it was an excuse to put off chores and dealing with others until morning, or until the sounds of whistles brought me to wakefulness.

I assumed it was just the echo of a dream, then, or Mevrou Huiseveldt's snoring or foul winds, when I thought again of the lions roaring that night on the veld. The canvas of the tent quivered and then compressed like the head of a native's drum, except we were inside the drum. And then cannon fire landed so close it could only be the men coming to free us. The explosion of a shell thrust darkness from the tent. From the flash came the smell of sparks, not powder. It was lightning. The canvas took on an erratic pulse as the muscles of a storm flexed and recoiled and flexed harder.

"Get up, Lettie," Moeder called, loudly enough to awaken everyone in the tent. "Loosen the tent ropes . . . not all the way, just give them slack so the water runs off."

I ran out in my bedclothes, slipping with the first step outside, my arms up to the elbows in mud. I couldn't stay upright or regain traction, so I crawled around the picket of tent stakes, creating slack with the slip knots. I worked my way from windward to lee . . . until my wet night skirt twisted around my ankles, forming a hobble that pulled me down face-first. Relaxed lines would keep the storm from pulling up the stakes and taking it all away. But it left the tent pole unstable.

"Lettie," Moeder called from the middle of the tent. I could barely hear her over the whining ropes and clapping canvas. A lightning strike froze her image, like the flash from the photographer. I could see her arms raised, leaning into the pole. Willem knelt at the base of the pole while the Huiseveldts huddled on their bed and screamed. I shed my outer bedclothes, which had become a sodden anchor.

"Did I loosen too much?"

"No . . . but we have to hold the pole."

Above the clamoring storm rose shouts from the Van Zyls.

"Ma?"

"*Ja* . . . go."

The path across the row was a flowing stream. Amid the howls of straining tent ropes, I leaned into the wind to make progress. But mud pulled at me, sucking a shoe from my foot, and when I broke free, I fell forward. The wind had pulled out several of the Van Zyls' tent stakes and collapsed the windward side, so that I could not find the flap. I gave up and slid on my stomach beneath the tent wall, greasing my bedclothes tight to my body.

"The pole . . . I can't hold . . ."

The sick children groaned in the darkness, throats so constricted they struggled to scream.

"I've got it. . . . Tend the children."

With no purchase, my bare foot slid, leaving me on all fours, clinging to the pole. If it came down, the tent would become a sail and carry everything off. The floor of the tent was nearly as wet as the rows outside. I pulled myself hand over hand on the pole. I turned my feet at angles and dug in. I leaned into the wind; I could not fall again.

The children quieted as their grandmother gathered them on the drier side of the tent. They sat huddled, shivering with sickness under mud-caked blankets, listening to the storm and screams from outside. The pole slipped and struck my shoulder; my upraised hands had gone numb with lack of blood. I leaned against the pressure of the pole, holding it lower for a time, hugging it to my chest.

Lightning struck a hundred times, so near that it sizzled, the children gasping with each bolt. I pictured it striking the tent pole and frying me in place.

I thought of Moeder and the turpentine, and Oupa dealing with his thumb hanging loose without ever a word. I leaned in harder as the wind pushed the pole against me. I thought of little David, in the Dickens book, toiling in a warehouse at only ten. My feet slipped by bits through the night, stopping my heart every time, once awakening me from a quick sleep when I was nearly to my knees before I recovered.

I thought of Bina's working chants, making it all go easier, time passing in the lines of a song rather than in minutes. I started humming, trying to harmonize with the wind. I could not look back at the children or the old woman but knew they were looking at me, all of them, willing me to be strong.

And then it stopped, near dawn. I could not feel my feet or my hands, but everything else throbbed, so that I could hear my pulse in my neck. And above that pounding, the rhythmic wheezing of the children's struggling breaths.

AN UNNATURAL CALM FOLLOWED the torment of the night. I finally unclenched and tried to rub the knots from the muscles I had strained for so many hours. I restaked and tightened the ropes on the Van Zyl tent so that it would stand and then did the same with ours, pushing through air that still crackled with so much electricity that my hair sprouts stood out. Because we had loosened the ropes, the water had sluiced away from our tent and the inside was moist but not too thick with mud. I rolled into my blanket and shivered myself to sleep for a few hours.

When I woke, I was blind. Struck blind by God for my sins. Had I not paid a just penance through this awful night? I rubbed my face with still-throbbing hands, and dim light returned to my world. Mud had dried to my face and crusted over my lids while I slept. Relishing sight, I rose to fetch water. Queues would be long at the pump station, and it was barely above freezing.

I looked for my shoe outside the tent, but there was no sign of it. Walking with one shoe kept me off balance, and I considered taking the other off, too. But the mud that seeped between my toes was so cold that my foot went numb again. At some points I sank halfway to my knees.

The deluge had made the pump water a thick brown. The weight of the mud on my skirt threatened to pull it off. The families were awake when I returned, buckets half-empty from water spilling over the edges when I lost my footing.

Moeder sorted through the family's bedding, stretching blankets out with Willem holding one end, flapping them to dry them quicker. Cee-Cee was still asleep in a tight bundle.

"Moeder?" I tilted my head toward the Van Zyl tent.

"Of course."

The children quaked under sodden blankets, probably colder than if they had been naked. Ouma van Zyl stood but looked to be asleep with open eyes. Children gasped and then shivered, repeating the cycles. But they smiled at me.

"Can't get these things dry," she said.

The rain had stopped, but there was no sun, and nowhere to dry the bedding. Ouma van Zyl was helpless, and the children in piteous condition—no, perilous condition.

"Here. . . ." I scooped up armfuls of heavy blankets, leaving just one for the children. Within minutes I had shaken them and spread them on the closest fence, exposing them to the soft wind. It would take hours, but better than leaving them inside.

Women stared at me as I walked back to the Van Zyls.

"Where are they?" Ouma van Zyl asked.

"Drying on the fence."

"Will the guards punish me?"

"No . . . you had nothing to do with it. I can say they're mine."

I gestured to the children. "How will they make it through without dry blankets? Maybe you should get them to the hospital."

"The Death Tent?" she whispered.

"At least it might be dry there," I said, but I could not force her, and the children were sick enough that I knew it would be unfair to ask Moeder and the Huiseveldts to pull in tighter and allow them to stay with us.

"I'll go keep watch over your things in case a guard sees them. At least we can leave them out there until then. . . . It will be something."

"You should be wearing shoes, child," she yelled.

"The mud stole the one," I replied on my way out.

"You'll freeze."

"Too late."

It took an hour for a guard walking rounds to see the blankets and demand answers. If somebody had to discover them, I had hoped that it would be Maples. I could have reasoned with him. Perhaps he could have done something, overlooked it for a while. But it was a guard I had not seen. I could only hope it was not one alerted to our status with the commandant.

"I put them there," I volunteered when he approached. "Sick children need dry blankets."

"You know the rules—get them down."

"It's against the rules to dry wet blankets?"

"On the fence, it is—you know it is. The rules are posted everywhere."

"I can't read."

"You were told when you got here."

"I was sick with fever and could not hear when we got here."

"Get them down. . . . Can you hear that?"

"They're wet. . . . Where else can we get them out of the mud?"

"Your problem."

Ignorance didn't work; defiance was next.

"And if I don't?"

"You'll go into confinement. We have that here, too, you know. Or is that another of the things you don't know?"

"I'm already confined."

"I said 'confinement' . . . something for special offenders."

"Can't be much worse," I said.

"You'll be able to judge for yourself. Let us know what you think after a few days."

"Are you trying to frighten me?"

"Just warning you."

"I would welcome isolation. Isolation would be a holiday from the woman in our tent."

"Oh, without access to the latrine?"

I laughed. "This whole camp is a latrine."

"We can arrange punishments beyond that," he said, deepening his tone. "Afraid now?"

"I fear God." I stood as tall as possible until I realized that it made my bare foot visible. I had been numb long enough that they had stopped throbbing.

"You fear more than that."

"Well, yes, I do; I fear my *oupa* at times . . . but not the British. Not you, not your soldiers."

"Do you want to tell that to the commandant?"

That was an option I did not want to hear. But it made it clear the guard did not know of our "relationship" with the commandant.

"Do you want to tell him that you're putting a child in confinement because you can't scare her well enough?"

"He doesn't care. Trust me, he does not care."

"Good, then take me to the commandant's tent," I said, risking a bluff. "And I'll tell him that three sick children are about to die because they were not allowed to dry their blankets . . . and you were to blame."

"Fine."

"I want to see him . . . to look in his eyes. I want him to personally decide to put me in jail for the offense of drying wet blankets for sick children. I want to look at his desk, to see how big it is, to make sure I'll have room to lay out three dead children on it."

The guard looked me over.

"Insolent girl . . . what are you . . . twelve?"

"Are you mad? I'm fourteen . . . will be fifteen on my next birthday."

"You're small."

"So is the tsetse."

He had the nerve to smile. He looked at the fence, looked back at me again, and scanned the fence line. No other guards were in sight.

"All right . . . just this afternoon. I'll be back around in a couple hours and they'll have to be gone."

Within half an hour, a dozen more blankets were drying on the wire, with more families bringing out their bedding.

Moeder stood when I finally entered the sagging tent. She handed me a pair of black boots, shiny from what appeared to be a fresh dubbin treatment.

"Try these," she said.

I held the sole of one up to my mud-blackened foot. It was too large by several inches, but they showed very little wear.

"Where did you get these?"

"Ouma van Zyl. . . . She brought them over. . . . They were her daughter's. She said she's been saving them and wanted you to have them."

I padded them with rags and laced them tight; I spent the rest of my days in camp walking in a dead woman's boots.

28

September 1901, Concentration Camp

A distant whistle sounded, the first of the night. I scanned the dark rows to look for my uncle answering its grim call. I thought of the images he must carry from these nights when he was hailed by the whistle. And I wondered why so many seemed to die at night. Did they feel their day was done and it was time to let go? Having gone another day without relief, perhaps they found it easier to accept death as if it were just falling off to sleep. Could they not face the idea of another sunrise, another day?

I had reached the point where even I was bothered by all my questions. I hoped that someday my nature would allow me just to accept things as they happened, or spend less of my time sorting through the contents of my increasingly jumbled mind.

I kept my eyes turned upward even on the way back from the camp's edge, pretending I could use the stars to navigate through the identical rows of identical tents, down the identical muddy passages. Most were dark by this time of the night, but the tents of the ill were lit with candles or paraffin lamps, and they glowed like muted canvas lanterns. And when the candles guttered, the distorted shadows of the people seemed to dance. I imagined them as the Shadow People, spirits connected to the real people, but happier, dancing above their still forms.

Down one row, women gathered around a small fire, stirring a pot. The smell was of a warming poultice or the vile teas used to treat the sick. I kept a respectful distance as I passed, but then I came upon another cluster of women gathered at the next tent that glowed from within.

It was the *aasvoëls*, as Moeder called them, the vultures. They would pitch up without announcement or invitation, even in the deep night. Drawn by scent or evil instinct, they formed a loose black coven and pulled themselves in tighter near the tent door. They absorbed light, rendered heat, and served as death's relentless scouting party.

I slowed and circled, trying to study their faces so that I could give them scornful looks if I ever saw them during the day. But their black *kappies* hooded their faces, and only harsh sounds escaped from the faceless pack.

"Vultures," I shouted, but none turned, all focused on the tent door.

"Measles. . . . The mother should have made the little one drink goat-dung tea," one said.

"But where to get goat dung now? And wormword? Not in this camp."

"Why is there no blind over that child's eyes? The eyes burn with the measles."

"The strangling angel took a whole family last week," one said. "Throats swollen shut."

"Strangling angel?"

"*Ja* . . . bad."

"Better than some."

"*Ja* . . . praise God."

"Praise God.

"And a better deathbed."

Others harmonized assent, heads bobbing like black-feathered hens.

"Like the last child," another said. "God's gift."

More nodding and mumbles.

"Such a beautiful deathbed."

"The mother was so strong she hardly cried."

"True mother's love."

"But she cried enough," another said.

They passed judgment on the quality of the handling of the ill, on the death, and on the proportional grief of the family.

These women had gone mad.

Dear Lettie,

Yes, lice are everywhere. We have a large tank on this side just for boiling clothes and bedding to rid them of the vermin. I'm so happy to hear your brother and sister are well. Cee-Cee looks up to you so. Truly pleased about your reading and writing. I believe you have greatness in you, Lettie. You'll find it.

I have asked around as I might but have heard nothing about those who would question your "desirability." But I know they do watch. The only thing I heard about was a thing or two about our messenger that I can't write for obvious reasons. I will continue research. I love you, dear. Best to your brother, and kiss your little lamb of a sister.

Love,

Tante Hannah

I'd been foolish not taking Cee-Cee on walks with me. No, in truth, I'd been selfish. That had been my time to read, to clear my mind . . . to see Maples. It would be slower walking with Cee-Cee, but better, meaningful. In the tent we had the distraction of the Huiseveldts, and I had allowed us to lose much of the closeness we'd shared at home after the men had gone.

It would be good for her to get out when the weather allowed. We could have the time to walk alone together, I thought. I immediately wrote down that phrase: *alone together.* It would be time for us, the two of us, just as when Schalk had taken me for rides on outings, forging a closeness I'd never forget. There were only special people with whom you could feel alone together. I wanted to be sure Cee-Cee felt that way about me.

"Ceec . . . do you want to go with me?" I asked, heading out one afternoon.

"I'm still too small to carry water."

"No . . . just to walk . . . the two of us. . . . Is it all right, Ma?"

"Not far."

It was a clear afternoon, although brisk.

"Look at the sky, Ceec," I said. "So vivid."

"Looks like home," she said.

"You're right . . . same sky."

Some women who passed could not help stopping and petting her curly hair, which had darkened a shade in the past year or so, as Moeder predicted it would.

She wanted to talk about home and Vader and Schalk, so we did, but I wasn't sure it was good for either of us. She said she could not remember much of home.

"Miss them?" she asked.

"Of course . . . very much . . . Schalk especially."

"Me, too."

I held one of her hands; she held her doll, Lollie, with the other.

"You worry about them?" she asked.

Hmmm. What to say?

"*Ja*, sometimes . . . but they're strong and brave."

She looked at other little girls we neared, wanting to approach them but not comfortable.

"We'll bring Rachel next time," she said.

I did not want to bring Rachel. "Yes . . . maybe."

"She's sad since Klaas left," she said.

"Yes, we all are," I said.

"She misses him."

"We all do."

"What's that?" She pointed to a fire burning a short distance outside the fence.

I could see only the rising smoke.

But up ahead were Maples and another guard. I usually walked past him when he was not alone. I could not tell whether he saw me. If he came this way by himself, I would introduce Cee-Cee to him. It would be good for her to see that the British aren't all hateful, destructive savages.

But what if he said something and she repeated it to Moeder? I couldn't risk it.

"Time to go back, Ceec," I said. "Remember, Moeder didn't want us to go far."

She smiled. She looked tired from the walk, anyway.

MAPLES'S EYES SAGGED AT the edges and his smile produced no warmth. I had hoped he would lift my spirits, but he looked more grim than I felt. I did not need disappointment from him. I almost turned around or simply walked past him this time.

"Wait, Lettie . . . peace," he said.

"Peace," I answered. I had to stop.

"Have you talked to any Englishwomen?" he asked me.

Where would I talk to Englishwomen? "The nurses?"

"No . . . a visitor . . . Hobhouse," he said. "Emily Hobhouse."

"No." I hadn't heard the woman's name. Surely he would hear about the visit of a British woman before I would.

"She's from Cornwall, and she's raising a stir back home," Maples said. "Got my Betty in a fit."

"How?"

"She's been down here nosing around."

"A British woman visiting the camps? Why?"

"Making trouble." He pulled an envelope from his pocket and un-folded several pages of a letter. I could see the feminine writing.

"Betty said this woman has been putting articles in the papers and giving speeches in Parliament about the conditions in the camps, and Betty now thinks I'm an animal," he said. "Says the women aren't refu-gees but prisoners."

That point was beyond dispute. That was just now an item of news in England? "Have you told her nothing?"

"I never share much because she would worry or, worse, would tell Mum, and Mum would worry even more than she already does," he said. "I usually complain about the weather and the food and tell her how much I miss her and all the things we will do when I get home."

"But nothing about the war?"

"Don't want her to know."

"She doesn't ask?"

"Not really . . . just asks after my health," he said. "I don't think she wants to know, either. But now . . . I would rather she heard it from me . . . to get our side of it."

"What does this woman say?"

"Well, this Hobhouse has been to different camps. . . . Said some are run better than others, but most of them are bits of hell."

"That's what I heard from my friend Janetta. . . . Some are worse. . . . Some much worse."

He read from the letter. "Here's what Betty says: Disease, malnutrition, high fatality rates among children . . . starving, poor medical care . . . not getting soap for sanitary purposes."

I had taken conditions for granted so long that they seemed normal, merely the way things were, and to get from day to day you stopped expecting things you knew you couldn't have. I hated to think of it that way. But Moeder's attitude had conditioned me. We dealt. We moved on. Strange that it took a woman from England to remind me.

"Betty is learning things about other camps that I don't even know about . . . worse conditions . . . abuse."

"This woman is telling other Brits about this?"

"Telling Parliament . . . telling the newspapers . . ."

"Good," I said. "Maybe they'll do something about it once they hear about it from one of their own."

"She's rounding up supporters . . . trying to raise political pressure to stop the war. Betty said one of the members of Parliament said we've been using 'methods of barbarism' and conducting a war against women and children."

Yes, exactly.

"Also talks about farm burnings."

The pages of the letter shook in his hands.

"They didn't know about it before?" It had been more than a year.

He didn't answer. Maybe this woman could help our cause. Maybe she was helping everyone's cause.

"Wouldn't the end of the war be a good thing for you?" I asked.

He looked wounded.

"Yes . . . of course," he said. "But like this? I joined because Betty's father thought I wasn't good enough for her. I joined because I thought it would impress her. And now she thinks I'm some kind of animal."

"You're not an animal," I said. He touched my shoulder, and I leaned into his touch.

I would ask about Miss Hobhouse. I hoped she would come to our camp. I would love to talk to her. She might have questions for me, but not as many as I would have for her. I would tell her everything. She would have to beg me to stop. I would go through my journal for her and tell her everything. Not about Maples, but everything else. She might want to print my journal, and I'd be famous in England. It would be my first book.

He folded the letter and turned away. He leaned the rifle on the fence and reached into his pack.

"Here, I have something for you." He handed me a small package wrapped in brown paper with a twine string in a bowknot. I hoped it was another book, but it was a different shape. I looked at it and considered its weight. It was thick and heavy. I untied the twine and put it in my pocket to keep, then carefully unwound the paper.

It was a candle, one of the biggest I'd seen in a long time. My legs buckled.

"In case you want to sit up."

I went dizzy, and my mind filled with possibilities.

He wanted to sit up with me. He had come to respect our ways and knew my parents would appreciate this as proof he wanted to be one of us. The flame would reflect off his red hair . . .

"Wait, there's really no place for us to sit up in the tent," I said. "No privacy for us."

"What?" he said. "There are no boys here for you, anyway . . . are there?"

I realized that I'd said "us," but he'd said "you." Damn me as a foolish child, I thought. I tried to think of anything that might make my face not show disappointment. I knew I failed.

"Maybe when you get home . . . when this is over . . . boys will come to your home," he said. "I saw the candle sitting in a guard tent and thought about you and that sitting-up tradition you folks have. I took it. . . . Thought you'd need it someday."

"Of course . . . someday."

29

September 1901, Concentration Camp

The sound of the match scrape and the flash of a brave little flame carried ominous meaning.

"Ma?"

"Checking on Cecelia." She used her full given name.

She had not been noticeably unwell, but her little bird-chirp voice had grown softer, with a catch in it at times. She did not complain, and there were no symptoms to consider. Not really. How do you distinguish daily fatigue and hunger from something more serious? She gradually took to coughing a bit more and playing with her doll quietly in the tent. She was not as interested in my stories or songs. And when she did come close and want to hear them, they did not bring out her usual joyfulness. I was ashamed I hadn't noticed.

Another match flash. I saw my shadow on the tent wall. Moeder hummed. Sleep was no longer an option.

It had come on fast, in the past few days, with diarrhea leading to fever.

The scrape of another match. Cee-Cee's head rested on Moeder's lap.

When the fever took hold, Cee-Cee stopped taking food, only some beef tea, and then she had appetite for nothing. Moeder had not left the tent, and I was gone only for rations and water. This was not the togetherness I had planned. The weight of that guilt added to the cargo I already scarcely shouldered.

"Moeder . . . wait." From under my blankets, near my journal and books, I withdrew the package. "Here . . . I have a candle now."

"Where?"

"I found it."

"You found it wrapped in paper?"

"Found it like that . . . yes."

"Aletta? They could probably take us in for having this." Relief in having the candle overcame her worries and curiosity. "Light it . . . now. Let's try to clean her up a bit."

Under the steady light, Moeder examined Cee-Cee and then shook Willem awake.

"Willem . . . Willem."

It took several shakes to rouse him.

"What?"

"Go find the *dominee*," she said.

"Where?

"I don't know. . . . Find his tent."

"Lettie can go."

"I need her here," she said.

"He'll be asleep."

"Wake him if you have to."

He looked at me through half-closed eyes, trying to read how worried he should be. I tilted my head toward the door. Cee-Cee had heard Moeder send for the preacher.

"What now, Ma?" she asked.

"We're going to get you pretty for a visitor."

Her eyes closed and the sockets were made ghostly by the shadows of her cheekbones and brow. We had no soap to wash her.

It was the first time I had looked at Moeder in this light, too, and her face was nearly as gaunt as Cee-Cee's, with smoky gray circles around deepening eyes. Those eyes widened as she opened Cee-Cee's clothes. Cee-Cee's skin looked dark even by candlelight. I could count each rib, perhaps every bone. Her feet and knees seemed too large, with so little meat to cover the spindly bones of her legs. I had hugged her tightly during story time only a week before and could not believe her decline in so few days.

Moeder wiped her with a dry cloth, and skin sloughed in dark nuggets.

"Help me roll her over."

"This won't hurt, sissy," I said. "Give me Lollie and I'll take care of her."

I put her doll on the side of the cot and helped support her shoulders as she turned. The blades beneath felt thin and sharp, and I feared snapping a bone if we weren't delicate in her handling. The nodes of her spine could be counted, and we could see her hip bones clearly through the slack skin of her buttocks, which were flared red.

I could not look, and focused directly on her face, and petted her hair. "Would you like the *dominee* to tell you a story?"

She nodded and smiled with one side of her mouth, her lips dry white.

"Jairus's daughter," Moeder said. "The *dominee* will know that one from memory."

As Moeder cleaned her, Cee-Cee and I looked into each other's eyes. I tried to make mine as calm as I could by thinking peaceful thoughts. She squeezed hers tightly whenever Moeder rubbed a tender spot.

Willem returned with the *dominee* in less than half an hour. The man who had led us in psalms and hymns that night in the big tent draped his wet coat on the cot frame as Moeder covered Cecelia with a sheet.

"Who do we have here?"

"Cecelia," Moeder said. "Our little lamb."

"Well, isn't she just," he said, touching her hair.

He read a prayer of blessing and looked to Moeder to see whether that had been enough, and whether it had been presented with the proper gravity. I worried that more would frighten her.

"I think she would like to hear the story of Jairus's daughter," Moeder said.

The *dominee* understood.

He sat on the edge of the bed and told her of Jairus, whose daughter was very sick. So sick, in fact, that they sent for Jesus to bless her. Jesus was delayed, and when he arrived, he was told that the little girl had just expired. When the *dominee* said the word "expired," it was as if he were talking about some food that had gone bad rather than the end of a human life.

"But fret not," he added quickly.

As if angry at himself for being delayed, Jesus chased the family from the room and was alone with the girl.

"Jesus took her hand, and he said, 'Little girl, I say to you, arise.' And the little girl was not dead; she got up and walked."

Cecelia had been listening with closed eyes. When she smiled, it pulled her lips tight. She rested.

"Have you taken her to the hospital?" the *dominee* asked Moeder.

She shook her head forcefully. The idea of Cee-Cee's going to the hospital broke something in me, and I had to leave.

"Be strong for your sister, and don't cry in front of her," the *dominee* said, holding me by the shoulder near the tent door. "I tended a boy last night who told his mother a thing I'll never forget. You should both hear this."

I wiped my eyes on my sleeve. I didn't care whether he saw me.

"This little one had been sick a long time. . . . He said that he'd decided he was happy to go live with Jesus, because living here with us was too hard."

"But she'll . . . get . . . better," I said, having to suck in air between words.

He put his palm on the crown of my head.

From the door of our tent, we heard a voice. "Ah, true love."

We turned to see black-hooded faces peering inside the door flap.

"Regrets," the *dominee* said. "They seem to follow me, especially at night."

The vultures.

"Tend your sister," Moeder said to me, and she stepped through the tent flap. She had thoughts to share with women who believed they had a place with us at this time. I knew she felt they were beneath her scorn, but she was generous with it, anyway. I heard scuffling, and as I moved to the door, she stepped back in.

"The *dominee* chased them off," she said, disappointed.

Her face was brilliant red, and she held a torn black *kappie* in her hand.

WITHIN MINUTES, MOEDER SOMEHOW put a lid on her boiling emotions and assumed control. She positioned her lap beneath Cee-Cee's head and prepared to blow out the candle.

"Put yourself in order," she said to us. "And try to get some sleep."

Sleep? Not likely. Put myself in order? Yes. Just as Moeder had. Prepare for tomorrow. Quiet the voices. Focus. Tante Hannah knew how: create a wall of concentration against the invasion of thoughts.

Put myself in order: Yes. Freeze the images worth saving, like photographs fixed on paper, so that the good ones might be unchanged by time. But there was so little worth saving. The time inside the tent, time pacing the fence line, days that felt like the endless rows of tents themselves. We were restricted by the fences but imprisoned more by the infinite sameness. Discard that image.

Try, too, to forget Moeder's eyes. The look of them as she tended Cee-Cee would otherwise haunt. Had her eyes retreated, backing away from the things they'd seen? And the vessels that burst that day at the fence line were now a jagged web. But she remained unbending as the tent pole. That was the image to preserve.

Mevrou Huiseveldt wore her discontent like a coat she never removed. If I saved her image at all, it would be this: as sour as she continued to be, she had never once complained of an ailment since Klaas's death.

Willem was simple: I kept seeing him standing in front of the line of Tommies, viewed in profile, so thin, but with his jaw clenched so hard I could watch the muscles holding it tight. He was the image of defiance, even if foolishly so.

Janetta had been gone for months, yet I thought of her every day, thought of our walks, thought about her light breath on my cheek. And because it was her boldness that had introduced us to Maples, thinking of her made me think of him . . . his eyes . . . his red hair, which no longer offended me. I thought of him when I smelled the Dickens book. I thought of his way of speaking. . . . I heard him talking to me. . . . I heard him sigh. . . .

No . . . that was Cee-Cee.

"Moeder?"

"Go back to sleep," she said in the tone she used when praying. I would not bother them, perhaps she could rest. Moeder's voice calmed me. She hummed then and sang in whispers, the wind against the canvas muting most of it. I leaned closer to hear. It was "The Eagle Hymn," the one that Cee-Cee loved most. . . . *On eagles' wings we soar*. . . . Moeder had remembered. I smiled. There was an image to save: the depth of a mother's love that the vulture women would never understand.

Inspired by her, I prayed for the little one. I vowed to devote my days to her when she was better. I would finish Dickens with her. She had been good with her letters and would be writing soon. I would get more sheets of rules for her to start drawing on. We would walk and hug, and I would share my food with her because she was so thin. . . . No, discard that image.

But how to purge the image of her bones? How had I not noticed earlier? I felt my wrist. I did not imagine I had much meat there, anyway, even before, but my fingers easily went all the way around. We were all wasting. My soreness in the mornings might have been because there was so little now between my bones and the ground. I thought of my body's being ground down, day by day, and sifted into the soil at night.

Even this taking-stock process was exhausting, as thoughts refused to be marshaled, running loose, beyond control, grinding against one another, the friction and pressure creating heat. Breathing was like sucking syrupy air into my lungs, and every exhalation was steamy, and the tent swelled because of it. The top of the tent lost its point and grew round, and we all panted, sucking in thick air and exhaling steam. The canvas expanded and lifted up. . . . The tent ropes hummed . . . higher, more a whistle now, and the lines snapped like slingshots. . . . We rose, slowly at first, just inches above the ground, and then we were free . . . floating above the camp . . . the tent now round and white in the night sky. And below, the other tents pointed like shark teeth. I looked to Moeder and Willem, and they were swelling, too, and panting hot air, and we needed to keep exhaling or we'd be sucked back to earth, back to camp. Panting . . . panting . . . rising . . . never daring to look down. . . . We rose into the cooler air, and even as we did, I knew I was hallucinating, but it helped me finally float toward sleep.

MOEDER WHISPERED LOUDLY ENOUGH to stir me but no one else in the tent.

"Lettie, light the candle."

Not again, poor Cee-Cee.

Moeder held her on her lap.

"Oh no, Mama, no."

Moeder touched the tight curls.

"Ceec."

She opened her eyes when I said her name. They closed slowly and she released a raspy sigh.

I leaned over her and breathed in the tiny puff of air she had exhaled. I sucked in as much as I could, taking it deeply and holding it there, willing it into my blood. Hold it, hold it, hold it. I thought of Cee-Cee when she was a new baby, and when I held her hands and helped her walk toward Vader, and how we played and sang. Her breath was in my blood.

Hold it, hold it. I thought of the look of excitement in her eyes when I told her stories.

Hold it. Hold. . . . I wilted against the cot and had to exhale. The next breath carried only the scent of moldy canvas, fouled bedding, and the rest of us living in this small, miserable place.

Moeder lifted Cee-Cee's little arms from her sides to rest across her chest, the bones like brittle twigs in a loose paper bundle. The tent shuddered from a gust. Mevrou Huiseveldt snored without concern.

I shivered, and that awakened my morning hunger. But the smells soured it into nausea. Moeder pulled Cee-Cee up against her chest and rocked her, whispering something I could not hear against the fluttering canvas. Maybe it was a prayer or a song. I waited until she finished.

"What do we do, Moeder?"

"*Maak 'n plan*," she said. She sniffed at the air. "The wind should dry things and I can get to the reservoir to wash her dress," she said.

I thought of Cee-Cee's good dress and the times she'd worn it. I cried and did not care whom it woke.

"Lettie . . . calm . . . God's will," Moeder said. "God's will. . . . Never doubt. . . . Not a sparrow falls without his blessing."

"Not a sparrow falls," I repeated. Cee-Cee seemed exactly like a frail bird. But how did we let her fall? I bent to hug her and kiss her forehead.

"Pray for her soul," she said.

I mouthed words toward Cee-Cee but could not say them aloud without sobbing.

"Aletta, you have to get to the coffin maker. . . . If you're early, he might have wood today," she said. "If not, try to find some."

I stood, touched her shoulder and then her cheek. I heard that the Pienaars had buried their little boy in a cloth shroud because there was no wood.

"Yes, Ma."

"Go."

I shook my blanket and wrapped it tight as I could stand. The tent ropes moaned in the predawn. Through a rift in the fast clouds I saw a few stars, but the wind pulled a veil across them. I listened for activity in neighbors' tents. I knew Ouma van Zyl had nothing. Other than shaking canvas, there was silence from the Van Tonders'. If they were able to sleep, I would not disturb.

I looked toward the reservoir but hadn't seen anything that way. I walked to the east; Maples would not be on duty yet, I didn't think, but if I saw him he might have ideas.

The sounds of an uneventful morning seeped from the next tent. I cleared my throat, seeking permission to enter. A group was circled, holding hands. They stopped their prayer, opened their eyes, and welcomed my entry.

My words were thick.

". . . lost my sister . . . coffin . . . wood."

"Go to the coffin maker." The oldest woman pointed farther to the east. "God be praised, child."

The wind folded back the brim of my *kappie* and carried the stench from the latrine pits. My gut tightened again and I pulled my blanket over my nose and cursed into it.

It was still short of full dawn, but a dozen stood in single file outside the coffin maker's tent, as they might have at a shop in town, waiting to buy goods.

The last in the row turned. "Only cloths," she said.

The line moved quickly, some heading to the morgue tent, others just back to their families to prepare for services.

"My baby sister died," I told the man. "My mother sent me."

"No wood . . . no coffins," he said. "If you can find wood, I'll build one, but there's none in camp. None for miles."

"My mother sent me," I repeated.

He held up a square piece of canvas, part of a tattered tent.

"If she's small, this will do," he said.

I remembered how Cee-Cee would hide under her quilt at home, giving herself away with her giggling. The canvas piece was half the size of her quilt. She would fit.

I stood taller and focused on the man's eyes, stressing my situation. He seemed familiar with the look.

"I am a carpenter," he said. "A carpenter with no wood. What can I do?" We both squinted against the wind. He folded the canvas piece and handed it to me.

When I reached the tent, Willem sat at the far side with Rachel, who mouthed her porridge next to Cecelia's body. They prayed and sang weary hymns through the morning until Willem moved away and pulled himself inside his blanket.

Moeder returned from the reservoir with Cee-Cee's still-moist dress. I helped change her.

We gathered for the walk to the cemetery, a group from a nearby tent falling in behind, eyes down, carrying a young boy on a blanket. He was dressed in a black suit, a white scarf tied under his jaw to keep his mouth from falling open as they walked.

By the time our silent convoy reached the table-flat rise of land at the edge of the camp, several other groups were gathered around mounds and shallow clefts in the earth.

Two of the older men approached Moeder and offered to dig, their heads lowered, holding shovels across their chests like rifles. One apologized that the site was not ready; they never knew how many would be needed each day.

We stood like a windbreak of trees along one side. When a small trench was rent in the rocky ground, the *dominee* finishing up at a nearby grave was called to oversee the service for us. He recognized Moeder but could not remember Cecelia's name.

He opened his book and thumbed through the readings.

> Out of the depths of misery,
> I cry with heart and mouth
> To thee who can send salvation
> Oh Lord, look upon my pain.

We could scarcely hear him above the wind but recognized the verse. We repeated the final line of the stanza. Lord, look upon my pain, we said. Amen.

I expected more, but other groups waited. The preacher nodded his head to the diggers, who shoveled the rocks gently onto the small bundle. It sounded so loud, like those stormy days on the veld when the first stones of hail touch ground, slowly to start, before drumming louder, and then sometimes striking with enough force to bring down grown sheep. I took Moeder's skirt in my fist; she placed her palms over my ears until the sound was gone.

"A marker?" Moeder asked.

"No wood," said one of the men, stacking the final stones on the uneven mound. He retrieved a bottle from a mealie sack. He gathered soil and small rocks to pour into the bottle to weigh it down.

"Write her name on this." He handed a piece of paper and a pencil nub to Moeder.

"A bottle?"

The man nodded, beard blown horizontal.

The pastor offered his Bible so that she could use it to hold the paper flat. She paused.

Cecilia Venter

"Lammetjie"

Geboren February 1897

Overleden September 1901

She tucked the paper into the bottle and wedged it among the rocks that topped the small mound. Grit from a distant place stung our faces. I turned from it and saw several other families in mute clusters, planting other children beneath bottles, waiting for the preacher to offer words that would be carried off by the wind.

PART III

The Water and the Blood

30

October 1901, Concentration Camp

Living on the veld taught nothing about the real value of space, creating the illusion that it was limitless. The great open distances of our land, which had once felt like a warm invitation, now stretched out on the other side of the camp's fence like a cruel taunt. After weeks of slipping beneath the surface of an imaginary river as a means of withdrawal, a storm provided an alternate escape. I drew close to the tent wall and put my ear to the canvas, which in my mind became the sail of a great ship. When it fluttered, I was upon the open sea, shouting orders to my men, who pulled the sails taut to speed us away to wherever my mind commanded. I sailed to countries and islands Oupa Gideon had mentioned, places that sounded so foreign I doubted they were real. Zamboanga—after all, how silly did he think me? People came to the harbor to see the first ship captained by a woman. And I was treated to meals of fruits and meats and sweets and glorious liver.

We would be off again when the ropes resumed singing to a beat set by clapping canvas. And for a while, I was not merely adrift in the current of time; I was the one in control, the one steering the giant, spinning wheel. I plotted our course by the stars and by whim. And I took Oupa Gideon with me so that he could learn the sea as his grandfather had. Behind that wheel, we drank coffee and ate hard biscuits, and half our world was the night sky.

I might spend an entire afternoon "sailing" and only return to my family once the air grew still in the evening. When I stood, my legs wobbled from having been at sea. I was glad to have surrendered touch with the earth that had been pulling so hard at my bones.

When there were no sea winds to fill my tent-sail, I pulled up my blanket and saw myself in front of a classroom, all eyes focused on me, shaping little minds with my words. I loved the control a teacher had over their view of the world. Could there be a position of greater power than steering children's minds?

Sometimes when I dozed in my private space, I thought of times when I had gone riding with Schalk and it felt like floating through the tall, dry grasses. I could feel the animal's great warmth coming up through me, and feel the way I moved against it with each stride. I'd rock as we galloped, and post into a canter. Rock and post: I could ride forever, rocking to the motion of the horse, warming, rocking . . . faster . . . feeling so good.

"Lettie . . . stop," Moeder said. "Wake up and pray."

She woke me so forcefully it felt as if I had been thrown from the horse.

I resented having my pleasant escape disrupted and wanted to snap at her, but I blinked myself awake and prayed as she ordered. And I did so with a sincere heart. But my prayers changed in ways I could not share with her. What would I say? Yes, Moeder, I count my blessings as never before and appreciate God's gracious gifts. But now I also tally the cost.

When it had been cold, I thanked God for the next warm day. But I knew it would bring the flies that could drive me mad with their inescapable buzzing, biting, and clustering at my eyes and ears.

I then thanked him for the blessing of wind that drove the flies away, but it carried grit that could tear away skin. After the drought brought so much dust that our faces turned gray and our noses caked, I blessed the rain that he gave. I would hold my arms open to feel it wash the dust from my body and know with certainty that God himself had sent it down. And then it would turn the soil into glue and cause the latrines to fill and overflow, and the stench would be so complete that I prayed that God would take my sense of smell.

I was blessed to have my family but paid for it with the agony of loss. And soon they'd have to deal with my death. My body was shutting down, and from what I'd seen, it would happen one process at a time and come quickly.

Thankfully, I was now able to withdraw my body into my mind, to pull it all into such a tight place that I was certain I had disappeared. *Let me hide myself in thee*, I sang in my mind. It got easier and easier to drift away like that. But increasingly difficult to return.

So many questions still came to mind that I could not voice, especially as there was such little conversation now. At times Moeder communicated with little more than looks and gestures, as if words would clutter the small tent. I spent more time watching her, studying her subtly. I used to be able to see my reflection in her eyes, but now they absorbed light. It was so much harder to read her face now, as it seemed she wore a leather mask, with deepening lines and hollows and shadows.

She sat on the cot, fingering the hem of the doll's dress. I remembered sitting next to her when she stitched the lace ruffle to the bottom. I had named the doll Lollie for a reason I could not remember, and she had slept with me every night until I passed her on to Cee-Cee, once she needed a nighttime friend more than I did.

For all the hugging Lollie had endured, the stitching had held up well. Moeder had used the same color of green thread she had given to Vader when he left for war two years earlier. I expected Moeder thought about Vader's stitched arm even as she fingered the dress of the doll that had belonged to her daughter, to *their* daughter. Maybe someday there would be another child, a new sister. I tried to recall how old Moeder was. How long would the war go on? How late can women have children? But the figures did not fall into place.

Moeder called Rachel to her cot.

"Here," she said, handing her the doll. "You can play with Lollie."

Rachel and Cee-Cee had played with her together, and Rachel had at times tried to snatch it away when Cee-Cee wasn't holding it, leading to a scrap. How could she give it to Rachel, as if rewarding her for Cee-Cee's death?

I knew I was being unchristian again. After all, how long would the doll be hers before getting passed along to the next child? How many little girls would this doll outlast? Giving away Lollie was Moeder's sign that we were all going to try to move on. She was right; we can't forever cling to our little dolls.

But what else was going through her mind? Would she try to get word to Vader about Cee-Cee? Vader held a firm rein on his emotions, like most men. But I was sure none of us should ever tell him about Cecelia's final days. If he knew now, it would cause him to act the fool in battle, to attack the British by himself. Maybe that would be a good thing. But I could see him trying to ride into this camp alone, firing his weapons with both hands, if only for the chance to say a prayer at her grave.

I suspected that Moeder saw everything that had happened as the fault of Oom Sarel. Vader would have to learn of this later, or maybe never. I knew she was thinking of ways to find strength and pass it along to us. Nothing is unbearable, praise be to God. She had said that many times when we first got to camp. But less often since.

I lifted my eyes, but instead of the heavens, I saw our elongated and distorted shadows on the canvas pointing to the tent peak. It made us look thinner. I looked at myself . . . my wasting arms . . . another sign of death. I had suspected it for at least two months, and now I knew I would be the next to go. I would fade to a trace and then disappear, like a written word rubbed slowly from a page.

Moeder would tend me. Willem would go fetch the *dominee*. They would clean me raw and wash my pinafore and wrap me in canvas and carry me to the hill, where they would drop me in a hole and stuff my name in a bottle.

Dear Tante,

Cee-Cee died. It came on quickly. She didn't even seem sick, just tired. Passed in Moeder's arms. She's buried on the hill. She has no marker. But if you want to go pray over her, you might as well pick any of the mounds, God will know which is hers. I should have noticed her getting sick and we could have done something sooner. She was like my little girl and I didn't do enough to save her. Moeder said that "not a sparrow falls without God's blessing," but I feel as if I should have caught her.

I try to remember her every minute so that she won't disappear. I feel as if I should hate somebody for her death, to make somebody pay, but I don't know who. All I can do is question myself. I haven't been righteous and I worry that taking Cee-Cee was God's punishment.

Sorry to have to tell you this way.

Love,

Lettie

"Betty, the silly goose, sent me this," Maples said, holding up a strange knit hat that seemed designed to conceal everything but the wearer's eyes.

"I could have used that after the lice," I said. "But I need to tell—"

"It's a balaclava . . . because I'll need it in the cold. She still doesn't understand the Southern Hemisphere."

There was so much I had prepared to tell him, about Cee-Cee and her final days, but he gave me no room to start. I handed him my note to Tante Hannah. I no longer scanned the area for suspicious guards or women or the commandant's spies. I didn't care anymore. Take me, isolate me. . . . It would make the day different from the last.

"You should be happy she sent it."

"I am . . . but I won't need it for months. She thinks it's about to turn cold here."

"You'll be happy you have it . . ." I was going to say "next July," but I did not want to think of the British still being here next winter. It had been almost two years.

"I still have a hard time thinking about the heat of Christmas and the snow in July," he said. "That doesn't seem right."

"You have your right, we have ours."

"I suppose," he said. "You'd have the same troubles if you visited England. Do you think you'll ever visit? . . . We could take you around."

Visit England? Of course . . . I'll attend school there . . . Oxford . . . Cambridge. . . . Wait . . . he said "we" could take you around. We? Betty would be with him? No, I did not need this Betty to show me the sights of Great Britain. He's going to have to learn to get over Betty.

"I want to go to England to see the stars. It's a different sky there, did you know?"

"Uh . . . hadn't thought about that," he said. "I suppose that's true."

"I want to someday see the Great Bear, the constellation that points to the north . . . a ship captain's best friend, my *oupa* . . . my grandfather . . . told me."

"Does he know sailing?"

"Learned of it . . . stars and such . . . from his grandfather, who used to sail around the world."

"Dutch?"

"Yes . . . Dutch . . . great sailors."

"We had wars with the Dutch . . . at some point," he said. "I was never that sharp with history."

"You've had wars with everyone."

"Well . . . not everyone."

"You have a history of taking over other people's countries," I said. "You could point at a map with your eyes closed and hit one of them."

"That's why they call it an empire," he said, thrusting his shoulders back.

"And you're doing it for their good. . . . They're all so happy to be part of your empire," I said.

"They're better for it, most of them," he said.

"Yes, you can see how much happier we've been since you came here. It's such a privilege to have you, and it will be nice of you to take all that gold out of our way. It has been so bothersome."

"Right . . . and your people . . . your history?"

"We keep moving to get away from people like the British, people who think it's their business to tell us what to do . . . how to live," I said. "We don't invade every chance we get."

"So there was nobody here when your people came this way?"

"No, it was wide open."

"Nobody?" He thrust out his jaw as a challenge.

"Just the natives."

"Exactly."

"Wait . . ."

"And your people had rifles and they had, what, spears?"

"I don't know what they had . . . but that was different."

"Oh? Did you take their land?"

He pressed in.

"They weren't . . . like us," I said. "They weren't really farmers."

"Did you take their land . . . maybe kill some of them?"

"There were wars . . . and they attacked . . ."

"Where were you when they attacked . . . on land that had been theirs?"

"We were trying to . . ."

"Oh . . . were they happy you showed up? Did they welcome you? I doubt it. See, we're not so different."

"You think you can talk . . . with the things the Tommies . . . the things you . . ." I stopped. The war wasn't his fault. What difference did it make now?

"I know . . . I know," he said. He put his hands out; he did not want to argue, either. "It's just all bad . . . and getting worse."

"Worse?"

He leaned in, lowering his voice. After having been called a spy several times, I finally felt like one. As he bent close, I noticed I was almost as tall as he was now.

"They're building blockhouses, connected by barbed wire, and driving the Boers into the fences."

I pictured the men and thought of them as sheep, helpless.

"Burning the farms wasn't enough?"

"They decided your boys could keep this going forever if they wanted," he said. "Hiding, attacking, hiding . . . being a nuisance. They might never win the war, but they win in some ways just by keeping it going. There's some that won't ever quit. And that would mean we'd be here forever."

"The Bitter-Enders."

"Right."

"Won't give up for anything."

I knew Vader would be the last man standing if it came to it. He would take on the entire army. Half a million Tommies could surround him. Vader, Oupa, and Schalk would stand with their backs together and their rifles readied.

But to be driven into fences and gunned down? Would the only men left alive be those who had surrendered? What kind of country would that be? Nothing but quitters . . . Hands-Uppers? A whole country of them?

I had to go. I was fearful for the men but also sick at myself for not having stopped all this war talk and told him about Cee-Cee. I wanted to tell somebody about her. I wanted Maples to know about her. I wanted his comfort, his sympathy. But I decided I should get to the hospital as quickly as possible. I was dying.

Dearest Lettie,

I'm so deeply sorry. I'm sure there was nothing you could have done. She needed medical attention, and even that might not have been enough. Cee-Cee loved you more than anything.

I will tell you how I dealt with emotional losses. I embroidered. It caused me to focus on something that wasn't my grief. Perhaps your writing or your notes or your books would help you.

Because you will be wondering what I know about loss, I will tell you something no one else in the world knows . . . not even Oom. I've known the loss of a child. Four children. Four who were never born. One who died before he could breathe air; three others who never got that far. I don't know why. God's plan for me. I gave them each names and I pray for them every day. Oom knew about the first one, but it broke his heart so much I didn't tell him about the others. It is not the same as having had Cee-Cee to love for five years, but it is something I feel each day.

Let's pray for each other, sweet Lettie.

Your loving Tante Hannah

Bina could have explained it to me and might have had some *muti* as a cure. I assumed that she and her women had the same systems, but I had no way to be certain. She might have known my problem before I said anything. She often knew things about me before I did. After Cee-Cee died, I realized that I hadn't been bothered . . . how many months . . . three? . . . I had lost track.

And once I started worrying, it consumed me. What does it mean?

What caused it? Something I did? Food poisoning? Some women said that the British had poisoned the food. Could they put chemicals in the rations that would affect women's cycles—maybe as a way to kill off our breed? This was one thing I did not even share with my journal.

I found myself wearing down when I walked to the edge of the camp. That had to be a signal of something. I prayed at all times and in all places, even in the latrine. Had God done this to me as a tax upon my sinful thoughts?

Janetta would have known something about the problem or would have gone with me to the hospital. I almost asked Moeder a dozen times. But I could not shape the words and force them out. I would not allow myself to die without a fight, but I was too much a coward to tell my mother.

The British nurses at the hospital tent seemed my only option. They would not know me. They were trained for such things, I suspected. A nurse could take me in and tell me how long I had to live, and those left in our tent would not have my illness thrust in their faces. But what kind of examination would this require? A nurse, perhaps, but a doctor . . . never. I would run.

I expected the nurses would have no time for me with so many sick children needing attention. I would walk toward the hospital marquee and circle at a distance until I was able to subtly bump into a nurse going to work. Or I might see one outside the tent. I would comment on the weather, and she might recognize some symptom. I had never been to a hospital or been examined by a nurse. But I could do this.

Two guards stood near the tent, and mothers clustered nearby, waiting for word of their children. They were kept out except for short periods. My hands shook from nerves. I had heard women saying that this was a place where doctors pretended to help but instead hastened deaths as part of a plan to bring about our extermination. And the nurses, they said, were here only to find husbands, to marry an officer or a doctor.

Several nurses came out together in stained aprons, short red capes, and straw boaters atop pinned-up hair. They walked past the group of mothers while another nurse stopped to talk. I eased toward the fringe of their circle so that the nurse might walk past me when she finished her updates. She provided reports as calmly as possible. Some women confronted her, and others abused the guards; some raised howls, and others turned away, silent. The nurse nodded her head solemnly with each report, respectful of their grief but not participating.

Having worked her way through the mothers, she stepped toward me. "And you?"

"*Ja* . . . hallo."

"A question?"

"I . . ."

"You've stopped having your cycle and you're afraid to ask your mother about it."

The woman was a medical genius.

"Am I dying?"

"No."

"Oh, praise God. Am I sick?"

"Probably . . . it's usually a sign of poor health, but it's common here. Your cycles will probably come back and you'll be fine."

"I'm not the only one?"

"No . . . half a dozen a week. They all stand outside looking lost . . . like you."

"So . . . I am not dying?"

"Not from that."

"Why . . . why now?"

"Living here. Bad food, stress . . . happens all the time, particularly to the young girls. We didn't know this would be something that developed in camps like this. Probably something we need to keep track of and study. Our understanding of medicine grows from times like these. I think in your case, you're not getting enough good food. You thought all sorts of horrible things, didn't you?"

"Yes."

"Natural."

"Do I need . . . what . . . an exam?"

"How are you otherwise?" She felt my neck, beneath my jaw, asked me to cough. She looked in my mouth, turning my head toward the sun. She took my face in her hands and looked in my eyes. What else can she see in there? . . . Can she read my thoughts, too? Am I that open? She looked at the edges of my *kappie*.

"Lice?"

"Not anymore."

"Common," she said.

She felt my shoulders and then my arms.

"You're malnourished, but healthy . . . surprisingly. Think of it this way: your body knows it can't do everything anymore, and it has to make some decisions. It is still trying to grow, in addition to everything else."

I thought of Cee-Cee, her breath in my blood, deep in the vessels, and my obligation to carry it for her. I needed to stay healthy.

"Are you much weaker?" she asked.

I hadn't thought about a degree of such a thing; something that happens so gradually is hard to notice. When I thought back, I couldn't summon the small things, but only the big things, the violent storms, the floods, the dust and winds that wore me down. "I don't know about weakened," I said. "It's more like I've eroded."

She nodded.

"You could have come in and seen us, you know," she said.

"I was . . ."

"Afraid?"

"*Ja.*"

"You'd heard we were terrible."

"*Ja*, the women at the reservoir said . . ."

". . . children only come here to die."

"*Ja.*"

"Most children aren't brought here until they're about to die and it's too late for us to do anything about it."

Cee-Cee.

"Or they've been treated by some folk remedy or witch-doctor cure."

"*Muti.*"

"What . . . yes . . . some tribal medicine, folk treatments. Some of it seems helpful. . . . Some of it is ridiculous."

Her accent was different from Maples's, making every word with an *r* turn into a lengthy growl. I found I kept saying "pardon" . . . forcing her to repeat herself.

"I'm sorry, I have a hard time understanding," I said.

"Many do. . . . I'm from Scotland."

She pulled a hard candy from her apron and gave it to me. I took it without thinking. She opened one for herself, too.

"Are you with the Undesirables?"

"I don't like that word."

"Little wonder . . . how's *Irreconcilables*?"

She pronounced the word in more syllables than I could count, and it rattled the hard candy against her teeth.

"Better."

"Don't like any of the names, do you?"

"No."

"I just wish this would be over," she said.

"Me, too."

Neither one of us took sides on the outcome, only craving an end.

"Would you tell me something? The truth?"

Oh, God, what could she want of me? I had to be careful. This might be how they get information: we get sick and frightened, and they make us talk. Maybe that's what happened with Oom Sarel. They don't do it with things in the food or with firing squads; they use our fears against us.

"That depends."

She laughed.

"What do you think would happen if the nurses tried to make rounds of the tents . . . to do exams?" she asked. "We don't have enough medicine for everybody, nor enough nurses, really, but I was thinking we might give it a try. Experiment, so to say. It's not like we have a great deal of time, but we could answer questions like yours pretty quickly. That kind of thing could settle a lot of anxious minds."

I thought of my mother's most likely response. She would not allow this woman in the tent. I turned my head, not wanting to insult her.

"Right . . . that's what I thought. Have you lost family?"

I thought of Cee-Cee, blood of my blood, but said nothing.

"I'm thinking about becoming a nurse," I said, although I had not considered it until it sprang from my mouth. Maybe it was her uniform, or the powers she seemed to have, or her helping nature. It seemed as if she had cured me with only a few words. It would be a calling that was helpful, compassionate.

She took me seriously.

"Wonderful," she said. "You can start right away."

"Truly?"

"Yes . . . not as a nurse . . . but as a helper."

"Really?"

"I could let you start training as a volunteer if you wanted," she said. "We can use all the help we can get. To be honest, I think you should do everything you can to stay out of this place. You're healthy now, more or less. You should try to stay clean. Stay out of crowds of children. But if you're serious, come back. Or if you have any troubles, come back. What's your name?"

"Aletta Venter."

"Mine is Agnes. Nice to meet you."

"Seriously . . . I could help?"

"Seriously, yes, very seriously. But you have to see what we do first, what it's like in there, and decide if it's worth it to you."

I looked past her shoulder at the door of the tent, and the women gathered near the guards. I recognized the tall woman coming out from the tent, heading our way.

"Tante Hannah?"

31

October 1901, Concentration Camp

My sister died," I said without allowing Maples to get out a word. "She was the most wonderful little person."

I described her hair and her voice and the way she would sit on my lap when I read to her. My bottom lip quivered so much that I had to repeat some words. "Dickens . . . yes . . . Dickens . . . I was reading Dickens to her. And I wrote stories for her and we sang . . . sang . . . songs together. She had such a pure little heart. And it all came on so fast it just ate her up."

By the time I finished, I had to suck in a breath to push out each word, and I then cried myself empty.

"I hate this camp," he said.

"I hate this camp, too," I said.

Three women walked near, and I turned my back to them; Maples pointed at the fence as if scolding me for a violation.

"I'm sorry," he said when they had passed.

"Nobody's fault," I said. The words tasted false, and I realized I had said them only because he looked so upset.

"It is our fault," he said. "I hate it here."

"Can you go back?"

"Home? No."

"No . . . out there."

"No, no." He stepped back from me. "They won't let me."

"Tell me."

"I can't."

"I told you . . . about Cecelia."

"I've never said any of this . . ."

"I need to hear about it all."

He turned and walked down the fence line. I followed.

"Yes," I said to his back.

"Not this."

I still couldn't decide whether he was the enemy or just another person who had been pulled into something he hated as much as we did.

"Not now . . . your sister . . . you're grieving."

"I need to know it all."

"I hate being a part of this. "

"I want everything horrible out at once," I said.

He looked like Willem after being caught in mischief.

"The first thing I ever saw killed was a horse. . . . I could not believe somebody could shoot a horse," he said. "First day under fire. It makes sense that if they were shooting soldiers, a horse might get hit. But this one crumpled. . . . Legs just stopped running. . . . Body kept flying forward. It let out this horrible scream. The first man I saw killed just dropped cold on the spot . . . not a peep . . . small hole in his chest. But that horse kicked and wailed. It was pitiful."

Maples turned away, and I just looked at the back of his helmet and his thin shoulders. The hem of his tunic trailed loose threads.

"More," I said.

"Horses just kept getting shot. At every skirmish. And they'd heat up out in the sun and bloat and turn black and stink to heaven's gate. And then they'd die in the river by the dozens and we'd be so thirsty the men would drink the water and then be racked with dysentery."

He turned, his face tightened as if drying out.

"The horses . . . you're bothered by the horses?"

"I love horses," he said.

"What about the men? What about the farms?"

"Yes . . . exactly . . . I saw it all."

There it was. He was one of them after all.

"Did you burn farms and houses?"

He dropped his eyes.

"You did, didn't you?"

I could see only the top of his helmet now.

"I could have killed those men who came to our farm. . . . They took joy in it."

"I know. Some in my column did, too. Something got into some of them."

"The devil."

"Maybe. Yes . . . the devil . . . it felt like that when they lost control."

"Nobody invited them."

"I know. . . . No, I don't know. . . . War is one thing. . . . This was something . . . else."

"Why didn't you stop?"

"I tried. . . . I asked for a transfer. . . . My major assigned me the stock. He put me in the squad that had to kill the sheep or cattle or pigs . . . all of them. Had to stab them with bayonets. Hundreds a day.

Blood and squeals all day. I could hear them all night. And then we took the dead sheep and threw them down the wells to foul the water for any of the commando units that might come through later and think they could get fresh water.

"*Let the water and the blood,*" I said without melody.

"Sometimes the kaffirs would come fighting to the family's defense and we'd have to push them back or chase them down. . . . Sometimes they were happy to turn on the Boers and help us in any way. You never knew."

He leaned even closer to continue his unburdening.

"There were times when we were practically starving, too," he said. "Marching thirty miles in a day, burning sun, beyond supply lines, living without rations."

"You shouldn't be here," I reminded.

"I know . . . but we are."

"Leave."

"One day, a squad of us were sent to a small farm," he said. "Just a woman inside . . . old . . . her men gone, no one else at home. She said we looked awful and offered us milk. She had one cow and apologized that it hardly produced anymore."

"Fine Christian."

"More than that . . . a saint," he said. "She said her husband was dead and she just had one son on commando. . . . She hadn't seen nor heard from him for months. She spoke his name and asked if we had seen him, as if we were all introduced to each other at the start of the war. She said she prayed every day that God held him in his protective hand. She held her hands like a cup, or a little nest."

"And you burned her farm . . ."

"There were only seven or eight of us, and she brought milk for all of us."

I feared the rest of the story.

"Our orders were to burn the farm and bring any stock back to the garrison. But she had only the one cow."

"You burned her farm . . ."

"Without even threatening her, she said we could slaughter her cow for food . . . even though we were the enemy, we were God's children and we were starving."

"So you slaughtered her cow and then burned her farm . . ."

"We asked her about her kindness . . . unbelievable kindness. And grace . . . such grace. She said she imagined if her son was fighting in England. If he was starving . . . she hoped that some Englishwoman would have the heart to sacrifice her last cow to help him survive."

I knew women like that. Tante Hannah would probably do that. But I also knew many who would have shot him between the eyes. Moeder, for one.

"And then you burned her farm . . ."

"No, we didn't. We thanked her. Some of the men even gave her little things from home that they were carrying. And we took the cow back to the main column."

"You didn't burn her farm?"

"No, we did not."

"Good." A thimbleful of my faith in humankind was restored.

He tightened his mouth, words caught on the threshold of speech.

"*Ja?*"

"The following day . . . another troop scouted in that direction . . . and burned the woman out."

I thought I was beyond being sickened. It turned out I was not. We were silent for several moments, looking out through the fence.

"So how did that get you into this camp? They didn't think you were savage enough?"

"That's what they decided. I kept getting sick at every farm; the men kept mocking me, but I couldn't stop. I kept telling them it was stomach trouble from bad water. They finally sent me to the doctor and I told him the truth. He told the major to get me out of there . . . didn't want me around the other men."

"So now you guard women and children."

"I don't like this, either . . . but it's not"—he searched for the word—"as savage."

"How do you live with this?"

He considered it and shook his head a time or two before answering. "I can't."

WILLEM HAD GONE SILENT. He had lost his playmate and then his sister, and he was unwilling to invest in me anymore. I made no attempt to teach him. Concentration was difficult for all of us, and it seemed pointless. He had solved the most important mathematics problem of his life, in the face of the commandant, so the teaching he had received was considered a success already.

He had his back to me, to all of us, his hat pulled low, but I could see his ears moving, betraying the motion of his jaws. He was chewing, slowly, like a cow.

"What do you have?" I whispered.

He would not turn.

"Are you hiding food?"

Silence.

"Willem?"

"Mmmm?"

I crawled closer.

"Willem . . . you can tell me. I won't take it. . . . I won't tell Moeder. You can trust me."

He turned and opened his mouth, showing a thick gray bolus, and some blood at his gum line.

"What is that?"

I couldn't understand what he said.

"What?"

"*Riempie*," he said.

"From where?"

"Stool."

"From your stool?"

"*Ja . . .*"

I looked for his little stool in that wedge of the tent that he had claimed as his area. Half the tanned ox-hide strapping had been peeled from it.

"You can't eat that."

"Not eating . . . chewing."

"Does it taste good?"

"Hmph-um." He shook his head.

"Why?"

He moved the mass to one cheek to speak: "Feels like eating."

I groaned, but no one looked our way.

"Biltong," he said.

"Like biltong?"

He nodded.

"But what about your stool?"

He lifted his shoulders up to his ears.

"It will make you sick."

"Hmph-um."

He pulled a short piece from his pocket and held it out to me.

"No . . . you keep it. But thank you."

I would write this in my journal. Willem, now nearly as thin as the legs of his stool, gnawed on ox-hide strips to be reminded of chewing meat. Were boots next? Leather? Tent canvas? Anything to give him the feeling that he was eating? I felt the opposite; I had such little appetite.

But when Moeder turned, she saw Willem looking at me through an air of guilt. His bleeding gums oozed at the corners of his mouth.

"Hey, little soldier," I said, trying to explain the blood. "Everybody loses their teeth."

Moeder waved him closer and examined his mouth. She found bloody holes. His permanent teeth were falling out.

"Maybe we need supper early today," she said.

The stringy tinned beef would do him no good. That challenged anyone with well-rooted teeth.

She opened the ration bin and took out the small bag of mealie meal and the pinch sack of salt.

"Porridge," I said. "Perfect for Willem."

I brought the water bucket to Moeder.

"We should try it cold tonight," she said. "It would be good for us to get used to it cold, just mixed with a little water and salt."

Willem sniffed. Moeder moved her eyes toward the pot. We had no way to heat water.

FRETFUL WOMEN CLOSED TIGHT around the guards at the front of the hospital tent. They talked at once, frantic, some pawing at the men's tunics. The guards were deaf to their begging and unmoved by taunts and curses. The women glared when I approached, resentful of my health.

"Nurse Agnes said I could help here," I told the guards.

"Wait here."

The women stirred at the word "help." Was I there to help the children or to help the British? They began talking at once to me, as if I could somehow solve their problems or could help them gain entrance. I erased all expression, gesturing in a way that implied I could not understand them.

It was another outing about which I misled Moeder. These outings were growing more common, and I swallowed back rising bile every time I deceived her. I was growing used to the taste. I expected her to block a trip to the hospital because of exposure to illness and to the British. It was easier just to leave while she was preoccupied. I was not sure she would notice my absence, anyway.

Nurse Agnes appeared, her cape covered in fluids, and her hair coming unpinned. But she was stiff backed and strong voiced. "Aletta . . . good to see you. . . . I have only a few minutes, but I'll show you our little hospital. Your aunt Hannah told me about you and what a wonderful young woman you are. She is a great help here. She loves the children. She works more hours than any of us. She almost never goes back to her own tent."

"I didn't know she was helping here," I said.

"For months," she said.

There were dozens lying in low cots, mostly children, a few elderly. Some areas were separated by portable drapes.

"Measles." She pointed to one portion that was quarantined and then gestured in sequence around the large tent. "Pneumonia, dysentery, whooping cough . . . typhus in that corner."

"I've seen them all," I told her.

"Just living in this camp should cover half the classes you'd need to get through nursing school."

"Plus diphtheria," I said. "I've seen that, too."

"They've developed antitoxins for that, but we don't have any yet," she said. "Medicine in the twentieth century . . . so fascinating . . . all the new ways to heal people."

I had not even thought of its being a different century. It sounded so modern. But this tent did not look modern and efficient; some of the children did not even have cots, just blankets on the ground. Coughing and murmurs and low moans arose from the choir of the ill. A few white-skirted nurses floated between the cots like weary ghosts.

"See what it would be like if every mother was allowed in here?" she said. "I'm sorry, but there'd be no room to work. They would be underfoot. I hate to see them out there, and feel for them. And for the children in here, too, it's heartbreaking. I know they think we're witches, but it's impossible. I can't imagine how hard it would be to understand if it was your child sick in here. But there's no choice. We couldn't even walk in here, and fifty women coming in and out would spread so much infection it would turn into a plague."

"Plague?" I thought of the Middle Ages in Europe. "From rats?"

"No . . . diseases," she said. "It's another problem nobody understood when they brought you all here. You have lived so long out there on your own, so isolated, that you've lost natural immunities to so many things that wouldn't bother people in cities . . . children particularly."

"So . . . what about me . . . my immunities?"

"Something to think about. Be clean, wash your hands. . . . We have soap here. Be careful what you handle. It turns out that nurses stay remarkably healthy . . . build up immunities to just about everything. We always seem on the verge of being sick but rarely come down with anything too serious."

They did not look robust, but they were not as thin as most of our women.

"Did all the nurses volunteer to come here?" I could not imagine why.

"It's a job. Some of them thought it would be a holiday, or a chance to meet an officer . . . that's true," she said. "I thought the war might be the best place to learn surgical nursing. I liked the idea of nursing soldiers. I was surprised they sent me to a camp instead of a field unit. But work is work. Sometimes it feels like we're doing some good; sometimes I wonder."

"They pay you?"

"Ten pounds a month."

"How can I help?"

"The next time you come back, I'll introduce you. You'll do whatever a nurse asks, mostly getting things for them, or sponging off patients, or sometimes just talking to them. Everything you can do to help a nurse allows her to spend that time with a patient. There will be dirty work, too, cleaning up messes . . . sorry."

She rolled a half-dozen *r*'s through the word "sorry," and it had more substance.

"I've done it before."

"And you know you'll see bad things," she added. "But you have to stay strong while you're here. You can do anything you have to once you leave, but you can't come apart in front of them. That's the last thing they need . . . that any of us need."

I understood.

"You've seen bad things already . . ."

I nodded. "I'll get to see Tante Hannah?"

"Of course, she'll be so excited," she said. "We use her husband, Sarel, too."

"I saw him one night . . . pulling the cart."

"Yes . . . he still does that, but he works here, for us, too. He's one of the best helpers we have because there's nothing he won't do."

Oom Sarel at the hospital? "What?"

"It's not a pleasant job, but he offered," she said. "He collects the messes of the typhus patients and carts it all outside the camp, where he burns it in big barrels when the wind is blowing away from us. I can't imagine how hideous it must be, and really very dangerous, but he volunteered. Certainly no one else wants to do it. We all think he's a hero."

MAPLES SHIFTED HIS EYES toward the fence and turned his back to me when I approached. I didn't understand. I had been so upset with him that I'd avoided him for a few days. But thinking I'd offended him caused my chin to sink to my chest. He looked back and moved his head as if trying to pull me closer with a gesture. I stepped to his side. From his pocket he pulled a graying handkerchief covering a lump bigger than a man's fist.

"I thought you could use it more than me," he said.

I held it in both hands, feeling a familiar weight and density but allowing anticipation to build. I peeled back the corners of the handkerchief to reveal a glorious brown potato. I had not seen one in more than a year, or was it two? I wanted to bite into it raw. I lifted it to my nose and it smelled of the earth.

"I'm sorry. . . . I could get just the one . . ."

I turned away; I couldn't look at him. I stared at the potato.

"Thank you."

"Don't let anybody see it."

"Moeder?"

"Of course . . . but just your family."

"Where did you get it . . . how?"

"It was headed for the officers, I suspect."

I rolled it over, examining it.

"Won't this get you in more trouble?"

"It could if you don't put it away and go."

I slipped it in the pocket of my pinafore as I scanned for anyone who might have watched. I spun to thank him again, to run up to him and hug him with both arms, but he was walking along the fence line in the other direction, rifle at his shoulder, as if marching in a parade.

I dared not look at anyone I passed, fearing I might give away the secret in my pocket. I felt its weight against my thigh as I walked. No one had ever given me a more valuable present.

The tent was quiet; the Huiseveldts were on their side. I had not thought of them. I remembered the way we shared with neighbors after animals were butchered, but that was in times of surplus, and as much as we talked about the value of sharing, we did so because the meat would go bad if we did not, and the act came with the expectation of sharing in return. This was different. It was not a pig or kudu. This was a potato.

I stood in front of Moeder with my back to everyone else.

"Look . . ." I held it in front of me with both hands.

She choked off a sound and looked over her shoulder at the others. "Where . . ."

"Someone gave it to me . . ."

"Tante? Oom?"

"No."

I feared greater protest, but she was overtaken by the sight. She scrubbed it like a family treasure.

"Not raw," I said. "Not tonight."

She questioned without speaking.

"Come here, little soldier," I said to Willem. "Get the pot, Moeder."

I took out my *African Farm* book and positioned an empty tin beneath the pot. I ripped a few pages from the book, the sound of tearing paper filling the tent.

"Match?"

"Lettie, no," Moeder said.

I lit a few pages, and the flare warmed my fingers.

"That won't be enough," Moeder said.

"The whole book might."

Willem edged close.

"Here, Willem, I'll tear them. . . . You put them in, just a page or two at a time," I said. "Wait until one is almost burned down and then light the next one with it. Don't hurry."

With responsibility for such an important task, Willem grew serious, and we formed a tight circle.

"Lettie . . . are you sure?" Moeder asked.

"I know this book almost by heart."

I scanned pages as I tore them from the book, reading passages that I had marked as favorites, thinking my reading would keep Willem at a steady pace.

"*'When I am grown up,' she said, 'I shall wear real diamonds.'*"

The paper flamed quickly, and Willem startled, almost tipping the pot.

"Careful," Moeder said, dropping a few pinches of salt into the water, the smoke and smell of the burning paper climbing the sides of the pot.

"*It seemed as though Death had known and loved the old man, so gently it touched him. . . . So it . . . sealed the eyes that they might not weep again; and then the short sleep of time was melted into the long, long sleep of eternity.*"

I extended the words "long . . . long" and "eternity" to hold off Willem.

Moeder eased the potato into the center of the pot as gently as if bathing a newborn.

"Didn't the minister tell me, when I was confirmed, not to read any book except my Bible and hymn-book, that the devil was in all the rest?"

My tongue swelled at the smell, so that it was difficult to read. Moeder leaned over the pot but knew it was too early.

"Overhead it was one of those brilliant southern nights when . . . the Milky-Way is a belt of sharp frosted silver."

I was almost halfway through the book.

"We need more at a time," she said.

"The troubles of the young are soon over; they leave no external mark. If you wound the tree in its youth, the bark will quickly cover the gash; but when the tree is very old, peeling the bark off, and looking carefully, you will see the scar there still."

"Save that page, Lettie," Moeder said. "It's beautiful."

I shook my head. "I've written some of these down in my journal." I peeled more pages from the binding.

"Oh, my darling, I think of you all night, all day. I think of nothing else, love, nothing else."

Moeder looked alarmed by the passage but withheld comment, returning her focus to the small flames. I ripped out the pages in larger portions now, and the smell of the warming potato overtook the scent of burning paper. Mevrou Huiseveldt sniffed so loudly we could hear. She'd been watching all along. I didn't care. I could easily deny her a part of this . . . payment for all the sleepless nights and complaints.

"So age succeeds age, and dream succeeds dream, and the joy of the dreamer no man knoweth but he who dreameth."

Only the cover remained now; I ripped it at the spine of the book.

"Wait," Moeder said. "The binding may be gum. . . . We might need to eat that later."

I put it aside.

With a spoon, Moeder rescued the potato and positioned it in the middle of a plate. She sliced it in half lengthwise, the steamy mist of scent rising from the incision. The halves fell open.

"Ohhh," Willem said. It drew Rachel to stand over us, Mevrou Huiseveldt holding vigil from her cot.

Moeder then made three slices crossways through the two halves. She sprinkled most of our weekly salt ration across the pieces, the salt reflecting like tiny diamonds on the soft, golden pulp. We sat silent, pulling the smell into our lungs, my stomach begging loudly enough that all could hear.

She held the plate out in my direction. I placed a piece on my tongue and allowed the salty warmth to fill my mouth; I dared not chew. She held the plate out to Willem, and he studied the pieces and took the largest. Rachel had retreated to the cot with her mother. Moeder held the plate toward Rachel, who put down Lollie and looked to her mother for approval. She used both hands to lift the small piece, placing one beneath it as if holding an invisible plate in case it fell.

"What do you say, Rachel?" The little girl looked at her mother and bobbed her head sincerely, not willing to open her mouth to voice appreciation.

"Here," Moeder said, extending the plate toward Mevrou Huiseveldt. "Mathilda . . ."

Mevrou Huiseveldt looked to the top of the tent, wiped her eyes, and took the next piece.

"Thank you," she said. She knew the words after all.

Moeder took a small end piece for herself and cut the last piece in two for Willem and me. I looked at the others; all sat with eyes closed, absorbing the potato more than eating it. . . . It felt like a holiday.

I panicked when I realized we had not blessed the food. But I didn't know whether a simple blessing was enough for an occasion like this. We should have sworn a solemn vow on the spot to recognize the Miracle of the Potato each year.

I thought of my favorite meals at home and I knew I had never cherished any as much as this. Without having recognized it, I had always admired the versatile potato. Moeder cooked potatoes in so many different ways, but they had been afterthoughts, something to fill up on after enjoying the flavor of the meat that was the foundation of our meals. I had never taken time to think about a simple potato, to understand how delicious a single mouthful could taste. How I wished we had butter, and then immediately felt like an ingrate for even thinking of such a luxury.

The tent was still the rest of the night, but each face, in turn, offered me a brief smile before returning to quiet thoughtfulness. It wasn't until the next day that Moeder thought to ask me again about the potato's journey to our tent.

32

November 1901, Concentration Camp

M y inner war never relented, conscience and guilt battling for dominion. Oupa always preached that we were to live by "the Word of God," but in quiet moments, Moeder had a different message: "People can bend the Holy Word to their own purposes," she said. "You should let your own conscience be your guide." When she said that, she was trusting that I had one that worked. But I'd failed her. I was weak.

I had known for months that Moeder would ask the question, and I had prepared a series of responses that evolved over time. But it arrived in a form I had not expected, and I felt ambushed.

"Who is your guard?" she asked.

"My guard?"

"Your guard."

"I don't have a guard to myself. . . . I don't understand. . . . They guard all of us."

"Aletta . . . a woman doing wash asked me what I knew about 'your guard, '" she said. "She looked at me as if it was a well-known fact. So, who is 'your guard'?"

None of my prepared excuses involved someone's telling my mother before I could. And certainly no one had the right to call him "my guard," although just hearing that caused me to shudder with what felt like ownership.

"I've been meaning to tell you, Moeder, but haven't because you've been so busy and there's been . . . so much. I knew you would worry, and there really was no need. I was thinking all along it would be better for you if I didn't tell you."

"You were doing it for my benefit?" she said. "Nonsense."

"Since I don't have a school to go to, I have talked a few times with a British guard about educational things . . . books . . . geography . . . that sort of thing."

Silence. I knew what she was thinking.

"No, that's not it, Ma, he's not handsome . . . not at all . . . a boy, really, not much older than Schalk. And short. I've been learning about British culture . . . and Dickens. . . . That's where I got the Dickens book."

She looked at me with a strained focus I hadn't seen directed my way before, and when I finished my explanation she said the most punishing words I could have heard.

"I trusted you."

Not stones, these words, but daggers. I did not change my expression or breathing, but my eyes filled immediately. I would not look away from her. I deserved this. She had trusted me and I had failed. She expected more of me. She thought I could be as strong as she was, but I knew I never could. And she could probably never understand that.

"I wanted to let you get out . . . meet girls your age . . . walk . . . read. . . . I felt you earned that . . . but this?"

"I did walk and read, and I met Janetta."

"The British are the enemy. . . . Have you forgotten? Think about what they've done . . . what they're doing."

"Moeder, he hates his army and this war as much as we do," I said. "He says so all the time. He sympathizes with us."

"We don't want his sympathy. We want him gone. He has a rifle, doesn't he? He's a camp guard, isn't he?"

She stopped, inhaled so deeply her chest rose, and turned in a slow circle around me, like an animal studying my weakness.

"I want you to answer this: What would your father say? What would your brother say?"

"I know . . . and Oupa."

"The British are trying their best to kill your father and brother," she said. "This man, this boy, this guard . . . he would shoot at them . . . and probably at us."

I looked into her eyes, my own as wide as I could make them, trying without words to communicate how sorry I was. But getting to know Maples had been the only good thing about this camp.

"He gave me the potato," I said. "He gave *us* the potato."

I thought it would calm her, but she looked stricken.

"Ma, the potato . . . remember the potato? . . . He didn't have to do that. . . . He took a risk . . . to help us. . . . He could be an . . . an . . . ally."

"He's the enemy," she shouted. "We don't take anything from enemies."

"He might help get a message to the men if we needed . . . get more food for us."

"Or he could report us."

"He wouldn't."

"If it was to his benefit, he would."

"The potato . . . he could have eaten it."

"But you said you visit with him for the culture . . . books. . . . Is that what you're telling me?"

"*Ja* . . . Moeder . . . *ja*." She knew. What point lying, now? "Mostly."

"How long?"

"Not long."

"If you know so much about his character, you've already spent too much time with him," she said. "If you'll lie about this, how can I trust you anymore?"

"I'm being smart, Moeder. Maybe he could help us get out, or help us get transferred to a better camp . . . or a better tent. . . . They can do those things. . . . It happens," I said, slanting my eyes toward Mevrou Huiseveldt. "It's smart to use him. It's what the men are doing . . . out-foxing the British at every turn. We should, too. We have to be smarter than them. Use them for our good. It's their weakness, not ours."

I had not even rehearsed these points; they were born of pressure. I could tell Moeder listened when I mentioned using them, outsmarting them.

"I have to think," she announced, and she went back to her sewing. She looked up a time or two and shook her head at me. I should have told her sooner. It would have been different if I could have worked into it. She would have respected my honesty. Maybe.

"And did you visit with him when you were fetching water?" She broke the silence with an accusing tone.

"I was getting water. . . . I was . . . always . . . but I sometimes walked past him. . . . We started talking about books and things."

She didn't speak for hours. I stewed in bubbling guilt, thinking about all she had done, all she had been through. She had believed in me; she had trusted me. Can a person ever regain that?

"Where is he?" she said. It had been so long since she had spoken that it took me a few moments to understand.

"Who?"

"Show me."

"What?"

"Him . . . the guard."

"I don't know. . . . How would I know?"

She glared.

"Fine."

I prayed he would not be at his usual station as I led her in that direction.

He saw us coming.

"Peace," he said.

"You teach him that?" she asked me.

"Private Maples . . . this is my mother."

"Mrs. Venter? Hello, I'm Thomas Maples," he said. "Pleased to meet you."

"I see no reason for you to talk to my daughter."

"I only—"

"I don't want to hear your explanations. Stay away from her."

"We only—"

"I don't want you talking to her."

"Ma, I thought—"

"Did Aletta tell you that your men threatened to shoot her younger brother? Did she tell you about her little sister?"

"I know. . . . I'm so sorry."

"Did she tell you about the commandant threatening us for no reason? Stay away from my daughter. You see her coming, you walk away."

"But I have places I have to be," Maples said. "Or I'll get brought up."

"Fine, stay here then. It means I will have no trouble finding you if I need to come after you. You should be ashamed."

"I am," he said. "I am ashamed. I hate it. I hate being here. I hate guarding women. I hate everything about it. Nothing you could say could make it worse than it is."

He brought both hands to his chest.

"If I could go back and not join . . . yes . . . I would do that," he continued. "I would never come here. I would work in a mill and never pick up a rifle my whole life."

He took the rifle off his shoulder and held it out to her as if to make it a present: "Take it."

Moeder was speechless, disarmed. I knew he had shot at our men and he had burned farms, but he was just a boy. I felt sorry for him. God may grant forgiveness, but I doubted Moeder was of that mind. I was surprised when she did not take the rifle and shoot him dead.

"I don't want you talking to her," she said. "Do you understand?"

She took my arm and turned us back toward the tent.

"Moeder, he said I remind him of his little sister."

"You're Schalk's little sister, and you're only fourteen."

"Moeder, I'm not thinking about—"

"You're lying again, but it doesn't matter what you're thinking. It matters what he's thinking."

"Moeder, he has a girlfriend back home . . . Betty. . . . He loves her, he told me. . . . He tells me that all the time."

"He's not a boy, Lettie, he looks like a boy, but he's not a boy, he's a soldier, and he's away from his home and his girl. And he's British. . . . You cannot trust him."

She held my face and spoke words between pauses: "He . . . is . . . the . . . enemy."

"But he told me he would try to help us if he could. Anything. In any way. He has said that often. Any way. And I have proof that he can be trusted."

We walked without discussion until we neared the tent.

"Go inside," she said. "And stay there. I have a few more things I need to say to Private Maples."

I considered following her, sneaking up on them, trying to hear what she was saying, and watching to see whether she would take his rifle and shoot him down and then try to free the camp somehow. Would she finally go mad? Had she already?

IT FLOWED WITHOUT THOUGHT, word after word, another lengthy guilt-fueled confession that was straight from the heart and mostly true. It started with "Moeder, I vow to be better. There are some things I have to tell you . . ."

She responded with the look I'd seen when I was about to pour turpentine on her bloody hands.

I told her about going to the hospital and how I now wanted to become a nurse. I said some idealistic phrases about wanting "to help our people in a time of great need" and "doing God's work." And by the way, I would be seeing Tante Hannah there because she was also "doing God's work." And I went there in the first place because I had "a health problem that made me think I was dying but I'm not."

She listened without remark.

"Tante Hannah is not the devil, she's just married to him, and she is family, and Oupa Gideon taught that nothing is more important than family . . . and . . . I will never again betray your trust."

"Fine," she said. One word. I was certain I heard it, but I did not even see her lips move.

"It's all right?"

"Fine," she said. "Health problem?"

"Every month."

"You went to the hospital?"

"*Ja*, I'm fine . . . just . . . not as fine as I might be."

"Why didn't you tell me?"

I opened my mouth to answer but did not. We communicated in silence, just looking into each other's eyes for a minute. Or maybe it was an hour.

"It's good they could help you," she said.

"They just talked to me," I said. "I met a nurse who was nice and she asked if I wanted to help. Can I help? It would be helping our people . . . helping our little ones."

"*Ja*."

I rushed to her before she could finish, and pressed my cheek to her cheek.

"And if you want to talk to your guard . . . about books . . . that's fine . . . just not long . . . and only where people can see, but not where too many people can see."

Was this her first attempt at a joke?

"Wait . . . Ma . . . have you given up on me?"

"No . . . you're growing up. . . . That happens with or without my permission."

. . .

I WAS PROUD TO defend Tante Hannah to my mother. I could not imagine Tante Hannah's life with Oom Sarel and the shame she must have felt, all the while knowing that the contempt for him painted her with a stain that might never be washed clean.

If we are who we are through others, as Bina said, who are you when you have no "others"? Who did Tante Hannah have? Oom Sarel? Not really. He had paid her so little attention even before the war. She had no children, no friends. The hospital was a chance to work in the place of greatest need during our most desperate time.

Tante was at the far end of the tent when I entered that afternoon. Nurse Agnes told me she was cleaning the mouths of typhus patients and I should stay away. But I approached and watched from a short distance. She had a pleasant tone with them, as she always did with us. And when they opened their mouths for her to examine, the sight was hideous, lips cracked, gums bleeding, teeth hanging by their nerves.

She saw me and smiled but said nothing until she finished the row and aggressively washed her hands in a basin.

"Hallo, dear." She hugged me with both arms. "You're so tall."

"I just seem that way because I'm thinner," I said.

"No . . . you're growing, too."

She hugged me again and we stepped outside the tent and away from the guards.

"Your note about Cecelia broke my heart," she said. "I'm so sorry."

"Your note broke my heart, too," I said.

Guilt surged again; I no longer had the chance to be close to Cee-Cee. I hugged Tante hard.

"You can talk about it if you want," she said.

"Not yet."

She gave me the same look I had perfected in those cases when words were not strong enough to carry the weight of sympathy.

"I didn't tell you about my working here in a note because of what you might have heard about the hospital tent. We do good here. And I'm glad you're going to help."

"I might want to be a nurse."

"What about being a writer?"

"Maybe . . . still . . ."

"You can do it if you want. . . . You have more to write about now."

I looked toward the tent.

"Does your mother know you're here?"

"*Ja*. She approved it."

"She did?"

"Said it was fine."

"That was the word she used? Does she know I'm here?"

"Yes, fine."

"I'm glad you told her the truth."

"Of course."

We nodded in unison. Both of us were afraid of Moeder.

"How is she?"

I tried to think of the perfect description. Grieving silently. Planning. Plotting.

"Unbowed," I said. That was the word I'd arrived at years ago, and it was only more fitting.

"Always," Hannah said. "But you're still worried about her?"

"I shouldn't talk about it."

The tent emitted a groan, and we moved farther from the door.

"No, you shouldn't," she said. "But I should."

I considered how important Tante Hannah was to me, and how much had been shared through our brief notes, but I would always defend Moeder.

"I love your mother. . . . We were very close. . . . Did you know that?"

More than a year in the camp had drained from me the capacity to be stunned, but this was a surprise.

"We were. . . . We talked all the time . . . two young wives," she said. "And every time she had a child, I felt worse for not having one . . ."

"And Oom Sarel blamed you . . ."

"I'll shoulder it as my fault . . . my failure . . . my resentment."

I wished I could cry for her. I wanted to show her how sorry I was, but it took so much now.

"Lettie, I didn't know about what happened with Oom Sarel until I got here. I didn't know you were all taken from home until I saw the smoke. . . . You were gone when I got there and Bina told me."

"Bina?"

"She came to our house that night, but the Tommies were there for us the next morning. . . . They ran her off."

"Did they burn your place?"

"No . . . I should have known something from that. They took everything of value, but they didn't burn it. When I got here, they led me to a tent, and Oom Sarel was already inside. That was the first I heard of what had happened."

"Can you tell me?"

"I'm not sure I really know. . . . He was hurt. . . . They brought him in . . . and he signed the paper so he could get treatment."

"He put his hands up and left Vader and Schalk and Oupa out there to fight."

"Yes . . . but he . . ."

Again, we nodded at each other. I hated that it sounded as if I thought Tante Hannah was responsible.

"Lettie . . . if I had known, I would have run . . . gone with Bina to live in the caves, or somewhere on the veld. I would not have come here. I would have left earlier with my mother. I should have listened to her . . ."

I wanted her to blame Oom Sarel; I would have felt better if she had laid it all at his feet. But she did not.

"Or I should have come here . . . but with you."

I wondered how Moeder would have reacted to that and how that might have changed things. The currents pulled at me again. Was I betraying Moeder by even talking to Tante Hannah? By being sympathetic? By even considering Oom Sarel's reasons?

Enough.

"Do you like working here?"

"I do . . . very much. I keep telling the doctors that if they need anybody to do any fancy stitchwork to close wounds, I'm the one for the job."

We both laughed.

"What about the British . . . working with the British?"

"One doctor is good and one is horrible; most of the nurses are wonderful. You met Agnes; she's the best . . . very compassionate, and so strong. They're good to me because they know I'll work around the clock."

"Doesn't it wear?"

"There is so much need."

I knew that was true.

"I wasn't able to find anything about who might be watching you or informing," she said.

"Oom?" I said it in a whisper.

"No . . . no . . . I'm certain. He loves you."

"I don't care who it is anymore," I said.

A nurse called her: "Sister Hannah?" She smiled at the sound. She held up one finger.

"Are you sure you want to help here?" she asked.

"I think so."

"Lettie . . . I think you should know what happens in here."

"I know. . . . Some die."

"Lettie . . . you have to know before you decide. . . . Eighteen passed in one night."

I could not imagine. Eighteen souls. Eighteen burials. I closed my eyes and everything felt heavy, as if the moon had suddenly stopped pulling at me, only the earth. Tante Hannah lifted her stained apron to her face. How could a person say such a thing in a normal voice and another absorb the fact with an accepting mind? What kind of place was this that such things could be said without needing to be screamed? Where was the rage this would trigger in any other part of the world? What had happened to us, to our weary, weary souls, that eighteen deaths in one night caused no hysteria, no wild ravings? I remembered being sickened to the core when the Tommies killed a dozen of our chickens. But now I could hear of eighteen children dying in one night and just nod my head.

"One night we lost only two and we felt as if we should have a celebration," Tante Hannah said. "A young lady should not see that. Some of the nurses, grown women, have to leave. Doctors, too. We've gone through several. . . . The work is too much, or they feel helpless."

"I'm a woman . . ."

She looked at me.

"So you are. . . . Nurse Agnes said you are welcome to help anytime you can. And I know I will love to see you whenever you do."

I had one question, but it would not have been fair to ask, and I would have been afraid of the answer: Would Cee-Cee have lived if we'd brought her in?

I FETCHED WATER AND changed bedding and fought tears. I tried to smile when I brought water or tea to children, and I concentrated on their eyes when I changed bedding so that I would not stare at the way their skin clung to their bones, because it reminded me of Cee-Cee. But when I started seeing her in each one of them, my spine went soft.

Tante Hannah was there the whole time, but we talked only later, and she brought Nurse Agnes to me. She had been right: the hospital might have been too much. At least for this first day.

"That's enough for now," Agnes said.

"Do I not look well or something?" I asked. "You're both staring at me."

"You should sit," Tante said.

"I can do this."

Agnes led me to a chair.

"You look wobbly," she said. "It takes time, and it's hard work, and the first day is the hardest."

"I can do this," I said, and I tried to stand. Tante Hannah held me in place.

"You might be able to do something else more important outside the tent that I can't do, and your *tante* can't do," Agnes said. It took seconds for her to expel the short word "do," and it came in waves, and I felt I could ride it, float on it . . . and I slumped forward.

"Put your head down, Lettie," Hannah said.

As I lowered my head toward my knees, Agnes spoke near my ear. I answered toward my boots.

"Would you like to be my assistant?"

"I would. . . . Doing what?"

"Would you talk to girls in the camp for me?"

"I would. . . . Talk about what?"

"Would you ask them how they are doing, whether they're having troubles, whether they might be having the same kind of troubles that you were having, and tell them they don't have to worry?"

"I could do that. . . . wait . . . say those things to strangers?" I shook my head slightly but that made the ground shift beneath me.

"I know . . . it might be hard at first . . . but it is important. You don't want others to be as worried about their health as you were, do you?"

"No, I don't." Deep breaths brought some clarity. "Would they talk to me?"

"Would you have talked to another girl about your problems? More likely than talking to your mother, am I right? You'd do it sooner than you would come in here and talk to us."

I smiled at the ground.

"We'll talk about it more in a day or two. . . . I'll tell you everything that you would have to tell them. . . . It will be very important. The more they'll talk to you, the more likely they'll be to trust us if they come down with something more serious."

Tante Hannah leaned down. "You could help save lives, Lettie."

I told Moeder that I was to be an important nurse's assistant, and she asked a number of questions with genuine interest and no judgment. For all the disappointment and times I had been unworthy of her trust, she still had the strength to say these words to me: "I'm proud of you."

I felt like singing. But I spared them.

33

November 1901, Concentration Camp

Maples charged at me at a gallop, rifle slung and clattering behind his back. Women walking past stopped to be certain I was not in danger. My memory flashed to the soldiers who charged into our house . . . how long ago?

"Look." He held out a letter; the writing wasn't Tante Hannah's.

"From Betty?"

I reached to take it, but he pulled it back and started reading.

"My dear Tommy."

He closed it in thirds as if he could no longer look at it. He bent his head, composing himself.

"Yes?" I said.

Head down so his helmet bill covered his eyes, he opened the letter again.

"She starts out with the usual 'hope you are well's' and then tells me that we are over. Finished."

"No . . . why?"

"She has read all the things in the newspapers and said she's disappointed in me," he said. "She said she could understand me fighting but couldn't see how I could guard women and children. Didn't mind me getting shot at, but can't tolerate my standing guard."

He deserved better. "I could not imagine one of our women turning her back on a man fighting for his country," I said. "I can understand leaving him only if he did *not* fight for his country."

It was another example of how our women were superior to British women. I would stress this point another day. But this was a time for understanding.

"Yes . . . exactly. She doesn't think I'm the man I was. Of course I'm not; who would be?"

"She doesn't understand you."

"Not at all."

"Have you told her about . . . everything?"

"Not much . . . I'm not proud . . . getting transferred . . . no . . . I didn't explain that to her."

"She has no idea what you've been through. You're better off without her."

"Better off?"

"This was her chance to show her loyalty. How long did it last? She turned away at the first sign of hardship."

"She must have somebody else. I would wager anything."

He needed compassion. I put down my buckets and came close, closer, and hugged him, feeling the rifle and its steely mechanisms across his back.

He pulled back and shuffled the pages of the letter until he got to the end. "Look. . . . Read the last line."

I read aloud: "Best of luck in the future."

"Can you believe that? Like I was some stranger who was trying to find work. Best of luck? Best of luck stayin' alive? Best of luck fighting a war . . . living without her? What future? What future do I have?"

He asked as if I was supposed to answer, but I had no idea of anybody's future.

"What future?" he asked again.

"Here . . . let me look." I studied the note.

I tilted my head from side to side, taking time to show I was considering a response. "She writes in a pleasant hand."

He leaned his head back so I could see his moist eyes, and I wished I could take back the last remark. He put the letter back in his tunic and dragged his nose across his sleeve.

"After all I've gone through . . . now what?" he asked.

"You're asking me?"

"You're a woman . . ."

What could I tell him? No, I'm not heartsore she broke it off? It was the best news I had heard in a long time. I was so happy I had to force myself not to show it.

I had two empty buckets and had to get to the pump. But when I tried to step around him, he stopped me.

"Can you stay a little longer? I don't want to be alone."

"All right." I put down the buckets again.

"I don't think your mother will mind."

"You talked?" I pretended ignorance.

"We did . . . handsome woman . . . delicate features," he said.

"Delicate? She's made of iron." I was offended; I was the one who was delicate. He did not sense my offense. "I thought she hated you."

"I'm looking into some things for her."

I waited.

"Fine, but don't tell her I told you. . . . She wants me to ask around for information on your uncle Sarel," he said. "And then she wants me to find a way to get her over to the Joiners' camp."

"She wants to go there?"

"Very much."

"Why?"

"It seems she wants to find your uncle."

"And . . ."

"And she wants to kill him."

"She said that? She told you? Why would she tell a British guard something like that?"

"Because she wants me to help her do it."

I STUDIED MOEDER AFTER Maples's remark, trying to sense murderous intent. I knew she could generate the necessary rage, and she also had the ability to craft a plan. She had withdrawn from us for some time, I realized now, but had done so in a clever way that we didn't notice. By giving me more rein to walk whenever I chose, and easing back on some of Willem's rules, she earned more private time for herself. Loosening her hold on us was a way of gaining separation while staying in the same place.

But morally? She was absolutely devout, but "righteous vengeance" was a term I had heard her use several times, as if laying out a biblical excuse. She might consider it her "bounden duty," as she used to say, to cleanse the family name. I thought of the way Willem and Klaas had made wild plans to kill guards. They were just boys at play, but Moeder would be an actual threat. She might have been listening to their plans while pretending to ignore them at the time. I shuddered at the risk she took in not only telling Maples but enlisting his help.

I couldn't ask or even hint that I knew. She was pulling back and hardening over with a shell, and I suspected her of working through options in her mind with the same tenacity that Willem chewed his *riempies*.

She needed my help. Not with her plans for Oom Sarel, but in avoiding a family disaster. I did not care what happened to him. I had no respect for the man. Tante Hannah would be freed by his absence—whatever the cause. But I feared an attempt would only get Moeder in trouble and leave Willem and me in this camp on our own. Then I would have to be Willem's mother and someday have to explain it all to Vader and Schalk. How could I take over? I didn't even know how to cook.

I needed to draw her out, to occupy her mind. I could not talk about the men, it would fuel her anger. Family was out of the question. The past? The future? No topic seemed safe.

Someone was playing the concertina again, another dirge, slow and mournful. Even muted by canvas, it came from close enough that we could follow the melody, but it was still far enough away that it seemed carried by wind from a distance. Once again, a few bars of light dance music were added, as if the concertina were playing itself just for a moment to remind everyone that it was not only an instrument of mourning.

"Would it be all right if I tried to find who is playing?" I asked Moeder. Maybe I could persade whoever it was to play something joyful.

She did not consent but did not forbid; she might not have even heard me. By the time I stood and wrapped the blanket around my shoulders, the music was finished and there was no point.

"I wish we could hear more," I said.

She looked up.

"Ma, do you think you could play the concertina?"

The question breached her wall of thoughts; her expression softened.

"I don't know . . . maybe . . . once I figured it out."

"I miss your playing the organ. . . . You play so wonderfully."

At times I saw her fingers move as if dancing upon invisible keys.

"What is it like when you play music, Ma?"

"No . . . Lettie . . ."

"You can remember songs even without the music, can't you?"

"Um-hmm."

"You could play even without the keys in front of you, can't you?"

"Um-hmm."

"Could you play one with your fingers in the air and hum the notes?"

"No."

"Please . . . imagine the keys. . . . They felt so smooth and cool whenever I touched them. . . . I can only guess how wonderful they felt to you. The way they responded to your touch, the way you controlled the mood of everyone in the room with just the touch of your fingertips."

"Ma, please," Willem said.

"It was always so perfect, even when you didn't have music . . . like your fingers had their own memory. . . . You must have played for a long time, since you were young. . . . Do you remember, Ma?"

She put her hands out in front of her, fingers bent, so thin now.

"Play it, Moeder, I want to remember the way it sounded in the parlor. . . . Only you can do that."

She moved her head with the silent beat. And then hummed softly.

"I remember those nights, Ma . . . the hymns and the other songs you played afterward. . . . I loved them most in the evenings when it rained and the house was cool and smelled fresh . . . or when we could smell *koeksisters* and were waiting to eat them once you finished playing. You had such power to make us happy."

She moved her feet now, up and back, as if on the bellows pedals. I hummed breathy notes along with her.

"I remember once . . . when the men were gone, Moeder . . . you played a song you loved. . . . You leaned against the edge of the organ, your stomach against the keyboard, and it looked like you were a part of the instrument, like you were taking the music in, feeling it deep inside you."

She stopped. I had said the wrong thing. I was trying to help, to take her mind from the tent, and I had said something wrong.

She opened her eyes; they were gray again and cold.

"Ma . . ."

"*Ja.*"

"Close your eyes a moment."

She looked, closed them, opened them suspiciously, and then closed them. I leaned in and kissed her on the forehead, exactly in the middle, and then once on each cheek.

I HAD BEEN A woeful big sister to Willem. I think I was jealous of him and whatever that quality was that sometimes allowed young boys to have the strength of grown men. He was so absolutely fearless. Fearless and defiant. He made such an effort to be a man that I came to expect it of him, even though he was so young. I'd seen him stand up to British rifles, and later he never complained even when teeth fell from his head. But I was so impatient with him whenever he acted as he should, like a little boy. He had always been thin, but now he'd become prickly as a sweet-thorn branch, and it seemed he forever speared me with his elbows and knees, and the bone-against-bone contact was painful enough to bring tears.

But when he was defiant on my behalf . . . I loved him so, and never more than the night he tore into Mevrou Huiseveldt in a way we all wished we could. It was so inappropriate and disrespectful, and all the more glorious because of it. The little man rose up for us all.

At some point in the usual hour of crying and sobbing before Mevrou Huiseveldt commenced her noisy sleep, Willem walked to her cot and shouted one word: "Stop." He could not have yelled louder; it might have awakened those sleeping in tents several rows away.

I could see only shadows from the moonlight seeping through the canvas. I saw Mevrou Huiseveldt sit up, curious and then stunned.

"What?"

"Stop . . . woman . . . stop . . ."

"Who do you—"

"We're all sad . . . we're all tired . . . but none of us can sleep because of you."

She slapped his face.

Willem laughed. He tilted his head back and laughed as if roaring.

She slapped him again, with her palm cupped, so that it sounded even louder. It knocked him back a step, but he laughed again, equally loud, and stepped back within her range to invite another.

Moeder was there before a third slap could land.

"Don't you touch my son."

"He can't speak that way to me."

"No . . . he can't . . . but I'll take care of that . . . not you."

Mevrou Huiseveldt began shouting incoherently, waving her arms at Moeder. "Hunger . . . Klaas . . . my Jan . . ." Words emerged between wails and violent inhalations.

Rachel backed away from her mother.

"Beef . . . mealie . . . you . . ." She pointed at me repeatedly, as if with a knife, shouting nonsense. "You . . ."

Moeder lowered her volume but hardened her tone.

"If the men were this weak, we'd have lost the country in the first week. . . . Don't you think the rest of us have suffered?"

"Suffer . . . suffer . . ."

"A year in this tent . . . when have you ever thanked Aletta for carrying your water every day? Not once. Not a single time. If you'd even said a word one time about it, that would be enough."

"Lettie . . . water . . . photo . . ." She held both arms open to me now. Her mind was gone.

"It's hard enough . . . without your crying and snoring," Moeder said, cutting with controlled comments. "Praise God, your snoring could shake him from his holy throne. Roll over. Roll over, woman. I pray at night for you to roll over."

Moeder sounded like Oupa, so stern she overpowered the woman's wails. It was the only way to get her attention.

"But he . . . he can't talk . . ." Mevrou Huiseveldt pointed at Willem.

"Willem, come here. . . . Apologize," Moeder said.

"Will not."

"Willem . . . now!" He looked so tall as he strutted to her cot again. "Sorry."

Mevrou Huiseveldt broke out sobbing again.

"Now . . . don't touch my son again," Moeder said. She moved Willem directly in front of the woman's cot and slapped him hard across the back of the head. And then did it again. His head snapped back on his reedy neck both times. I knew that Willem would not allow himself to cry. It must have embarrassed Mevrou Huiseveldt to see him take the beating without a sound.

"And don't think you got away with it," Moeder said, causing the woman to soften her cries. "I had been so sure my brother-in-law was the informant that I overlooked the obvious. I should have known from the start."

"What?"

"It was you lying to the guards . . . the informant . . . the one who made up the stories for the commandant that we were sending letters to the men. That Willem was making plans to kill guards. . . . He was just playing with Klaas."

I leaned as close as I could. I needed to hear this.

"What?" Mevrou Huiseveldt said.

"It was you . . . trying to get us shot or hanged or at least taken out of this tent," Moeder said.

"No . . . I wouldn't . . . why would you think—"

"Because the commandant said an informant told him that letters to spies were coming from this tent."

"*Ja* . . . but . . . I didn't—"

"But they only searched through our things," Moeder said. "They didn't touch a thing of yours or your family's."

The woman answered with a series of coughs.

"So be quiet . . . and go back to sleep," Moeder said.

It was several hours before she started snoring again. I remember the night because Moeder's shadow seemed to glow in the darkness, her figure vibrating with rage.

A NIGHTMARE WOKE ME to the sound of snoring. Willem's outburst had accomplished nothing except to earn him a headache from repeated blows. As I did every time I woke now, I felt my head, tracing rows through my hair like raking tender grass sprouts. Any irritation? Blood? Detecting the nits early might prevent another outbreak.

Perhaps that was one piece of advice I could give other girls in camp that might help them, and help me get to know them; it would earn their trust, and they would feel more comfortable with other topics. They would tell their friends and seek me out, and maybe they'd call me Sister Aletta. Eating? Nutrition? There was not much I could say. They had no options. Cleanliness? *Ja*, keep yourself clean. Oh, no, so sorry, we don't have soap.

I was interested in what Nurse Agnes would tell me about my work with girls in camp. I wished Janetta were with me. She would be perfect for this, so open with others, and wise. Because no matter how much the nurse might instruct me, it would benefit none if I was too reluctant to share it. The girls I saw were all thin and worn, so many with dark eyes. I had stopped using Moeder's mirror . . . my mirror. In fact, I asked Moeder to keep it for me, safe in her bag.

I was not convinced I had the energy to help Sister Agnes, but I would try to make it so. I would pay attention and learn. Caring for others would cause me to be less focused on myself. I brought a page of rules so that I could take down things they might tell me at the hospital.

As I neared, Tante Hannah ran to me. I had never seen her run, and it seemed a painful exercise. She clutched her arms against her chest as she swayed with steps so long that the front of her skirts flew up. She didn't hug me this time but clutched my shoulders and focused her eyes on mine.

"Your father and Schalk are fine, " she said.

Vader and Schalk were fine. Her eyes bore in with such force I heard nothing after that.

"That's good," I said.

She shook my shoulders.

"Aletta . . . did you hear me? Oupa Gideon's been killed."

"What?"

"I'm sorry. There was no other way to say it."

"Schalk and Vader?"

"The last we heard, they are fine . . . as far as we know."

"Oupa Gideon . . . my *oupa*?" I yelled. "How?"

"I don't know. . . . His name appeared on a list. A soldier told Oom Sarel that he was killed in battle," Hannah said. "That's all we know."

"Vader and Schalk?"

"Yes, both alive, at least that day. It was almost a month ago."

Tante Hannah's *kappie* was pinched too tight, or her face was swollen, or my eyes distorted it all.

"I'm sorry, Lettie. Oom Sarel is frantic."

I pushed her away, hard. I hated her for the news. For being married to Oom Sarel. But I had no air in me to scream.

"Moeder . . . Willem."

"I would have told them, Lettie, but I knew she wouldn't talk to me. This was the only way I could . . ."

The women at the front of the tent intruded with cold eyes. I raised my lip to them.

"You had to know . . . Lettie."

Yes. I had to know. And now they had to know.

Tante's face shifted again, becoming openings and angles. She talked, but I did not hear. I had to go. I had to tell them. I shuffled, my dress gritty against my skin, my feet slipping inside my boots. I felt the air part against my face as I pressed through it. I had the paper and I should have written down what I would say before I had to speak it, but I could not form the words. I wanted to walk, to trace the fence line, again and again, to wear a path in the ground, deeper and deeper until I disappeared or the entire camp sunk in on itself.

I was afraid to stop thinking about Oupa for even a minute for fear I'd lose his spirit, his immense shadow. Oupa was a part of everything. The smell of his pipe, the scratch of his whiskers, his voice, the things he'd taught me. Hold on to his spirit—that was Bina's lesson.

I reached the tent and walked to the back side, trying to convince myself that there was no longer a door, that there was no way I could enter. I looked up, imagining Oupa in heaven; he was looking down, watching me. Tell me what to say, Oupa. Help me tell them, Oupa.

I would tell Moeder exactly as Tante Hannah had told me. Word has come. . . . Vader and Schalk are not hurt. Oupa Gideon died in battle. Word has come. . . . How had the words come? They just arrived, heavy and cruel, slow and indirect, but with force. They'd been handled by the British, passed on to the traitors, and then dumped in a small pile at my feet by a sorrowful woman. I had to carry them and put them in order and polish them as best I could before giving them to my family.

That was the best I could prepare. Willem was at Moeder's side when I entered. I could not speak. She read the look on my face, rose, and led me outside the tent with her hand on my lower back. I whispered it to her, using Tante Hannah's words. And she responded as I had: Vader and Schalk are well?

"Yes, but Oupa is gone. No . . . he died. He isn't just gone. He's dead. He's been gone a long time, but now he's dead." I only confused her with extra words. "Oupa Gideon . . . is dead. Shot dead."

I turned so that I would not have to look at her face. I knew she'd never loved Oupa the way I had. If she was in pain, I did not want to see it. If she was not, I did not want to see that, either.

"Willem?" I said.

"Lettie . . . no, you walk if you want. . . . I'll tell him."

Moeder was strong for us; I would show her that I could be, too. I put an arm around Willem's shoulders, and he struggled against me. Moeder told him, and his body tensed and began shaking as I held him with both arms. His shaking caused me to shake as well, and his crying made me cry, too.

34

November 1901, Concentration Camp

More stars flashed than I could remember, honoring Oupa or mocking me. Oupa would never be on a *stoep* with me again; he would not be there to teach my children the history of the stars. He would not lift them from their beds or transport them or, in the whispered voice of God, tell stories of our ancestors sailing ships around the Cape. That would be up to me. But they would not know the smell of his pipe or the scratch of his whiskers or the gravity of his immense faith.

The wind passed the latrines on its way to me, and the sour juices in my stomach bubbled up to my throat. It was happening so often that a sore had burned through back there, making it hard to swallow and causing me to try to clear my throat dozens of times a day, as if I were drying up. It bothered me most when I tilted my head back to look up.

The stars reflected memories this night, so I tried to look beyond them, above the sky. I'd been told by the *dominee* that the dead were in heaven and they looked down on us. They watched us. They lived through us. Wouldn't they want me to try to find them? I looked for Cee-Cee's face, perhaps in the shape of a cloud. One small cloud with soft edges might have been Cee-Cee's hair . . . and a wispy gray one pulled by the wind could have been Oupa's beard. Klaas, and Janetta's brother . . . were they up there watching? Did Ouma van Zyl's daughter look down at me and wonder about this girl wearing her boots?

In the way I imagined the men all healthy and clean and well fed, singing around a campfire at night, the dead of my acquaintance were once again happy and whole as they looked down. Could they help us? Could they watch out for us? Guide us? Should I pray to them as I did to God, or were they all together listening and watching at the same time? Did they watch me even when I did not want them to?

Looking up grew painful. I focused instead on the land. Cloud shadows raced across the grass like a ghost herd of springbok, taunting me with their freedom. They enjoyed whatever was the opposite of a being fenced in a "place of concentration."

I started back to the tent. I doubted I would sleep, but I would try for a short time before rising at daybreak to write and help Moeder deal with Willem, and grind more hours from another day.

Within a few steps, I scolded myself for acting the child. This isn't me, I convinced myself. I would go to the hospital tent in the morning and try to help, to do good work. I would think of a scripture from Oupa about the value of helping others, and it would honor him. Good works give glory to the Father, or something along those lines. I could not remember exactly, but it inspired me.

A whistle blew on the far side of camp. I turned in that direction for just a step or two. I heard a rustle at the closest tent flap, followed by a crash, and I was knocked to the ground.

"Bloody hell," a man said.

The stench consumed me.

"What . . ."

It was a Tommy guard . . . and the smell . . .

"Bloody buckets," he said, scrambling to his feet. He'd stumbled on a slop bucket, kicked it all over me, and fallen at my feet.

"What are you doing?"

"None of your business. . . . What are you doing out?"

"Using the latrine."

"So was I."

I got to my feet. It was horrid. I had to use my skirt hem to wipe the filth from my face. My clothes were covered in night soil.

"You're a liar."

"A woman needed help."

"Liar. Sinful liar. Shameful liar. Abuser."

I fired words as they presented themselves to me.

"That's enough, you're lucky I don't report you."

"You're lucky I don't report *you*."

"I was invited to that tent. Go ask her. Go. Go ask her."

I did not hear complaints from the tent. But that meant nothing. He could not be trusted. But he was off, apparently deciding I needed no further threats. I had no idea what I would do with my clothes until morning. My boots barely cleared the ground with my steps. I tried looking up at the sky again but needed to keep my eyes on the ground in case more pails reached out to me in the darkness.

I did not bother to keep quiet as I returned to the tent and climbed under my blanket. I didn't care if I was caught and punished. What would be the punishment? Beaten? Fine. I deserved it. It would break the monotony. It would be human contact. Except that I was disgusted by humans and wanted less contact with them rather than more. And disgust was a feeling other than grief, at least. Now, I almost hoped I'd be beaten. But Mevrou Huiseveldt was snoring so loudly no one could hear me

"God . . . make that woman stop snoring," I said, thinking of Willem's outburst. No one heard.

I wanted to read, to get lost in a book, and thought about lighting what was left of the candle from Maples. It was hard even to think of him when I smelled as I did. Thank God it hadn't been him sneaking out of that woman's tent. And thank God he hadn't shown up in our tent, given his recent interest in my mother. I had to tell him about the guard I'd just seen. Maybe he would know him and could report him—if anybody cared anymore about guards' behavior.

I left again at dawn to try to get my clothes washed and bring back water for the family. No sense waiting until they awakened. I could not sleep.

As I hoped, Moeder had questions when I returned.

"I was worried about you," she said.

"I was getting water. See the bucket?"

"Lettie . . . I can see. . . . I didn't know where you were."

"You were asleep. Why would I wake you if you can sleep? You don't need to keep track of me. I'm an adult."

"I do need . . ."

"I was out last night, almost all night, and you didn't know about it, and I got in no trouble."

My tone begged for discipline.

"I went out to watch the stars. And I can only see them at night. And I can't see them through a canvas tent. Did you want me to wake you up . . . or try to find a way to look at stars during the daytime?

Or don't I have the right to look at the stars? Is that something they're going to take away next?"

"Lettie, it's all right."

"It is for you. . . . You didn't love Oupa the way I did."

"Lettie . . . I loved him."

"I wanted to look at the sky to mourn him, or to talk to him the way I used to. You couldn't know. None of you know how close we were. We had secrets. . . . I can tell you now that he's gone."

"Lettie . . . respect."

"No . . . he used to sneak in and carry me out onto the *stoep* at night and teach me about the stars when everybody else was asleep. He wanted me to know so I could pass it on through the family. He picked me. I was the chosen one."

"I know."

"You know?"

"We could hear you."

"You knew?"

"He used to do it with Schalk when he was younger, too. They loved the time together. They acted as if it was their secret, too."

He did it with Schalk? Neither ever said a word.

"He used to say that was their special time together," she said.

"Bastard."

She gasped, but I kept going.

"Did Schalk get to everything first? Did Oupa do all the same things with him? The way Oupa used to say, 'Let's watch the stars,' rather than 'Let's look at the stars,' as if they were about to perform. Did he say it that way to Schalk, too?"

"Aletta."

"He lied to me," I shouted. "Oupa was a liar."

"Aletta . . . respect the dead."

"Why?"

"Lettie, calm. . . . Praise the Lord. . . . Be good."

"Be good? Be good? Or what? Be good for what? What will I get if I don't? How will I be punished? Bad food? Lice?"

"Lettie . . . no . . ."

Across the tent, Rachel Huiseveldt began singing a repetitive song to the doll to mask the sounds of our dispute. I boiled at the disrespect and snatched the doll from her arms. I marched to Moeder and held it in her face, just inches away, and shook her into a crazed dance.

"How could you give this to her without asking me? She's not family. This was my doll. It was made for me. I gave it to Cee-Cee. . . . It was MY present to Cee-Cee. My doll . . . my decision who should have it . . . not yours. It should have come back to me. Don't you think I would have liked it? A reminder of her? A reminder of me? Something to keep in the family."

"I thought you were too big . . ."

"You could have asked. . . . You should have asked. . . . But you always think being silent means being strong. Well . . . sometimes we need more from you."

Rachel froze.

"What else do I have of Cee-Cee? Nothing. What else do I have of me when I was little?" I pulled the doll from Moeder's face and hugged it to my chest. It had been months since I had said so many words at once. "What else do I have?"

"Go lie down." Moeder said it calmly. "Take your doll and lie down. We'll talk later. Go . . . it's all right for now. Lie down with Lollie. You're right; she was your doll. She is your doll. I should have asked."

Mevrou Huiseveldt grasped the sobbing Rachel by the shoulders, and they turned together toward the tent wall.

I took the doll and crawled under my blanket. I turned away and held the doll close. I told the doll a story that she'd heard before.

MOEDER'S BROOCH WAS IN my hand when I left the tent. I suppose I lifted it from her private things, but I could not recall thinking through the decision to take it or completing the act. I did not pin it at my throat, as Moeder wore it, because the collar of my dress was so slack. I pinned it to my pinafore, at my left chest, like a war medal.

I wanted Maples to see it and compliment me. But he did not notice. The magic it worked on Vader did not translate to an English guard.

"Betty," he said, his voice a whisper. He stared at me.

"It's Lettie . . ."

"Lettie . . . that's what I said."

"Are you all right?"

"News . . . don't know if you should tell your mother. You can if you think you should."

"Tell her what?"

"About your uncle . . ."

"Tell me. . . . I'll decide."

"Some guard . . . talked with prisoners. . . . Your uncle wasn't wounded. . . . Broke his shoulder when he was thrown from his horse . . ."

"I know . . ."

"Came in under a white flag."

We suspected.

"Had bones sticking through the skin. . . . Out of his mind with pain. They wouldn't treat him unless he gave information."

"And he did?"

"He did. . . . They already knew the commando was nearby since he could not have ridden far. But he pointed in the direction. . . . They found the commando the next day."

"The commando unit with our men in it?"

"Don't know who, but that makes sense."

"Boers, though?"

"That's the story we got."

"Does that mean he gave up the location of our men, his own brother and father?"

"Maybe, but it's possible he sent our men into an ambush. . . . The Boers were behind rocks and came out firing when they got there. Could have been either, I suppose."

"Don't tell my mother," I said. "Not yet. She doesn't need to know this. . . . It would do none of us any good. Maybe he was trying to help."

"I want to tell her."

"No, she'll go try to kill Oom Sarel."

"She wants to, anyway, and I'm going to help."

"How?"

"Can't tell. . . . Working on it."

"No, nothing good can—"

"Has to be soon," he interrupted, voice lower still. "I'm leaving."

"A transfer?"

"Leaving."

"Where?"

"Home . . . to Betty."

"But Betty said . . ."

"I know, but she'll want me when I show up. She'll see. She'll feel different when she sees I would quit the army and come all the way home to see her. Even her father will be impressed."

"Not if you quit like this."

"Can't wait."

"Not yet . . . not now. . . . Maybe it will end soon."

"I'll escape."

"You'll escape? That's not an escape. You're a guard."

"A prisoner . . . too," he said.

He repeated himself and rocked quickly, shifting his weight.

"I'll just leave my rifle and go . . ."

"You'll need your rifle."

"Better not to have it. . . . I wouldn't know who to shoot. And your men wouldn't think they had to shoot me if I don't have it."

"You don't know where to go."

"Doesn't matter. . . . Away from the savages."

"Savages?"

"All of them . . . out there . . . in here."

"No . . . they'll see you and shoot you. I know they will. One side or the other."

He stepped closer.

"Come with me."

"I can't . . . Moeder . . . Willem . . ."

"Bring them."

"No . . ."

"We'll all escape. We'll go to England."

He pulled at my arm.

"Not like this."

"You'll come."

"Not like this."

He pulled at my arm until it felt he was pressing into my bones. He leaned in harder, kissing me, pressing so that my teeth pinched my lips.

"Stop."

"Betty . . . Lettie . . . ," he mumbled, and he was gone.

WE BURNED THE DICTIONARY that night to heat water, stopping at *M* to save the rest for the next night. I did not look at the words before they turned to ash. The ones I needed I already knew, the rest were more valuable as fuel. We no longer bothered waiting until dark to try to sleep but just curled up and slipped off whenever we could. We almost never talked, certainly not bothering with full sentences when a few words would do, and never invested even those few words when gestures sufficed. There was no energy for courtesy. We simply retreated to the portions of the tent that were ours and pulled ourselves in tight. Except for Willem and Rachel, who started sitting together. Somehow they came to feel important to each other.

I slipped Moeder's brooch back into her bag when she had gone to the latrine, and if she noticed it had been gone, she never bothered to discipline me. It didn't work, anyway. I thought through the things Maples had said, as I did every time we talked, reading meaning into every word. But he was so confused. He had asked me to go with him. At least I thought he had. But there were currents of his own that he needed to fight, and they had caused him to come adrift. I warmed at the thought of his kiss and wanted another. But gentler.

Was it possible for him to leave, or for me to go along? I stacked up thoughts on either side to measure them, but they no longer stayed where I put them; they appeared and faded and took different shapes. I thought of my family and home and surrendering anything that reminded me of reality.

I walked in a fine dress beneath a giant hat alive with ostrich plumes; I would blink at all who passed. I ambled beside Maples, arm-in-arm. I pointed at the Tower Bridge, my hand heavy with the ring he'd given me—a diamond sunk in a gold band. It sparkled like a star. Schalk had joked at my expense, but he supported my decision to move to England and

marry Maples. Willem tried to kill my new husband but his slingshot broke.
Moeder and Vader? Well, they only wanted me to be happy.

IT WAS A THICK night that never cooled. There were fewer
people in the tent now, but it felt tighter from the heat. I fought to take
in air. I had to be free from the tent—to walk, to stir the air around me.

Moeder heard me.

"Lettie?"

I left without answering, and if she asked more of me, I did not
hear. I walked to the nearest fence line. I leaned my face close so that
my eyes were inside a wire square, so that no fence was visible. It was
like being outside. I could see the shape of a black *kopje* against the
blue-black sky, like the head of some giant emerging from the ground.
I wanted to walk there and climb to the top and look down on all this.
But standing so long had become an effort and I leaned into the fence
for support, and my face ached from the pressure against the wire.

A breeze fluttered tent canvases, but it just carried more heavy air. I
started to look up and scolded myself for my lack of discipline. I didn't
want to think about Oupa, and Orion would force me to. I resented
the stars for being so predictable, following their paths as if nothing
had happened, and the moon for showing its smug unchanging face.

"Peace."

Would I think of Oupa every time I smelled a pipe, too? Or ate
rusks dipped in coffee? My throat swelled and burned, making it harder
to manage the thick air. I'd been light headed for weeks, without focused thoughts. I should have prayed but didn't. Moeder prayed for us
and the men every morning and night, but I only mouthed the words.

"Peace, Aletta."

The voices again.

"I don't sleep now . . . like you. . . . I walk the camp . . . like you. . . . I hoped I'd find you."

"Maples?"

"I've been lonely."

"I have, too."

"Tell me about your grandfather," he said. How nice that he wanted to know.

"My *oupa*—a great man."

"I'm sorry."

"Thank you."

"I didn't do it," he said.

"I know you didn't."

"You miss him already?"

I leaned toward him; it was him, not a phantom voice. He put his rifle on the fence and pulled me in. I cried a wet spot onto his shoulder. I leaned back, but he held tight. It was wonderful, like riding the horse, but too warm, too close.

"Your hair did come back thicker," he said. "I told you."

He kissed the top of my head.

"Maples . . . ," I said.

"Tommy . . . ," he said.

My head felt light again, and breaths were gained only with struggle. He held me too tight.

"Maples . . . ," I said.

"Call me Tommy," he said.

He leaned against me harder, and the wire bit into my shoulder bones.

"Maples . . . ," I said as he pressed against my chest.

"You're fine . . ."

He squeezed the breath from me, raising a groan I could feel at the back of my throat.

"Quiet now," he said, placing a hand to my mouth, calluses scraping my lips, his hands tasting of metal and rifle oil.

"I want . . . ," he said.

I twisted my head away from his hand. "Maples . . . please stop, you're hurting me."

"Tommy . . . Tommy," he said, pressing so hard my head went back. Pleiades above . . . *which turns the shadow of death into the morning . . .* my pinafore pulled aside . . . air swept across my legs . . .

"Betty," he said. I couldn't breathe. A whistle blew. I bit his hand and tasted blood and meat. He backed a step. I bent deeply for air.

He looked up, his eyes reflecting night light. He groaned now. I followed his eyes as they dipped toward his stomach. His tunic was dark, then darker. He stood tall, then arched. And from his chest came the scrape of metal against bone, as when the men butchered game. With a gurgling sigh Maples slumped.

A sharp edge reflected in front of me, glinting and glinting, reflecting the moon. The steel point tilted upward and away from my vision, and the person behind the bayonet, holding the rifle, took shape in the darkness.

"Are you all right?"

"Moeder?"

My legs gave out, and I fell on Maples. He flexed with a jolt, and I shouted, and he went still. I shook him. He didn't move. I punched him on the back with my right hand, then both hands.

"Get up . . . Maples . . ."

I punched his shoulder blades, my hands wet and sticky.

"Moeder, you killed Maples."

"Lettie . . . stop . . . quiet. . . . I know who it was. I saw what he was doing. I heard you tell him to stop. He was not about to stop. He was crazed."

She leaned his rifle on the fence and came to me. I punched at her, too, then wrapped my arms around her waist. They encircled her. I shook so hard I nearly pulled her over.

"Dear merciful God, forgive me," she whispered. "We have to plan, we have to get rid of him."

"Get rid of him?"

"Lettie . . . they know you were close. . . . They'll come for us first thing."

She was right. And if he simply disappeared, they'd think he had gone off—exactly as he was planning.

"Get back to your tent . . . both of you. . . . I'll take care of this."

A man snatched the rifle from the fence.

"Go . . . now . . . go . . . ," he insisted in a harsh whisper.

"You . . ." Moeder inhaled the word.

"Go . . . Lettie . . . take her. . . . Go now."

"How did you . . . ?"

"I follow her . . . on her walks . . . many nights . . . to look out for her in case anything . . ."

"Oom Sarel . . . you followed me? Why didn't you . . ."

"I didn't want to frighten you. . . . You made it clear you didn't want to see me. . . . Now hurry. . . . I'll get rid of him. . . . I'll take him on my cart and burn him in my barrel. . . . No one goes there. . . . No one ever comes near me. . . . No one ever asks questions. . . . But you have to go now."

"Wait." Moeder tried to take the rifle from him.

"Go, Susanna. Think—they'll hang both of you if they come . . . and shoot me. This will work. But you have to go now."

His appearance had stunned us, so that I hadn't thought of what trouble we'd face being rid of Maples's body.

"Sarel . . . ," Moeder said, "are you certain?"

"*Ja*, go. They're used to seeing me go out there with my cart and barrel day and night. . . . No one wants to come near me."

Moeder scanned the darkness, took my arm, and pulled me to the tent. My chest ached from the pounding of my heart. I strained for air, as if underwater.

"Settle," Moeder said calmly. She petted my head as we clung to each other on her cot. I pulled tight against her. I was breathing three times to each of her breaths. Lighted flecks flashed when I closed my eyes. I slowed my breath to match hers, and the storm in my chest stilled.

I was to blame for it all. For talking to Maples in the first place. For leaving the tent. For not following the rules. I would take responsibility before she could start.

"I know . . . it was my fault," I said. "All of it . . . Maples . . ."

"Stop. . . . It was not your fault," she said. "He was the one who attacked you, Lettie, it's his fault he's dead."

I wanted to make excuses for Maples. His girlfriend. The war. He wasn't made for this. He had gone mad. I had, too. It really wasn't him. It wasn't any of us.

We held each other, sorting through thoughts.

"What is his burn barrel?" Moeder asked.

I told her of Oom Sarel's jobs, carting bodies in the night, and taking typhus waste from the hospital and burning it in barrels outside the camp.

"It is a good plan," she said. If he could get Maples to the barrel, no one would find him. I tried to think of the path to the far side of camp and how Oom Sarel would manage the cart with his bad shoulder, given the weight of the body.

We prayed from our hearts, and Moeder called for the Bible. I lit the candle that Maples had given me, and she read from Romans: *"He is the servant of God, an avenger who carries out God's wrath on the wrongdoer."*

She read passages at random after that, softly, so that no one else awakened. I listened to the words for hours but kept seeing Maples, and his sad eyes, and I thought of his words and his mouth and his callused hands and his chocolate. And everything was more confused, except for those few things that felt more clear. I shook my head to concentrate on Moeder's words, on her prayers. Focus. God and wrath and wrongdoer. Yes. Her face now lifted to heaven, I could see the words as she spoke, drifting, gathering above us, rising like the thin smoke on the nights we burned the book of words. Wrath and wrongdoer . . . Maples and his green eyes . . . and I focused on her prayer again, and the words emerged slowly and were so heavy she had to strain to be rid of them, and she aimed them to heaven, but they arced down slowly to my ears.

I shook my head again and pinched my eyes. I noticed that it had grown light and blew out the candle.

We slept for a few hours, perhaps, when a blast rolled across camp with such force it seemed the tents shook. We clutched each other in unison. It sounded like the thunderclaps on stormy nights on the veld . . . if five or six of them had struck at once.

I backed in tightly against her. We both knew it was a firing squad, and it caused me to shake again. She pulled me close and hummed in a whisper I could feel against my neck. I recognized the song: "Rock of Ages."

PART IV

Alone Together

35

May–June 1902, Venter Farm

Memory lies, and its cruelest deceit is allowing us to believe that things go on whole and unchanged. While in camp, I had thought of home as many times as there were stars. But I had not thought of the farm as it was burning, nor imagined how it might look after the British had picked clean its bones. The weight of memories from a lifetime in the building suppressed the images of the final flaming minutes.

When we started for home, I pictured my room and my bed and the parlor and kitchen as they had been. And through the long day's walk from where we had been deposited, I thought of sleeping the night in comfort. I misplaced the word for being alone and took a dozen steps before recalling it. I thought of Moeder playing the organ, and the smell of cooking luring me toward the kitchen.

The outline of the blue gum tree was the first to form in my vision, and then the thorn tree, a jagged silhouette against the evening sun. And between them stood a tall, straight man with sloped shoulders. It was Oupa Gideon, taller than ever. He stood alone. He had made it home. Thank you, God. I would never doubt again. It had all been a lie. A mistake.

"Ma . . . Willem . . . it's Oupa."

"Where?"

I pointed.

"Lettie . . ."

I lifted my skirt and ran in his direction. Oupa rose as I got closer, growing taller and taller. It was so like Oupa. So tall, so lean, so strong.

Lungs failing, I bent to suck in air. When I tilted up, my vision cleared. Between the two trees and above the foundation stood the stone hearth and chimney, the only part of the house left intact and upright. I sunk to the path. I rose only when Moeder and Willem pulled at my arms and brought me to my feet.

"It's not Oupa, Lettie," Willem said. "He's dead . . . remember? Shot."

Willem surged ahead with energy from some reservoir I lacked. He had started sorting through the shattered leavings before we reached the *stoep*. The stairs were unbroken, and the foundation mostly unharmed. But the floor sparkled with pieces of our life: shattered china, glass crystals from the hutch, and glass shards from the cracked photo frames. Each of our footfalls ground the pieces smaller. Moeder and I stopped after only a few steps and surveyed the room.

Nothing I could see was of value, just pieces of things. The organ was a jumbled pile, with the largest bits gone to the British or other scavenging jackals. The bellows and some keys were visible in the dimming light.

"We'll get another," Willem said, taking Moeder's arm.

She lifted both hands in front of her, fingers curled.

"We will . . . Moeder," I added.

"More important things first," she said, dropping her arms to her side.

We stood still, held in place by the sound of broken things.

She stomped her feet. "The foundation seems sound," she said.

"We can build on it," I said.

Moeder turned in a slow dance.

"They had less to start," she said. "Everything was brought here or built here."

I waited for her to expand, to reassure us that if they could do it back then, we could, too, now. But I was glad she did not because I did not know how to build an organ or make delicate teacups. These things at our feet had been family things, antique and irreplaceable.

We had some rations from the British and were told we could get some seeds, maize, and the like, from the Repatriation Board. However, I could not see Moeder approaching the British with her hand out. It would be one of the things that I would do to spare her the indignity. I would be the one in the family to deal with them. I had a history of accepting things from them.

The evening light died in an instant, as if a candle had been blown out, and the night was clear and not too cold. We backed into a corner where the hearth held together short wings of two side walls. A thin moon reflected off mica flecks in the hearthstones, and across the way, the curved iron headboard of Moeder's bed leaned against a fallen wall stud, its reflection like an animal skeleton.

We had heard nothing of our men but had seen others plodding to their homes as we made our way. It had been so long. I was desperate to see Schalk. I thought at first that I could not imagine Moeder's longing for Vader, but then realized that, yes, I could. Now I could.

The place reeked of rain-soaked ash, but I picked up the scent of overnight fires from native kraals. I prayed for Bina, for her health and safe return. I listened for drums but heard none, feeling only the rhythm of my throbbing feet. Although exhausted, I found I could not sleep without the sound of Mevrou Huiseveldt's snoring. The woman plagued me still, even in her absence. I laughed into the darkness at the thought. I untied the dead woman's boots that had delivered me home, and finally slept without dreams.

Tante Hannah woke us with a tentative "hallo" from the stairs. I ran to her, and Willem followed. We were wet with night dew, but she gathered us in and squeezed. She smiled at Moeder.

"I've been home for a few days," she said. "Roof and walls still standing. . . . Everything looted . . . except my stitchwork on the walls. Everything broken or taken . . . except the stitchwork. I am happy . . . and insulted."

We laughed softly, and once we started, we each looked around out of habit. But there was no one there to offend. We continued talking, getting louder, testing our limits. Even Moeder.

After the morning of the rifle shots in camp, Moeder and I did not speak of Maples nor Oom Sarel. It was the only firing squad we'd ever heard, but it was the talk of the camp for months, triggering rumors and speculation among the women. We were both alert to the tent flap, certain the commandant would march in to take us for a date with the firing squad for our part in Maples's death. All it would have taken was one word from Oom Sarel, maybe as he tried to bargain for his life he had relented and told them that it had been us. Or perhaps someone who had seen me with Maples had made some connection. But each day that passed without our being taken grew less stressful, and my appreciation for Oom Sarel grew in proportion. I came to realize that I had admired Maples's desire to back away from the savagery of the war—the same attitude that we found so objectionable in Oom Sarel.

Moeder asked about my well-being, and when I assured her I was fine each time, the questions came less often. She continued to look into my mind through my eyes. I was not fine, of course; I had many things to think through, and she seemed to trust that I could.

Perhaps a week after the shots, Moeder and Hannah met at the fence. I stood back, outside the range of their voices. Tante Hannah gestured with her arms, first out wide, then folded at her chest. I saw the back of Moeder's *kappie* move slowly. Then Moeder gestured, hands upraised. They continued, nodding like guinea fowl. Tante Hannah pointed in my direction the way Oupa used to point to constellations, and Moeder turned to look.

I imagined they were filling in the parts of Oom Sarel's death that the other could not have known. I doubt either knew how Sarel got caught with Maples's body, or what he might have said by way of explanation. I thought of all that had happened that night, and wondered how Moeder could explain to Tante our part in it. She might be honest but not tell the truth, or present a truth that was not honest. I'd learned the two were not the same.

Tante kept touching her chest with crossed hands, as if trying to assure Moeder that every word was rooted in her heart. This was far more than the solemn exchange of grief and condolence that had become so common for us.

They talked for so long across the wire that I needed to sit on the ground. They bent closer to each other. Moeder looked to me and then turned back to Hannah. She folded her hands low on her stomach.

Tante Hannah's face softened and she teared up. She reached a hand through the fence, and Moeder accepted it with interlaced fingers. Their shoulders then bobbed as they cried. When the bobbing stopped, each turned away.

"Ma?"

"We'll talk later."

But we did not talk about those things. Not for the remaining few months in camp, and not for years after that. I did not know whether Moeder had found some peace with Tante or just could no longer shoulder the weight of hatred. Whatever settlement they had reached, it was obvious that Tante Hannah knew she would be welcome when she arrived at our house that morning.

"Please . . . come stay at my place," she said to Moeder. "We can keep out the weather, at least. We can all come back and work to rebuild yours in time. You are welcome in my home."

Moeder stood.

"Thank you," Moeder said, dipping her head. I studied her face, reading the emotion in those words.

Moeder turned to each compass point, looking at the debris in full daylight. It seemed worse than it had the night before. But the crunching sound did not frighten me in the light, as it was clear that there was nothing among the things at our feet that could not be done without. The past two years had proved that.

"This much remains . . . ," she said. "His will be praised."

"His will be praised," Tante Hannah repeated.

When I went to the open place that had once been my room, I found only one thing unbroken and worth keeping, the thimble that Tante Hannah had given me. I had thought it so meaningless when we left that I didn't bother to take it.

I DIDN'T WRITE IN my notebook the final month in camp, in that uncertain time after the war had ended but before we could make our way home—the only time I truly felt like a refugee. The last entries were made the Sunday morning we got the news. When Moeder had prayed on the night of the shots, she must have made promises that included our attendance at camp services, so we had started gathering with others for sermons by the *dominee*.

On this day, he read a poem that I wanted to study later—"The Reaper and the Flowers." It could have been written about the camp, he said, referring to the way the innocent children had been taken from us, harvested to heaven by mistake, like pretty little flowers among grain stalks. It was beautiful, better than most of the psalms we recited or sang. He was trying to make us feel better, but I did not think we needed reminders of our losses.

Before he finished the poem, the commandant stomped in and whispered to the preacher, who closed his eyes, bowed his head, and retreated from the cartridge-box pulpit that held his Bible.

"Peace is here," the commandant said.

"We won!" I said.

I could tell from the profile of Moeder's face that we had not won.

The commandant knew no specifics of the agreement except that it meant that our leaders had surrendered. "We are no longer enemies," he said.

Moeder mouthed a few words I could not hear.

"What?"

"A prayer."

Willem stood and moved from my side to directly in front of Moeder, looking up into her face.

"We're not going to die?" he asked.

Moeder dipped her head but did not answer. I suspected she did not want to make promises.

"But the war is over, Ma," I said.

"This part of it," she said.

The *dominee* returned and finished the poem, but I no longer liked it. There was something about angels taking the little flowers. I saw no angels come for Cee-Cee and could not see angels being any part of this place. The vision of angels flying in and lifting her away was beautiful. But it was an insult to the way she had really died, with such fear in her eyes. I thought of her last breath and hoped it was still in my blood, but I knew that it wasn't and that this fact didn't really matter as long as I held tight to her spirit.

The announcement caused me to think of Cee-Cee in ways I hadn't in months. When she died, I took my cues from Moeder. Be strong, in control. Do what you must to get through the day. Take the pain and put it away for later. I'd done that. But when the war had ended and the preacher finished the poem, "later" had arrived.

I'd thought of her death as the product of random illness rather than of war, as if it would have happened regardless of where we had been. But the war killed her as surely as any soldier who fell from bullet or bayonet. It killed her just as it did the others, without explanation or apology, and definitely without the involvement of angels.

It took Janetta's brother but not Janetta; Klaas but not Willem; Cee-Cee but not me. Some lived, some did not, and others just disappeared. Near the end, I walked past the Van Zyls' tent on my way for water, and it was gone as if taken by the wind. No word. No good-byes. Nothing but a circle worn in the soil.

. . .

MY ROOM AT TANTE Hannah's was larger than the tent in camp that had held seven of us, then six, then five. I had the room to myself, with a palette on the floor and an old quilt Tante had found. The space overwhelmed me at first; even the sound of my breathing echoed in the emptiness. I spent an hour each night getting comfortable, thankful there was no mud on my blanket, no wet canvas, no disease. A quilt in a dry, quiet room seemed like an unimaginable gift. I never wanted to speak the word "dank" again. And if others coughed, it was in another part of the house and I did not cover my nose and mouth and turn from them. But it took time before I stopped worrying that each sniffle or sore throat was the first symptom of a grave illness.

I dragged my bedding near the window so that I could sleep beneath it and smell the land and see the night sky, which I had started looking at again. It led to predictable thoughts, but I needed to invite good memories to return, if only to balance those unwanted ones that intruded on their own.

Willem stayed in Ouma Wilhelmina's old room. We had not heard from her, but Tante Hannah did not expect she would be moving back. Tante asked if I might like to go with her to visit her mother in Cape Town once we were "back on our feet," and I was excited by thoughts of the ocean and the ships in the harbor. We could ride the electric tram and maybe walk to the top of the flat mountain that overlooked everything. It would make our little *kopjes* seem like ant humps.

Moeder and Tante Hannah slept in the same bedroom. I could hear the sound of their voices at night but not their words.

And when the weather kept us from work on the house or in the fields, I sat with Tante Hannah at the kitchen table for "school." We tried sorting through the war's confusing aftermath. We studied the treaty, which so obviously ignored the question of the natives' standing.

We tried to anticipate what that could mean. There were so many of them, and now so few of us. What would happen when the British went home?

"Instability?" Tante questioned. We talked for hours about it, trying to see into the future, and never could find a path that seemed untroubled. And we read how the treaty granted us eventual self-governance over our republics, causing me to ask: Could the whole war have been avoided if they'd done that in the first place?

But all of Tante Hannah's books that I had loved were burned. So were mine, I told her. I did not tell her how. It made me wonder what happened to Maples's things. Would Betty be curious what had happened to her *David Copperfield*? Had they sent all his belongings home to his mother? Would they include the letters that Betty had sent him? I pictured them being shipped back to England inside the fancy chocolate tin with Queen Victoria on the top. How embarrassing that would be for him to have his mother see what Betty had written. I shook my head against foolish thoughts. Maples would not be embarrassed. He was nothing anymore.

It was only then that I remembered that he had a little sister, Annie, and I felt close to her. Somebody would have to tell her about her big brother, to shape words to say that he had died in the war, which was true but not honest. The family would presume he was a hero, and maybe the army would tell them that on purpose. The army probably said such things to the families of every dead soldier in every war. That's how they kept fooling men into signing up. It was part of the bigger untruth. No one would ever join again if mothers were told that their sons had died in a bloody stack of men in a ditch, or that they'd been stabbed by the mother of a girl they were assaulting in the night. I knew nothing of little Annie except that she deserved better.

We burned *David Copperfield* in thirds to heat three dinners. I tore the pages out quickly, and I thought of the meal as a present from little David, a brave little boy. He was British, but the war had not been his fault.

We knew it would take time to rebuild our little libraries. Without reading as a diversion, I was open to Tante Hannah's offer to teach me to stitch again. And this time I concentrated on doing it the way she suggested. When Moeder was working at our place one afternoon, Tante showed me a few of the stitchings she had carried with her for the duration of camp.

"These are my secret," she said. "I've never shown anyone . . . not even Oom Sarel." There were four of them, all with golden thread on white cloth, the stitching like beautiful handwriting. They bore names of people I did not know. Her unborn children.

I looked into her eyes, dry and clear, reconciled.

"You named them?"

"I did," she said. "Silly, maybe, but I had nothing else. As bad as it was for your mother to lose an unborn, she had you all when she lost hers."

"My mother? Cee-Cee wasn't an unborn."

"No, of course not, the child she lost when she sent you to my house—when she was butted by a sheep or something."

"She hurt her back. . . . It was her back. . . . It wasn't a baby. . . . She said she hurt her back."

"Lettie . . . I'm sorry. . . . I thought she told you," Tante Hannah said, pulling me close. "I'm sure she didn't want you to worry."

"But she told you?"

"That day when we met at the fence to talk about Oom Sarel; we got into so many things. She hadn't known how many times I had been through it, and what it had done to me. And I didn't know she had experienced that grief herself. It was part of what brought us together, I think."

One evening, Tante Hannah took down her "honeymoon" stitchery and removed it from the frame. With a small knife, she undid the knots and pulled out much of the scene of her imagined life, which had proved to be so very far from reality.

"I'll leave the children in the front," she said. "Because we can say they are you and Willem now." She stitched a new scene over the top on the same cloth, the home simpler and smaller. But the pattern of the old stitch marks showed in a shadowy outline. It always would, and I think it was important to her that it did.

She gave me a fresh cloth in case I wanted to start a piece of my own, but I did not, not yet. I wanted to spend time with her mastering the stitches first.

WE WORKED UNTIL COLLAPSE most days as we planted and hoed, and tore down parts of the house and barn that were beyond salvaging. Moeder outlasted us all.

As we worked, we fretted over our men. We had still not heard word of them, and our worries were the only thing that grew quickly on the farm. Nature had overtaken the land and was reluctant to turn it back, slamming us in succession with stormclouds of locusts and then a severe drought. It would be many growing seasons before things were right, and the losses from that time would never be recouped completely. Not only had plants died, but no seeds had been planted, no seedlings sprouted. As I heard from other families in our region, it seemed that nearly three years of war had had a similar effect on all our lives. Half a generation had perished; another half was unborn.

I found myself looking forward to the farm work, even the most tiring, and was eager to get to it in the mornings. And I surprised my- self by taking pleasure in the simple act of working alongside Moeder, shoulder to shoulder. At times we'd race. When I looked at the farm, and what we accomplished each day working it, I felt even more a part of it all.

Restlessness gripped me more than fatigue some evenings, and I walked as far as I could in one direction, trying to tear down even the memory of boundaries. A breeze tickled the hairs of my neck on one evening walk, and when I looked up I could see a horse shuffling at a speed slower than a man would walk. I asked myself whether it was my imagination again.

I turned in that direction and then ran faster than I thought I could. And the figure did not disappear; it was Schalk. His clothes were ripped and patched and hanging loose. Slumped in the saddle, his hat pulled low, he looked like an old man, but I could see the still-wispy beard clinging to his jawline. His pony did not even twitch its ears as I raced at them.

"We didn't know about you," I said. "We had no word."

"Ma? Willem? Cee-Cee?"

"Moeder and Willem . . . not Cee-Cee."

"No." He slumped on the horse's neck. "When?"

"September. Vader?"

"Yes . . . not Oupa."

"We heard. But Vader's fine?"

"He's unhurt."

I hugged his leg harder and could feel that some lean muscle still protected his bones. He had made it through. He put his hand on my head and petted my hair. He dismounted the strange little horse I did not recognize, and we held each other without a word until the horse nudged Schalk with its muzzle.

I told him Oom Sarel was gone, too. He stared hard, reading my face. Sharing had always been so easy between us, but like everything else, that would take time to rebuild. He led the horse by its bridle, and we took many strides before he said, "Later."

His skin was covered in sores. He saw me examining him.

"From having no salt, they say," he explained. He wore a burlap mealie sack over his shirt as a jacket.

"When is Vader coming home?" I asked.

"Later," he said again.

"What?"

"Let me say it once, when we're all together," he said. "Lettie . . . I don't think I want to do it more than once."

"You said he's all right."

"He is."

"And Tuma captured?"

"*Ja* . . . he was with the after-riders watching horses, and a unit got behind us and took everything . . . almost a year ago . . . nothing since . . . work camp, probably."

"We're at Tante Hannah's now . . ."

"Everyone?"

"Um-hmm."

"With Tante Hannah? Moeder, too?"

"It's good."

"Let's go there."

The saddle slipped as he tried to remount. He had to tighten the cinch on the withered pony. He pulled himself up and then took my arm and swung me up behind him. The knots of the horse's spine dug at me with each slow step. I felt guilty to be its burden and thought of getting down, but it was so good to be close to Schalk that I could not bring myself to pull away. I leaned in tighter, the rough burlap on my cheek, my fingers laced against the ladder of his ribs.

"Ma," I shouted as we neared, and I swung down from the horse to announce Schalk's return.

Willem appeared first, then Moeder. They held him in a bundle.

"Come inside," Tante Hannah said from the door, and she gathered him in.

Moeder looked past us, toward the trail. But she did not ask the question. Schalk waited until we quieted.

"They brought us in to turn over our weapons and sign the oath . . ."

Moeder shook her head and turned away.

"It said that we had to agree to acknowledge the terms of the sur-render and become British subjects," he said. "Surrendering wasn't enough. . . . We had to sign that we would be British subjects . . . an oath. Vader stood right behind me. . . . I signed it. . . . He shook my hand. . . . He said he could not. By then I had no choice."

"He's not coming home?" Willem asked.

"In time. . . . I'm not sure when."

"Where is he?" Willem asked.

"He said he thought some men would try to regroup in Madagascar."

"Madagascar?" I was stunned. "Why would he not come home to us?"

"Is he going to try to come back and fight?" Willem asked. "Can he keep the war going?"

Schalk raised his hands as a shield against more questions. But I had so many. What about Moeder? What about us?

"What did he say? At least tell us that," I said.

"He said that Moeder would understand."

She understood. We all knew she did. She probably expected it. That might have been why she said that the war wasn't completely over. But I did not understand. Not then. I thought it was foolish of Vader then. And I still thought it was foolish when he returned a year later, having gained nothing from his pride. But I was so happy to see him that I did not complain. Neither did Moeder.

BINA WAS BENT OVER, clearing weeds from the garden spot, when we got home from Tante Hannah's one morning. She was half her size, and her shoulders sloped; her robes were threadbare and dun. She worked slowly and had to use her hands on her knees to rise to standing. But it was her; we heard her singing almost as soon as we saw her.

"Bina," I shouted.

"Peace," she said.

"Peace," I answered. "I've been so worried."

"You knew I would come back to you," she said. "Come here, child."

She hugged me.

"More bones . . . same eyes," she said of me.

As it was each time we saw someone for the first time since the war, we exchanged our inventories.

"Tuma?"

She shook her head, looking from me to Moeder.

"Captured. . . . Made to work on the railroads. . . . So hungry he tried to eat off a buried carcass they dug up . . . rinderpest cow. . . . Died that night."

Moeder touched her hand and then squeezed. I closed in for another hug so quickly that I nearly knocked Moeder down. Bina patted my back to calm me. I wanted to comfort her, and she ended up consoling me.

"Tombi?" I asked.

"Taken to work for the British. No word."

She did not ask of Cee-Cee. I expected she knew there would be only one reason for her not being with us. And she waited until we offered information.

"You?" Moeder asked.

"Camp," Bina said. "That's all . . . camp."

"Was it like—" I started, but she wouldn't let me finish.

"Camp," she said, wanting no further discussion. She seemed only a fraction of herself. I could not imagine what hardships could have pared away half her body and such a giant portion of her energy.

"I could see you had been here. . . . I just started working," she said.

"We're at Tante Hannah's," I said.

I asked Moeder if she minded if I worked with Bina that day. When the others were gone, I told her things I could not tell Moeder or Schalk. I told her how often I had thought of her and her sayings and her songs, and how much they had helped me through the days. I wanted to put it in a way she would best understand.

"I carried you with me," I said.

She lifted her hands to her chest. "I carried you, too."

I told her about Maples, but without details. It was the first I had spoken of him. I told her the war made him lose his mind. She said that it did that to everyone, some more than others.

I did not tell her about Oom Sarel's surrendering, nothing except that he died in the camp. I owed him that.

"Tante?" she asked.

"She and Moeder are . . . good." I held my hands together.

"They need each other. You be good to Tante."

I explained that Oupa Gideon was lost. And that Vader was among those who would not be tamed. Nothing seemed to surprise her.

"He will come back," she said. "When it's right for him."

She sang as she worked, but she sounded so tired. She had lost her husband and, in some ways, her daughter, too. I thought of the Tommy that day at the farm trying to tell her it was not her war.

I listened to her song and then tried to join in. It was easier to sing with her than to sing the hymns, since her songs often had no tune and I didn't understand the words, anyway.

"Will you be all right?" I asked her. She stopped singing and looked at me and then across the veld. She raised her hand and fluttered her fingers, her reminder to be like the water. I thought it the perfect response.

"And your . . . people?" I gestured in the direction of her kraal. "What now?"

"I don't know," she said. "A beaten dog will someday bare its teeth."

It was another of her sayings I would remember. The next day, she somehow discovered a goat with bright yellow eyes and brought it to Tante Hannah's barn. She then came to stay with us.

SCHALK AGREED WITH MOEDER: everything should come down except the hearth and the flooring. I doubted it would ever feel new. I thought that a house might be like a tree, always carrying its old scars unseen beneath its bark. Schalk had taken over work on the house, along with his constant shadow, Willem, while Moeder and Bina and I worked the fields and Tante Hannah cooked and kept house at her place.

Schalk and Willem tried to make order of what was still good enough to use. Willem stacked the broken bricks that remained, and

Schalk cut and sized the few pieces of wood he could salvage. Since we had shelter for now at Tante Hannah's, Schalk convinced Moeder that we should concentrate on getting the crops and stock restored so that they might sustain us first, and take our time to rebuild the house properly. It would take longer but be more sound for the future.

After Willem collapsed in bed one night, Schalk and I walked, and when he pointed out the Southern Cross, it made us both think of Oupa.

"Let's watch the stars," I said.

We sat.

"Were you there when Oupa . . ."

"So quick . . . no suffering. . . . He couldn't even have known."

We watched the sky. I allowed time for him to tell me more, but he did not.

"Oom Sarel?" he asked.

"You first . . ."

"We didn't know. . . . Thought he was just captured . . . probably . . . or . . ."

"Or?"

Schalk seemed to examine my height, as if that would be a factor in whether he should share more.

"Oupa and Oom had a terrible fight," Schalk said. "Sarel had been in so much pain. He was thrown from his horse when it stepped in an antbear hole, and he broke his shoulder to pieces. It was purple and yellow, and you could see the bones in a lump where they were broken. Some men joked."

"Why?"

"To be cruel; they said that falling off a horse was the kind of thing a Tommy would do," Schalk said. "Pa wouldn't stand for the jokes; he pulled his rifle down on them and said the next joke would be the last. He included Oupa in that threat, but Oupa wouldn't stop. He kept calling him the antbear. Oom Sarel finally had enough, with the pain . . . and Oupa's comments."

"What happened?"

"Oom Sarel screamed in front of a group of men that Oupa should tell us all about the native girl that worked here after Ouma died, and something that he had seen between her and Oupa. And Oupa called him a coward . . . said he killed Ouma with his birth . . . coming into the world sideways . . . like it was all his fault even as a baby."

"Did you understand?"

"I don't know. . . . Lettie . . . they kept calling each other names."

"What did Pa do?"

"I don't think he had any idea. . . . We both watched them raging . . . Oom Sarel grabbing his shoulder all the while because the bones would grind when he yelled. The next day, Oom Sarel volunteered to scout, said he could do that. I helped him onto his horse. He never came back."

"Well, he ended up in camp . . . with Tante Hannah."

I did not say a word about Oom Sarel's death. If Schalk was curious, he did me the courtesy of not asking. Or maybe Moeder told him about it in a moment they shared. I did not tell him at all about Maples or his death or Moeder's involvement. I thought that only Moeder and I needed to know about that. I knew she must have given Tante Hannah some kind of explanation, but neither offered that story to me.

We stood and walked, and watched the sky as we did. He asked about Cee-Cee.

I weighed the details that he should know against those that would be burdens.

"Illness . . . we did all we could," I said. "She was a beautiful little lamb to the end. Just as she'd always been. You can remember her that way."

"Buried there?"

I told him about the bottle.

"We have to bring her home," he said in a way that invited my opinion.

I thought of us digging into the rocks and disturbing her. I knew I could not be there for that; I could not see that canvas bundle again.

"I think we need to let the ground heal up over her," I said. "She's resting there."

"Then at least I'll make a proper marker," he said.

I wanted Moeder to decide. After dinner, Schalk told her his idea.

"*Ja*, but later," she said.

He fashioned a board cross, the long piece angle-cut to a point. He spent almost a full day carving her name in the wood. But it was nearly another year before we went back to that place. We had been waiting for Vader, but he had still not returned and the time seemed right. The valley looked so small and barren except for grass; it was so hard to imagine hundreds of tents and thousands of people there. The cemetery was all that was unbothered, and the mounds were too many to count.

We had to split up to search through the bottles, Schalk carrying Cee-Cee's cross over his shoulder. There were so many bottles reflecting the light, as if some strange crop of glass had sprouted in this field. Rain had seeped through the corks of some of them, leaving the names nothing more than sad dark smudges. I felt guilty looking at them, as if disturbing their rest. But how else to know? Schalk was the one who found Cee-Cee's bottle. He hammered in the cross he'd built. Moeder offered a number of readings from the Bible, giving our little one a more proper service than her first. And when she finished, she placed the bottle in her small bag and brought it back home.

FROM BENEATH A LIGHTNING-STRUCK snag on the tallest nearby *kopje*, I could see all the way to where the weight of the massive sky pushed down the edges of the earth. The wind rose from those edges and bent the grasses in waves across the high plain. The brush rattled a warning that the breeze was climbing the hill. A hawk nearby rode the updraft toward thin horsetail clouds. The breeze carried the scent of all that it passed crossing the veld. I inhaled and held it deep.

I would come to the hilltop even though it was a long walk and there was still so much work that needed to be done on the farm. But Moeder always approved when I asked permission to get away for a while. Time had grown lighter again, less resistant to my passage through it, and I no longer had to plot against it. I lost track of the small increments that used to dominate my thoughts, and came to note only its larger cycles.

I spent an afternoon watching the leggy secretary bird catching snakes, tossing them in the air as if it were a game, and then pouncing on them with lethal claws. Birds had the gift of flight, and that had saved them during the war, I presumed.

To the west, afternoon warmth rose in pale shimmers. There were fewer springbok and impalas, and no lions; the lions had probably followed the antelope into some country away from the war. I told Schalk that I wanted to go back and spend a night camped in the bush with him again, just the two of us, or maybe bring Willem, too. I wanted to hear lions again; I wanted to hear them in the night and then fall fast asleep even as they roared. I wanted Schalk to see that I was now made of stronger stuff, hardened now, like kiln-fired clay.

Much of the veld had been burned, but it was coming back in spots, with the weeping love grass pioneering. Most of the rest was just scabland, anyway, which was still beautiful in the way its color changed during the day. I tried to write a description of the quality of light late in the afternoon but could not arrive at the fitting words.

I wrote bits about the grasses and the soil to which they were all rooted—the soil that reflected the sun and swallowed the floods, the soil that was rent by the farmers and the natives, the miners and the rivers and the grave diggers.

At times I studied my old notes. I could see how my writing had changed, the late entries pared down to scrawled fragments as I gradually lost my words. From the pencil marks and word combinations, I could sense those times when my mind had come untethered. I spent days sorting through the notes to decide what was hallucination and what was real. It was on that hilltop one afternoon that I decided that every bit of it was real.

I saw how silly I had been in the early notes about people, back when I tried to capture their identity with a few words. We were all so many things that fit together and then sometimes came apart. When a part was taken away, the other things that remained had to change shape to fill the space, like water. And we couldn't know what parts were the most important until the others fell away.

As I went through the notes, I sensed I'd been hollowed out. The camp had made me see the order of the things that we surrender. What goes first? Consideration? Compassion? Friendship? And then it gets down to faith, or maybe it's family and then faith, or maybe even memories. It was only when everything was taken away that you got to see what was at your core. And if you could hold on to that, that singular meaning, you went on; if you couldn't, the collapse was complete.

The words in the journal were what I carried home. They occupied space and had weight, and each was precious. I hoped writing would help me sort through the pieces that had broken off and find ways to put them back into place.

So, I might describe the way Klaas Huiseveldt died and his empty eyes were pulled open for a last photograph. But more important might be to tell how no one wanted to occupy that small portion of the tent where he liked to sleep and play. But when one of us finally did, it seemed all right.

I might write of Bina's sayings and her lessons about water and the vessels that carried it. Or maybe the need for holding on to the spirits of the dead. But the best example of those spirits were the sad, empty shadows of children that clouded Tante Hannah's every day, living only as gold thread on pieces of cloth.

I would tell of how Oupa Gideon had given me the gift of the night skies, although the stars never once guided me somewhere I needed to be. I would someday write about Oom Sarel and Vader and their relationship and their connection to their own father—and the secrets that were the sparking flint rock of their conflicts. But that would take a while to understand.

After all, I still did not understand the currents in my own mind, the sins and doubts and weaknesses, and the things I learned to feel although I sometimes wished I hadn't. And Moeder? It would take years to learn all she had gone through.

Some of our people could never forgive Tante Hannah's loyalty to Oom Sarel. It was said that an unburned farmhouse stood as the sign of a traitor. But Tante paid her toll. Her farm was in ruins, crops in cinders, and stock long dead.

Although my sleep was mostly sound, one common nightmare

replayed the scene the night that I was attacked; it was so real I could almost feel Maples's breath, and taste the blood from his hand in my mouth, and hear the scrape of metal on his ribs. The vision arose of both Maples and Oom Sarel, Moeder standing over them humming "Rock of Ages" just as she had that morning when we heard the rifle shots. *"Be of sin the double cure / Save from wrath and make me pure."* I woke feverish when I saw how perfectly it happened, a double cure, Maples and Sarel both dead, almost as if Moeder had planned the whole thing to work out exactly as it did.

I scolded myself for being suspicious of even my mother. In a way, I didn't care whether she had had a part in how it all happened near the end. When I thought of the times I was most near collapse—the day we arrived at camp, the day we buried Cee-Cee—she pulled us close and kept us standing. Straight as a post and rooted deeply, she was our strength.

But I supposed it was natural that the naive openness I had once carried had hardened into suspicion after seeing how others could treat us, how some were willing to simply march in and take what was ours. I didn't think any of us would forget that or tolerate any hint of it. I think most of us wanted, evermore, to be unbothered and apart.

I decided on one thing I would not write about: the war. At least not the battles. Someone else could write about the war's big stories. I would write only about my little part of it, the part I saw myself. We each had our own war.

Everything continued to change. I was back on the farm, yes, but very little was the same. There had been a war that took me from this spot, only to deposit me here again, a different person—far closer to the woman I would become than to the little girl I had been. Did we really go through so much just to return here? It seemed such a long and horrible path just to get home. But that was the real story of it all for me . . . that was my Great Trek.

We all built our truths to serve our needs. They were like our oaths and vows and covenants—all had been firm, but so few were permanent.

The lesson that came through this trek most intact was the one that Bina had taught me: deeds live. I learned that they not only lived but had to be carried.

I knew I would write about the night I spent on the veld with Vader and Schalk, the night I heard the lions and the drums. And how, at the time, I wanted nothing more than to have Vader comfort me and hold me and assure me all was well. I had hated that he refused to hug me close. But I saw his wisdom now. The best thing was for me to deal with the fear on my own, and once I learned that I could do it, it was a strength that would never leave me. For me, in the worst days, when everything else had been pared away, that remained.

The wind picked up again. I pulled a cochineal beetle off a prickly pear and squeezed it the way Schalk had shown me, so that its red-dye juices oozed. I dabbed the dye in spots on the back of my left hand, three in a row in the middle, and four others at cross corners. I blew on it to dry it, hoping the small constellation would seep into my skin and stay there forever.

But I knew it would fade.